MW01285374

The Odyssey of Sheba Smith

The Odyssey of Sheba Smith

Thomas E. Coughlin

Fitzgerald & LaChapelle Publishing, LLC

Copyright 2003 Thomas E. Coughlin
All rights reserved; no part of this publication may be reproduced,
stored in a retrievable system, or transmitted, in any form or by
any means—electronic, mechanical, photocopying, recording, or
otherwise—without the prior written permission of Thomas E. Coughlin.

Written, produced and printed in the United States of America

ISBN: 978-0-9666202-2-1

Cover Photography: Robert F. Hoffman, Nashua, New Hampshire

Cover Design: Lisa Atkins, Pelham, New Hampshire

Cover Location: Parson's Way, Kennebunkport, Maine

Cover Model: Amanda Riggas, whose Irish, Greek, and Native
(Blackfoot Tribe) American lineage make visible the character of Sheba

This book is a work of fiction. Names, characters and incidents are
products of the author's imagination or are used fictitiously. The
names of actual places were used largely with permission or as a point of
historical reference. Any resemblance to actual events, locales or persons,
living or dead, is entirely coincidental.

SECOND EDITION

Fitzgerald & LaChapelle Publishing, LLC
P.O. Box 352
Chester, NH 03036
(603) 669-6112

Dedication

For Mary Catherine Olenchuk
Sweet angel, you must know that the exploitation of
your innocence and trust continues to haunt the
collective soul of our region.

Acknowledgments

Lowell City Library, Kennebunk Town Library, Kennebunkport Town Library, The Lowell Sun, Dick Henry and the Maine Diner, Colonial Pharmacy, The Beachcomber, Wells High School, Wells Historical Society, William O. Thomson, Francine Tanguay, Richard Chasse, Dennis Tito, Manya Callahan and lastly the O'Neil family for allowing me to use The Stonehouse to adorn the front cover.

1

December 23, 1969

T HE HEAVY, BROWN DOOR CLOSED with a thud as the teenage girl
emerged from the house and out into the bitterly cold Maine
morning. A fresh inch of December snow crunched beneath her Keds
as she began the forty-yard walk from the house to the road. She
moved along one of two rutted paths, depressions in the ground from
years of vehicular travel. The driveway ran through an assortment of
junk cars, all in varying degrees of disrepair. The vehicle parked closest to the roadway was a 1962 Ford Falcon, which her father, but not
the state of Maine, considered roadworthy.

"Have a good day in school," came a voice from the doorway of
the house. Broderick Smith had slept through his daughter's morning
preparations but was awakened by the slamming of the door
seconds earlier. The young woman turned back to the wreck of a
building she called home and waved.

"Thank you, Daddy," she called back. Sheba Smith was a girl of
above average height and medium build. Born on Christmas in 1953,
she was only days away from her sixteenth birthday. He gestured to
her with a wave, then disappeared behind the paint-chipped door.

Sheba looked back at the house as she did on so many mornings,
waiting out the arrival of her bus. For more years than she cared to
count, she had endured the humiliation of being picked up in the
morning and dropped off in the afternoon in front of, as what she saw,
the most dilapidated structure in Wells, Maine. She imagined every set
of eyes inside the bus taking critical notice of her and her home. On
this morning, she tortured herself, looking down the driveway at the
formerly yellow structure, now scarred by chipped paint and mildew.
The two-story building had no less than two broken windows plugged
with rags. The chimney appeared to lean away from the house, and
most of the trim was in a state of advanced deterioration. To Sheba,

this building defined her in the eyes of the world, or at least her small corner of the world.

She glanced up the empty road to where her bus would shortly come into view. She could see for over a quarter of a mile in both directions. Sheba lived on one of the town's rural back roads, Burnt Mill Road, in Wells, west of Route 1 and hidden from the tourists who invaded the southern coast of Maine every summer. Sheba Smith's Maine was not what vacationers came to see and, for the most part, remained invisible to them. Burnt Mill Road was intersected by railroad tracks a short way up from Route 1. For this reason, the phrase "from the wrong side of the tracks" held a special meaning for her. With oceanfront homes and the finer colonials located east of the railroad tracks, she did not need a detailed explanation to convince her which side of the tracks she resided on. On this morning, she took comfort knowing there would soon be a weeklong rest from school and class work. The bitter, December air caused her to shiver as she moved about in an attempt to stay warm. Sheba was a pretty girl. However, her looks were of the unusual variety, not strange, just unusual. There was a wild look about her and it was most evident in her eyes. It was a combination of these wild, unusual looks, a surly disposition, and her dirt-poor wardrobe that dissuaded the young men of her school to even consider a relationship. Sheba Smith was a pretty girl, but not pretty enough to overcome these shortcomings.

As the bus pulled into view, a gust of wind blew snow down from an overhanging pine tree. Sheba pulled the hood of her coat up, covering her brown hair. Her feet, protected only by a pair of thick cotton socks and sneakers, were already numb from the cold. Seconds later, the yellow bus groaned and creaked to a stop and she made her way up the stairs and back to the fifth row, aisle seat, driver's side. Tossing her school bag onto the empty seat to her left, she immediately elevated her wet sneakers to the back of the seat in front of her. This was her daily ritual and the nonverbal message was clear: Sheba did not want company during her commute to school. She was one of those rare persons who was indifferent to popularity, or for that matter, acceptance. Earlier in the year, a freshman boy who had just moved to town happened into Sheba's seat in row five. When her half civil explanation of his slipup did not prompt any action on his part, he was lifted from the seat by his lapels and deposited on the floor in a heap. The flustered freshman protested the humiliation bitterly, from the seat of his pants, to an unresponsive Sheba before claiming another seat at the rear of the bus.

Sheba spent the better part of her thirty-minute bus ride planning her Christmas vacation. Her grandmother had invited her to spend Christmas Eve with her in Kennebunkport. Her father was scheduled to join the two the next day for dinner. Sheba was already looking forward to this quiet time with her only living relatives. On the day after Christmas she would begin the task of finding a job, a part-time job, to bring some much-needed additional income into the family. She knew summer employment would not be a problem, with countless waitress, chambermaid and salesclerk positions opening up for the tourist season. She planned to work a minimum of two jobs over the summer. It was not uncommon for her to lie in bed, dreaming of the good use the extra money would be put to in the coming months. But finding work in York County in the off-season was a different story altogether. Sheba would have to be diligent and lucky to secure any kind of employment at this time of the year.

The school bus arrived at Wells High School a few minutes after eight on this morning. The two-story, brick building sat a short distance back from Route 1. The building's most prominent features were the four broad, white columns facing the road, lending it a degree of dignity on a roadway otherwise dominated by weathered beach houses and rows of cookie-cutter housekeeping cottages. As Sheba exited the bus in front of the school, she was obligated to look off across Route 1, directly across the street, to the cemetery blanketed in snow. This had been her daily ritual for the past year and a half, since entering high school. The Smith family plot was there, along with other local names such as Littlefield, Gooch and Tripp, and beneath the snow rested her mother and older brother, there since a traffic accident plucked them from Sheba and her father. It was on a summer afternoon over nine years before that an oil truck had broadsided the family car at Four Corners in Kennebunk, killing her mother, her brother Billy, and the family German shepherd instantly. Miraculously, Sheba, seated in the back seat and away from the impact, had escaped with a minor concussion and a cut lip. Turning away from the cemetery, the sophomore allowed herself to be swept up in the flow of students making their way into the building. She entered the school in silence, choosing not to join in the chattering all around her.

Sheba followed the school's preopening bell rituals in her customary manner, her chin cradled in her hand and propped up by an elbow. Her posture gave the appearance of a teenager lost in faraway thought. In truth, the girl's lackadaisical posture and general lack of eye contact were a deception. Sheba Smith was a young woman with high intellectual curiosity. In junior high she was briefly thought to be a genius by a few educators. After all, here was a girl who passed in no written homework assignments and appeared to daydream her time away during classroom hours, yet still maintained A's and B's. In time, her teachers learned that her lack of eye contact did not represent detachment from lectures or class work material. A sense of fierce individualism coupled with a rebellious nature were behind her seemingly non-academic behavior. But away from the eyes of her teachers and peers, she read and absorbed the lessons presented to her.

It was midday when, having endured geometry, English, history and physics, she made her way downstairs for what she thought of as her last school lunch of 1969, or for that matter, of the 1960s altogether. Earlier that morning, Sheba had slapped together two bologna sandwiches. This and a glass of water would be her nourishment for the noon meal. As was her custom, she retreated to the far end of the cafeteria and a sparsely occupied table. Settling into a corner chair, she opened her geography book and stared down at a map of Asia.

About twenty minutes into an otherwise uneventful lunch period, Sheba's eyes caught sight of some unusual activity, as Felicia Blackburn and her usual entourage passed out leaflets to the crowd of teenagers. From a short stack of yellow papers, Felicia and her friends were hand-delivering a single sheet to each student. This was accompanied by a short commentary.

Felicia Blackburn, a statuesque brunette with a smile that left boys weak-kneed, seemed the personification of everything a superior gene pool could produce. In addition to being the most attractive female at Wells High School, Felicia could also list best grades, best dressed, most popular and most talented on her list of superlatives. The daughter of York County's most prominent and successful attorney, she was a young woman being groomed for success. Sheba was hard-pressed to remember the first time the two girls set eyes on one another but was sure their mutual dislike was born that very moment, a dislike that went largely unspoken. However, one small incident could have changed this a few days earlier.

The previous Friday, Sheba had struck a nerve in the pretty brunette when she raised her hand following a rare incorrect response by Felicia. Sheba went on to answer the question correctly in her usual nonchalant manner, barely raising her eyes from her desk. For someone unaccustomed to coming up short at anything, the experience left a thorn in Felicia's memory.

From her corner, Sheba's eyes followed Felicia as the girl progressed around the lunchroom. Sheba noticed that a number of students made a point of searching her out after glancing down at the leaflet. The distribution continued up and down the elongated tables throughout the room. Finally, with lunch period drawing to a close, Felicia thumbtacked one of the yellow leaflets to the bulletin board, in mock ceremonial fashion. She promptly left the room after flashing Sheba a sly grin. Sheba wasted no time gulping down the remainder of her sandwich. Hopping to her feet, she strode across the floor to the bulletin board, her eyes riveted to the yellow sheet just posted there.

It read: Wells High School – 1970 Sophomore Awards

    MOST TALENTED BOY – Ronnie Reno
    MOST TALENTED GIRL – Felicia Blackburn
    BEST DANCER, BOY – Bob Barbin
    BEST DANCER, GIRL – Patricia Betts
    MOST HANDSOME BOY – Sheba Smith
    PRETTIEST GIRL – Susanne Howell
    MOST LIKELY TO SUCCEED – Felicia Blackburn
    MOST LIKELY TO DIE PENNILESS – Sheba Smith

Sheba reached up and pulled down the list, having no desire to continue reading the group's venomous attempt at humor. Her tranquil mood from only moments before was replaced by a blend of hurt and rage. Felicia, her tight-knit group of companions probably only passive accomplices, had struck a nerve. What made the situation even more frustrating, she thought, was the difficulty of figuring out a meaningful response. Felicia was a self-assured female with no visible weaknesses. Looks, brains, poise, money, friends—she had them all, along with the total confidence that went with them.

By the time Sheba reached her classroom, it was three-quarters full. As usual, Felicia was holding court, surrounded by other teenagers who felt validation by her mere acceptance. Clearing the doorway, Sheba established eye contact with the attractive brunette.

"I hope you're not taking our list the wrong way," said Felicia coyly. Sheba did not respond. She chose to walk to her desk in silence, but not until she shot her tormentor an icy glance.

"Jesus, it's for your own good! Consider it a wake-up call from all of us. My God, the way you dress—your hair—your attitude! Oh, what the hell—I might as well come out and say it. You pretend like you don't want any friends, when the truth is no one wants to *be* your friend. You're weird and you're creepy, so don't delude yourself into thinking you're a loner by choice. You're creepy and no one wants to be around you. You're an embarrassment to the whole school."

Sheba found her head reeling from this onslaught as she tried to elicit a response. Sitting atop her desk, her gorgeous legs crossed and on display, Felicia's expression telegraphed the immense pleasure she was experiencing as she systematically picked her adversary apart. Drowning in this moment in time, Sheba fought back tears while considering a dash for the door. The attack was not over.

"Oh, and don't try to feed us all that crap about being poor."

"Take it easy, Fleece," suggested Ronnie Reno, almost under his breath.

"Shut up, Ronnie. This is long overdue," she snapped back. "Maybe, just maybe, your father might spend a little less time guzzling beer in Biddeford and use that money to buy you something decent, like clothes."

"Don't you dare talk about my father, not when you've got some low-life lawyer for an old man! At least my daddy makes his money the honest way, building things. He's not some lying slug, chiseling grandmothers out of their life savings for a living! How's it feel knowing all your fancy clothes and all come from your crooked old man bloodsucking the rest of us honest people?"

"Listen, you little bitch! I'll have you know my father does a great deal of pro bono work for the poor—but you wouldn't know anything about that!"

"For the poor, is it? Well, he should, he probably made them that way! License to steal—isn't that what they say amongst themselves? Well, *Fleece*, I say your old man's nothing more than a thief—except he gets to wear suspenders and a three-piece suit!" Sheba's tirade drew a scream from Felicia, just as Miss Maitland arrived for Spanish class.

"Unless someone in here is giving birth, that'll be enough of that," quipped the youthful teacher. "Miss Blackburn, would you care to express your anger verbally, so that we all might work toward some resolution?"

Felicia drew in her rage and gestured no. Shooting Sheba a final glare, the girl slammed open her textbook while friends whispered consolations. For her part, Sheba sat transfixed, considering her achievement. She had pierced the armor of the seemingly invincible Felicia Blackburn. She sat back at her desk, stunned by her own success. However, she knew this was only the beginning. She and Felicia were at war, and undoubtedly there would be more battles to come.

* * *

The exhilaration of her arrival home on the threshold of Christmas vacation was dampened when Sheba saw Jody Pease's pick-up truck in the driveway as she stepped down from the bus. Jody was a local carpenter and contractor of limited skills. For the past seven years he worked with Broderick Smith as his partner. Broderick's advanced carpentry skills allowed Pease to bid on jobs that he otherwise could not. What Pease brought to the partnership were contacts within southern Maine's business community. Armed with his double-pump handshake and a laugh as phony as a cavity in a set of dentures, he had found the two sufficient work to keep the bill collectors at arm's length. Pease was of average height, sporting a beer gut that hung over the belt of his trousers. A shock of oily, dirty-blond hair rested atop his puffy moon face. Lastly, Pease and Smith were drinking buddies, sometimes in the lounges and bars of Biddeford and Sanford, sometimes at the Smith residence in Wells.

Sheba entered the house to find her father and Pease sprawled out in the living room, each clutching a bottle of beer. A noisy space heater whirred away along the wall behind them.

"Hello, sweetheart—good day at school?" asked her father. Broderick Smith was tall, over six feet, with wide shoulders that tapered down to a narrow waist. Trim from years of manual labor, he walked around in a body one came to expect on a man of twenty-two. However, his biological age showed on his face, carved there through years of excessive drinking.

"I've had better, Daddy."

Pease looked on from a beat-up chair in the corner of the room. His eyes played up and down Sheba while she stood in the doorway. "I'll start putting something together for supper," she announced while approaching her father to plant a kiss on his forehead.

"Put a little extra on. I've invited Jody to join us."

Sheba glanced over at Pease who responded by raising his beer bottle in a mock salute.

"Don't forget, Daddy, I'm going to Nana's tomorrow and sleeping over." Sheba wasted no time excusing herself, making her way to the kitchen at the far end of the house. The men resumed talking as she passed through two drafty downstairs rooms before taking inventory of what they had stocked in the refrigerator. It was just after three o'clock, much too early to begin preparing supper.

She scampered up the back stairwell to her bedroom and flung her books on the floor. They would go undisturbed until the morning she returned to Wells High School in the following month of the following year of the following decade. With the sun dropping in the afternoon sky, the room lit up with horizontal beams of light. The girl fell backward onto her bed and began running pleasant thoughts through her mind. She joyously anticipated the challenge of job hunting after Christmas. She resolved not to put it off. On Friday, December 26th, she would go from business to business along Route 1.

From job hunting, Sheba's thoughts went back to the confrontation with Felicia Blackburn. It was a great relief knowing it would be nearly two weeks before school would reopen. With thoughts of high school came the image of Ronnie Reno. Sheba had been surprised when Ronnie attempted to calm his girlfriend during her assault earlier in the day. He had appeared upset by Felicia's verbal barrage and its initial effect on her. In truth, no matter how much disdain Sheba had for teenage boys or males in general, she reserved special status for Ronnie. He did not act the fool the way so many of the other boys in school did. Then, of course, he was the cutest sophomore at Wells High. It was Ronnie she brought into her nighttime thoughts and dreams, thoughts conjured up at bedtime as she lay awake under her bed covers. This was also the time she explored the pleasures her own body was capable of giving her. In the last few years, Sheba was amazed by the indescribable pleasure brought on by her own touch. For this reason, she longed for a mother, older sister, or even a close friend to speak with about these feelings.

2

IT WAS FOUR O'CLOCK when Sheba descended the stairs to the kitchen and began preparing supper. With Jody Pease joining the Smiths for their meal, she peeled extra potatoes. However, with less than a pound of hamburger in the house, she was forced to prepare the patties razor thin. A can of yellow beans rounded out the meal. She called the men to the table just after five o'clock.

Supper conversation was stunted with little said beyond the predictable. Near the end of the meal Jody slipped in a comment about knowing how the starving millions in Biafra felt. Sheba bit her tongue, holding back a caustic response. With their plates cleaned and no dessert on the horizon, the two men retreated back to the living room, where the better part of a case of Schlitz sat chilling in Jody's cooler. The teenager proceeded to clear the table, wash the dishes, and bring the kitchen back into a state of order. For her, the evening's itinerary was already in place. She would retire to her room, where a telephone book would provide her with the names and addresses of potential employers. She would start with restaurants and grocery stores in Wells. She would construct a map and systematically begin her job hunting the day after Christmas.

Jody and her father were parked in front of the TV set when Sheba slipped in to wish her dad a goodnight. Pease, now well into his pre-holiday drinking binge, made a half innocent crack about receiving a kiss just after his partner had. The girl left the room without comment and made her way upstairs. Outside, the wind's velocity increased and drove waves of frigid air against the side of the house, causing it to creak and shudder. Arriving back in her bedroom, Sheba set herself up at a writing desk in the corner after plugging in a space heater by the bed. She worked on her map for over an hour, then pulled out a well-worn copy of *The Collector*. She lost herself in the novel before noticing it was after nine o'clock. Her schedule for Wednesday was crowded, making an early retirement advisable. She returned the book to the top drawer of her desk before preparing for bed.

Sheba undressed, then slipped on a nightgown and heavy cotton socks. She did not feel comfortable leaving the space heater on throughout the night, so she protected herself from the cold with five layers of blankets, the nightgown and socks being a second line of defense. The oil supply at the house was low and her father kept the furnace on a minimal setting. With the room in darkness and the December wind howling by the window, she withdrew from the reality of her existence and wandered off into the world she created for herself within her mind. Inspired by a matinee at the Saxony Theatre in Kennebunkport a few years back when her grandmother brought her to see *Doctor Zhivago*, she created a romantic excursion within her imagination that she built upon in the darkness and privacy of her bedroom. On this night she did not deviate from her ongoing script.

* * *

Her now-familiar fantasy finds her wandering in the woods on a cold, November afternoon. The light is rapidly dissipating as snowflakes begin to fall and fill the forest. Stepping atop a cluster of fallen trees, her foot slips between two boughs, twisting her ankle in the process. Testing her foot, she knows she is in no condition to walk any distance. The snowfall intensifies. From behind her comes the sound of approaching footsteps. Sheba turns to see Ronnie Reno breaking through a clump of brush.

"Sheba, what are you doing out here?"

"I could ask you the same question, couldn't I? But the truth of the matter is, I'm friggin' lost. I've gotten turned around so many times, I can't tell west from east."

"Yeah, me too. And now the radio's sayin' there's this storm's come up — out of nowhere. They're sayin' a foot of snow before it stops tomorrow. This is November, for God sakes!"

Here Sheba explains to Ronnie how she cannot walk, with the twisted ankle and all, and Ronnie volunteers to carry her to safety. The snow continues to blow and pile up as he carries Sheba in his arms, her arm hooked around his neck. With the last of the afternoon light practically gone, they happen upon a log cabin. They have already given up hope of finding their way out of the woods when a critical decision is made. A window is forced in and the two teenagers must make do inside while the forest around them fills up with snow.

In protective fashion, the boy puts Sheba down on a couch directly in front of a fireplace. He assures her that they will be able to have a fire in a short time. There is an ample supply of firewood and wooden matches in the kitchen, and kindling wood, to have the fireplace roaring in ten minutes. Ronnie has also found a battery-powered radio in the kitchen, and an emergency weather report announces that the storm has been upgraded with snow accumulation of sixteen to twenty inches.

"There is nothing to worry about, Sheba," consoles Ronnie. "We have plenty of canned goods in the cupboard. There's a wood shed with plenty of dry wood just outside the door, and we can always melt snow for water."

By now, Sheba had slipped her hands beneath the covers with one positioned under her nightgown. Her breathing intensified as she moved deeper into her fantasy, accompanied by the feel of her fingers as she explored her own body.

"It's almost like we're Adam and Eve here together," he suggests as he slips down beside her on the couch. "It's probably not a bad idea if we draw from each other's body heat." The boy pulls his sweatshirt over his head, his tee shirt follows, then in one swift movement, he deposits his trousers in a heap in front of the fire. Slipping beside her, she feels his tightly muscled body envelope hers. His head rests against hers as their limbs tangle around one another. Sheba feels the warmth from his body all around her as Ronnie deliberately directs her mouth toward his and the two taste each other's lips.

As Sheba explored the most private regions of her body, currents of pleasure ran through her. She felt herself grow weaker from ecstasy. Her body was wet from the attention her fingers had extended and from the erotic journey her mind had taken her on. There was a faint, not unpleasant scent in the room from the ecstasy that surged through her. Her mind soared from the excitement of the moment. Suddenly, though, a creaking board from the hallway interrupted her exhilaration. It was followed by the sound of movement from her doorknob.

"Who is it?"

"It's Jody. I'll be heading out in a few minutes, and I just came up to wish you a Merry Christmas and a happy birthday. Can I come in?"

"Absolutely not! I don't think my father would be very happy if he knew you were up here."

The inebriated Pease pushed open the door, a moronic grin pasted to his face. "Listen, Sheba, you don't have to be so damn ornery every time you open your mouth." His speech was slurred from hours of drinking.

"I'll call my father," she threatened, raising her voice.

Pease continued forward, slowly moving toward the bed. "Your old man is passed out downstairs, dead to the world." Pease was standing directly above her. Sheba looked up and thought she detected a subtle change in his demeanor. "You know, it's not like you're one of James Bond's babes, or something. You're a little broad with a few too many pimples and who could bear to lose a few pounds—and I'm being kind. I won't even get into that bird's nest you call hair. So, where the hell do you get off being so damn uppity?"

"In case you've forgotten, you pervert, I'm fifteen years old!"

The man responded by lunging down, grabbing her wrists and pinning them to the pillow. As she struggled, he found her mouth with his. After kissing her, he briefly caught her upper lip between his teeth. She pulled her mouth away before he could exert serious pressure. When he brought his mouth down on hers a second time, she managed to free her right hand and strike him repeatedly in and around his eye. Stunned by the counterattack, Pease pulled back beyond arm's length, only to receive a sharp kick in the groin that she launched from beneath the covers. He gasped for air and sank in slow motion to his knees. Scrambling from the bed, Sheba grabbed a baseball bat that stood in the corner. She approached him as he knelt helplessly, still trying to catch his breath.

"I swear to God, I'll send you to the hospital with more concussions than they can count if you don't get out of my room—now!"

"Goddamn it, you little bitch!" he spat out, inspecting his left eye with his hand. "I'm goin', don't worry, I'm goin'. God, your room even smells like a French whorehouse."

"And you'd know all about that," she answered, the bat poised to strike.

"One thing before I go. Not a word to your old man about all this. I shouldn't have to remind you about who brings in all the work—and how you two would be starving without me. Don't do or say anything stupid."

Sheba did not answer. She motioned him from the room, then followed him downstairs to the front door. Pease, still bent over from her kick to his groin, turned back a final time, shooting her an angry glare, before stepping out into the cold night air. She threw the lock on the front door, then peeked into the living room. Broderick Smith was snoring loudly on the couch. Most rooms in the house were cold by this time. Sheba had literally seen her breath in the air while escorting Jody downstairs and through the rooms to the front door. Retrieving the blankets from his bed upstairs, she placed them over her father and turned off the space heater. That left nothing to do except kiss her dad goodnight for a second time and retire for the evening.

3

December 24, 1969

SHEBA WOKE UP EARLY the next morning to a frigid bedroom and forced herself out from under the warm blankets and onto the cold wooden floor. She looked forward to spending the night at her grandmother's house. She had not seen the woman since Thanksgiving Day. First, she packed a travel bag that included a change of clothes, wrapping Christmas presents for her father and grandmother. She had not fully recovered from the incident in her bedroom with Jody Pease the night before, so as a precaution Sheba brought her baseball bat downstairs to be added to the cargo for the trip to Kennebunkport. With packing completed, she took a sponge bath in the upstairs bathroom before making her way downstairs to the kitchen. There, she prepared for herself and her father a bacon-and-egg breakfast, again reminding him he was expected at Nana Lake's house at noontime on Christmas Day. Finally, she turned down a ride to Kennebunkport in the Falcon, choosing to walk and hitchhike the seven miles.

Route 1, where she would pick up meaningful traffic flow toward Kennebunkport, was approximately a ten-minute walk from the house. The day was overcast and not as chilly as the past few. Traffic was heavier than usual, owing to last-minute Christmas shoppers, as the girl set herself up at the junction of Route 1 and Burnt Mill Road and extended her thumb. Sheba was not an experienced hitchhiker, but even with no experience to fall back on, she quickly deduced that the baseball bat balanced on her shoulder was not helping her cause. So, five minutes into her venture, she changed strategy. She slipped the bat behind her, its handle resting on her buttocks and out of sight. The teenager then put a discreet hitch in her hip while the wind from passing cars swirled hair around her face. Less than a minute passed before a VW bus dusted in road salt screeched to a halt.

A young man with long, shaggy hair and a droopy brown beard

threw open the passenger door as Sheba ran up to the vehicle. She hopped into the front seat without a moment's hesitation, tossing her travel bag on the floor in front of her. The man's eyes opened in surprise as he surveyed his passenger.

"What's this?" he asked.

"Louisville Slugger—thirty-three inches—Del Ennis model," answered Sheba behind a devilish smile.

The man, looking to be in his early twenties, shook his head as the bus pulled back onto the road. There was silence within the cabin of the Volkswagen for a few moments. The man stole one, then a second glance across at his young passenger while she sat silently, her eyes riveted on him. "You are one strange, little bird."

She did not respond. Sheba's take on the fellow was that he was a flower child of sorts. The dashboard displayed colorful decals and peace symbols. His speech seemed foreign to Maine. He became noticeably unnerved as she stared at him from across the front seat. Then, only seconds into their drive, he abruptly turned the steering wheel and the vehicle came to a roaring halt by the side of the road.

"Man, I'm sorry, but you are really spookin' me out! I'll have to ask you to get out—please."

"You've got to be kidding. You're spooked by a fifteen-year-old girl?" They had traveled less than a mile. She angrily picked up her things and exited the bus, displaying her agitation. He glanced over at her and flashed the familiar two-fingered peace sign.

"Get bent, weirdo!" she called out before slamming the door closed. Unflustered, she went back to the stance that brought her success only minutes before and was rewarded seconds later. A woman heading all the way to Kennebunkport stopped and inquired about her final destination. This resulted in a connection and the girl was given a ride to her grandmother's front door, a half-mile beyond Dock Square on the road to Cape Porpoise.

The door to the small cape opened as Sheba exited the car, thanking the lady for her hospitality. Already in the doorway and prepared to greet her granddaughter was Dorothy Lake. Small in stature and noticeably stooped from osteoporosis, she raised her arms, beckoning to her grandchild. A broad grin lit Sheba's face as she broke into a trot. In seconds, the two were in an embrace on the elderly woman's porch.

* * *

Dorothy Lake was less than two years from her eightieth birthday. Written off as barren by the medical community following fruitless attempts at starting a family, Dorothy surprised everyone when she became pregnant in her late thirties, then gave birth to a healthy baby girl a few days after the stock market crash in 1929. Elaine would be her only child, a child Dorothy always referred to as her mysterious gift from God. Now, in Sheba, she saw the only surviving bounty from that small miracle. The loss of her daughter and grandson in a senseless car accident had shaken the woman's faith years before. Those closest to her, friends, neighbors, the folks from church, firmly believed that the better part of Dorothy Lake had died along with her daughter and grandson that summer day nine years ago.

"Come in, child, let's get you warm." Sheba followed her grandmother into the hallway, her arm draped affectionately around the elderly woman. "You're early, and that's just fine with me," said Dorothy, ushering Sheba toward a living room chair. The house was warm and meticulously clean. "Are you expecting the Red Sox?" The question was accompanied with a gesture toward the baseball bat.

"Travel insurance, Nana," came back the girl, with a mischievous grin.

"I'll put some hot water on for tea, unless you'd prefer coffee?"

"Tea'll be fine."

The old woman moved toward the kitchen but continued the conversation. "Child, we have an awful lot to talk about today, a great deal. That's why I invited you here to spend the night. I have things to talk to you about that your father cannot be a part of."

In the living room, Sheba was resting in a soft, comfortable chair and absorbing the warmth of the house. She was finding her grandmother's words curious.

"Nana, you're making my coming over sound so mysterious."

No response came from the kitchen, just the clang of utensils. The teenager found herself experiencing a measure of peace at the moment, with her head back and her eyes closed.

A short time after the whistle from the teapot, Dorothy re-entered the room balancing a tray carrying tea and an assortment of holiday cookies. Sheba sprang to her feet and helped her grandmother set up the refreshments. A minute later Dorothy sat stirring her beverage. She appeared to be gathering her thoughts.

"Granddaughter dear, if it were possible I would love to absolutely prepare you for everything you're about to hear, but I don't think that's possible—at least by me. I'm afraid your first reaction to what you'll hear from me over the next few hours will be the same as mine, when I heard it from my daddy almost sixty years ago. You see, sixty years ago my father, your great-grandfather, brought me out fishing and told me things I couldn't and wouldn't believe. And now—it's time to pass these things on to you. But child, as sure as I'm sitting here and Jesus is my savior, what you hear from me is what my daddy told me—and it is the truth."

Sheba sat in silence, transfixed by her grandmother's words. The old woman took a sip from her cup before continuing.

"First, a small piece of information you probably don't realize. We've had talks before about the mongrel blood line the Lake family has—and how we can claim to be Anglo, French, Dutch, Irish, Scottish, even a trace of German. Well, there's at least one more to add to the list, and that's Quintanok. They were a group of American Indians. Before the Europeans arrived on our shores, there was a band of people who lived here along the coast of Maine. They were a decent and hardworking people, tall and handsome in appearance. They lived here in peace with their neighbors, the Wawenocs. The Wawenocs were part of the Abenaki Nation. These people were known as the Quintanoks, and they numbered only about three hundred or so. Among the Quintanoks was a very special man by the name of Mowalk. Our ancestors tell us that Mowalk was close to the Great Spirit and that he spent hours and sometimes days at a time speaking to Him. Mowalk was known to go off from his people to a holy place, where he would talk with and worship the Great Spirit. On one occasion, when he returned from the holy place to the Quintanok camp, he was shocked to find a large number of his people dead, slaughtered by attackers. The dead were primarily men and boys and women beyond childbearing years. Following a visit to the camp of the Wawenocs where he spoke to their leaders, Mowalk deduced that a war party of savages from some distance away had descended on his people, catching them at rest and ill-prepared. The savages slaughtered all males, including children, and carried off the Quintanok females for breeding, servitude and pleasure. Mowalk, grief-stricken and despondent, returned to the holy place and asked the Great Spirit to lift the weight of this horrible act from his shoulders. When the Great Spirit saw the despair and grief of his beloved Mowalk, He decided to give His most obedient and loyal child the means to change the horrible events of the recent past. The Great Spirit directed Mowalk to come to the holy place on the night of the longest day. He was told that if he meditated on the people and places of the past, to a time before his own birth, he would be allowed to journey back to that time. The Great Spirit told him that he could then warn his people about the events in the future—and perhaps change the outcome of those events. Mowalk was advised that he would return to his own time when the moon was erased from the night sky—and that his work would have to be accomplished during the time allotted." The elderly woman stopped talking. She closed her eyes, appearing to be gathering recollections from far back in her memory.

"And what happened then, Nana?"

"When Mowalk returned from his journey back to the time of his ancestors, he was overjoyed to find his people at their camp. He learned that in his absence there had been an attack and some of the Quintanoks had been lost in battle. But, due to the band's policy of constant vigilance and of armed overnight guards, a practice dictated through a directive from a prophet sent by the Great Spirit many years before, the savages were defeated and driven off. And, so it was through the years, the Quintanoks were visited by holy men. These men would appear from out of the forest, unclothed and always bearing knowledge, direction and guidance. The visitations from these prophets came to be expected. On arrival, the holy men would be clothed and fed. The prophets would meet with the Quintanok leaders and give then council. Once convinced that the band's leadership understood the purpose and lesson of the visit, prophets would break all contact with the people. It was said that campfires would be visible on the side of Agamenticus after the prophet's departure until the moon was next erased from the night sky."

"Was Mowalk coming back to visit his people over and over?"

"No, but child, we mustn't get ahead of ourselves."

Dorothy took a break to offer her guest an additional cookie from the tray. Her granddaughter accepted, then settled back into her chair.

"Nana, this is a wonderful story."

"You mustn't think of this as just a story, child," chastised the woman. "Your great-grandfather told me all of this and there wasn't a hint of play in his voice. But I don't want to get ahead of myself. As I said, my daddy took me fishing one morning and told me things I've carried with me ever since. That day, as we sat fishing, he told me how he had heard everything from his father. Then he told me this incredible tale. It seems his father had told him about this mysterious rock and how this rock held special power for anyone who knew its secret. He told me about going there one night on the first day of summer, on the longest day of the year. He told me how everything was tied to the history of the Quintanoks and to Mowalk in particular. He went on to say that when Mowalk was given his gift from the Great Spirit, it didn't stop with him. The Great Spirit promised that as long as the blood of Mowalk flowed through the body of coming generations, the gift would not be taken back. And so it was, through the centuries, the secret of the gift was passed from one descendent to the next, the torch passed in the final days of one to the next. Sheba, your great-grandfather swore to me he went to the rock, Mowalk's sacred place, and woke up the next morning shivering on top of the great boulder, not a stitch of clothing on him. He said when he came down and made his way toward town he thought he sensed something strange. He laughed when he told me he stole clothes off of a clothesline so he could walk in public. There weren't any cars on the road back then, so teams of horses moving about was nothing unusual. But, my daddy said he soon noticed that there were no familiar faces and, in time, he heard people talking about the war and how well it was going—the Mexican War! He told me he spent the next few nights sleeping in the loft of a barn over in the lower village and eventually woke up one morning back on the rock and back in his own time. Sheba love, your great-grandfather told me all of this and said it was important that I never forget. He made me cry when he told me he wouldn't be around much longer and it had to be passed on to the next generation. He was a healthy man at the time but he said his end came to him in a dream. Five days later, they carried him from the woods, crushed to death in a lumbering accident." A sad expression came over Dorothy's face as she shared memories of her father with Sheba.

"Why are you telling me all of this, Nana?"

"Because it's time for you to know. Just as my father had described to me, I've been visited in a dream. It's time for the secret to be passed on. Late last week I was visited in a dream. So many of those who meant so much to me and that I loved—my Alfred, my parents, and grandparents, my best friend from school, the Reverend Grissom, they all came to me. It was just like my father described to me before he died. It's time to pass the secret and the power on to you. I've squandered the gift—not taken advantage of what was there. But Sheba, there was only one thing I saw worth going back for, and I saw that beyond my power. How could I have warned your mother about that horrible accident when I would have to go back before the time of my own birth, as Mowalk had been told to do? I couldn't see any way of changing the course of my little darlin's life and—I know I didn't fully believe the words of my father."

"Nana, you have to be wrong about all of this."

"Child, do not make the mistake I made. You have too much to gain from this incredible blessing. In my dream, when I saw all those

I loved and that had passed on before me—your mother and brother were not among them. I'm sure that means something. God is good in that He seems to be giving me a final Christmas and birthday with you. But, we cannot squander these few hours together. I must pass along everything I know. This is for no one's ears but yours—until the time that you will pass it along to the next of Mowalk's bloodline, God willing."

"I don't want to lose you, Nana," cried out Sheba.

"I've lived a full life, and the sight of those waiting for me makes me yearn for their company."

Sheba jumped from her chair and rushed to her grandmother's side, burying her face into her shoulder. The girl wept aloud as Dorothy stroked her hair.

"To find the holy place you must follow the road to the sea from Dock Square. You'll pass the Grande Manse, then continue to beyond spouting rock and blowing cave. At about a quarter of a mile from where the road separates itself from the sea, you'll turn left and go up into the woods. At no more than a hundred yards from the road you'll see a rock rising like a pulpit from the ground—probably dropped there by a glacier a million years ago. Atop that rock is Mowalk's holy place—where he spoke to the Great Spirit. Remember, our pact with Him can still be broken if a word of this is breathed outside of the bloodline. Do you hear me, child? It's me to you and someday you to one of your children or grandchildren—and to no one else." The elderly woman pulled her granddaughter's head up, staring deeply into her eyes. In her grandmother's face she saw a fragment of desperation behind the tired eyes and wrinkled skin.

"Nana, I'll do whatever it takes to reach my mother."

"My child, your life has been anything but a picnic over the last nine years—with no mother and all. Broderick, he's not a bad man. He's weak, but he's not bad. He's never been able to get over your momma. That doesn't make him bad, maybe just the opposite. I wish you could remember him from before the accident. Your brother, Billy, he deserves to live out his life. You have the power, young lady," she added, stroking Sheba's hair. Dorothy leaned forward and emptied the contents of the teapot into the two cups. "Child, I'll pass along everything else I can remember and then it's up to you to question me on anything you don't understand. Hopefully, I'll be able to answer any questions that come up. Your great-grandfather told me he used an old photograph taken before the Civil War to help him conjure up the image of when he wanted to go back to, the year, I mean. You could do the same. He also figures that he was only back a couple of days, three at the most. The new moon came very soon after he arrived. Oh, and this is very important. When you've managed to do what you set out to do, you must remove yourself from the people you've gone back to see. Remember, I told you how the prophets would leave the camp of the Quintanoks when they were sure the leaders understood the purpose of the visit—and how the prophets' fires would be visible on Mount Agamenticus until the moon was erased? Well, you'll have to be careful to do the same. Your great-grandfather compared it to the ripple in a pond from a stone, and how you must make the ripple as small as possible. Do what has to be done and say what has to be said, and remove yourself from the scene. The longer you stay around, the more chance you have of doing or undoing something you didn't intend to."

Silence descended upon the room as Sheba's mind raced out of control, first trying to comprehend the enormity of her grandmother's words, then dealing with her rational side, which reprimanded her for even considering its legitimacy. At present, her rational side was in full control of her feelings. It was evident her grandmother's age had caught up with her. However, it was also clear she firmly believed every word she said, and she would be crushed if Sheba did not at least appear to take her words seriously. Therefore, Sheba decided to earnestly question her grandmother on this whole matter. For all she knew, her grandmother would forget the whole incredible tale by the time the New Year rang in.

For the remainder of the afternoon, the revelation was left hanging in the air, each making references to it from time to time without any discussions. The conversation was directed to more timely matters, like Christmas and Sheba's sixteenth birthday. Sheba took the opportunity to quiz her grandmother on personal issues involving her mother. She was reminded of where the Lake family lived in the '40s and early '50s. Dorothy had moved to Kennebunkport from Wells shortly after her husband died in 1956. The two women had a light supper on Christmas Eve while already preparing for the Christmas Day feast the following afternoon. As the two sat across the kitchen table from one another that evening preparing a vegetable platter, Sheba brought back the revelation as the topic of conversation.

"Nana, knowing everything they did, what happened to the Quintanoks?"

"They adapted to conditions and situations as they were. That's what I was told. As the story was told to me, and that's all we have, a prophet directed them to mix their blood with the Europeans. He said that way their bloodline would flow forward. Intermarrying didn't prove to be real hard. I told you they were a handsome people. According to what my father told me, they were even able to pretty much avoid the worst of the smallpox and measles epidemics that ravaged some of the other tribes."

"Now, everything you told me about the holy place—how many times did you go and see it?"

"I'm embarrassed to say only once. But you have to remember, it wasn't all that long after my father told me that I met your grandfather. Between courting and making a home for us, there wasn't a whole lot of time." Although still highly skeptical, Sheba could not help being amazed at the detail and construction of her grandmother's incredible tale.

With the turkey prepared and stuffed, and all side dishes for the Christmas meal under control, the two women retired early on Christmas Eve. They decided no gifts would be exchanged until Broderick arrived the next day.

4

December 25, 1969

ON CHRISTMAS MORNING, Dorothy and Sheba rose early, placing the turkey in the oven before dawn. They attended Christmas service in town at the South Congregational Church after Dorothy's neighbor, Mrs. Bibber, promised to come over and baste the turkey every thirty minutes until they returned. The noon church bells from the village were still sounding when Broderick's Ford Falcon pulled up to the house for the Christmas celebration and the sixteenth birthday of daughter Sheba. Only happy remembrances were discussed at the small family gathering. Broderick went so far as to abstain from all alcohol, adding to the wholesomeness of the festivities. Among the combination of Christmas and birthday gifts, Sheba received a pair of water-repellent winter boots from her father and, from her grandmother, an assortment of camping items, including a sleeping bag and kerosene lantern. Sheba, Broderick and Dorothy spent a joyful holiday together. By the time the Smiths slipped on their coats in the front hall, it was nearly nine o'clock and the three all radiated a sense of familial warmth, the kind only arrived at on the most meaningful of occasions. As Broderick bounded down the steps and toward his car with the last of the presents, Sheba gave her grandmother a final kiss.

"I promise I'll visit over school vacation," she said.

"Remember everything I've told you, child," answered Dorothy, ignoring her granddaughter's words. Sheba looked deeply into her eyes but did not respond. She kissed the woman a final time, then sprinted out into the cold and toward the Falcon.

The car heater was just beginning to warm the air when she jumped into the front seat beside her father. On this evening, the ride back to Wells was a delight for the eyes, with Christmas lights shining from most windows. At this time of year, Dock Square in Kennebunkport took on a magical, fairy-tale appearance, and it was particularly enjoyable on this evening with few cars lining the roadway. When Sheba stared out through the windshield, she beheld a world covered with a blanket of snow, masking everything that was broken, dirty or worn out. She loved this time of the year.

"Daddy, tomorrow morning, bright and early, I'm going out job hunting. Just a part-time thing, you know, until school breaks in June."

"If you want or need a ride, I can save you some time."

"Daddy, you know how I feel about driving around in this car—in the daylight, anyway. Not until you get an inspection sticker."

"You don't have to be scared about us getting stopped, not anymore."

"What are you talking about?"

"I'm talking about something I picked up last week. Jody and I were grabbing a quick pop during lunch up in Biddeford, and this guy at the bar tells us how he hasn't had an inspection sticker on his car, a valid one anyway, in over two years."

"And how many tickets does he have in his glove compartment?"

"None, little Miss Know-it-all, and here's how he does it. If he sees a cop car coming toward him from the opposite direction, he rolls down his window and pounds the side of his car while singing. If the cop's parked on the side of the road, he starts pounding the top of his car—still singin' away. What happens is the cop's eyes are drawn to the unusual, to what's out of place. His eyes are drawn to the hand pounding on the car and away from the windshield. And of course, there ain't no law against singin'—not yet, anyway."

"I'm sorry, Daddy, but it sounds idiotic to me. I'll just hoof it tomorrow, if you don't mind."

"Suit yourself," he answered, while turning the car back onto Route 1. Sheba found her grandmother's words coming back to her and it triggered a question.

"Out of curiosity, Daddy, did Mama ever tell you anything about her having any Indian blood?"

"Indian blood! No, as far as I know, your mother was a WASP, pure and simple. Well, maybe some Scotch-Irish, too. I'm pretty sure if she had any Indian in her, she would have told me." Broderick's mood, which seemed upbeat only moments earlier, was changing before his daughter's eyes into a thoughtful, melancholy one. "You know, it's good to get out of the house on special days like this. Sheba, not a day goes by that I don't think of your mother. I do miss her terribly. But, it's the special days like Christmas that tear away at me the most." Sheba reached over, squeezing his arm affectionately. "I'm telling you, kiddo, if it weren't for you, I would have checked out a long time ago. You're what keeps me going. I couldn't leave you alone—not my little girl."

"Daddy, stop it."

"There are probably a lot of folks who think I'm drinking myself to death—and I probably am. But that takes time, enough time for my pretty, little girl to grow up and start her own family."

"Daddy, please stop talking like this!"

"It's just that I loved your mother so much. Maybe it makes me crazy, but I think there was one woman in the world—one perfect woman and no more, and your mother was that one. When she died, most of me died along with her—not to mention Billy. I don't know why God saw fit to do that to me—to us. A girl or boy needs a mother growing up, more than a father. It should have been me." The man was working himself into a state of despondency by now, tears beginning to hinder his sight.

"Please, Daddy, pull the car over," ordered Sheba.

He turned the Falcon off the road and coasted to a stop. There came the sound of frozen snow crunching beneath the tires.

"Mama and Billy are no doubt in heaven. You've got to stop thinking and talking about it in the wrong way and concentrate on knowing you'll see both of them again someday. Okay?" He nodded his head, almost childlike, in agreement. "There are some things you're better off not looking directly at—the sun is one, and death is another," Sheba added. Broderick stared out the car's front window, collecting his composure. Finally, with his demons adequately suppressed, he eased the vehicle back onto the road.

A snow shower materialized from the dark sky above them as the Falcon turned up the driveway and rolled toward the house. The old building sat in darkness and silence as the Smiths returned to it in the last hours of Christmas. It was ten years since the shattered excuse of a house had reverberated with the laughter of the Christmas season. Father and daughter paused in the hallway after unloading the car.

"Happy birthday, sweet sixteen," said Broderick, a melancholy tone still present in his voice.

"I love you, Daddy." Sheba did not wait for a reply. She bounded up the stairwell into the darkness. The cold, dark house sat like a monument to everything Christmas was not. Sheba quickly undressed in her darkened room and slipped between the covers on her bed, letting out a gasp when her bare skin made contact with the cold linen.

5

December 26, 1969

ON FRIDAY MORNING Sheba rose early and selected her wardrobe for the day. This meant a freshly washed pair of jeans and one of her best blouses. She slipped on her new winter boots for the first time, letting out a sigh of relief when the fit proved perfect. Her plan was to prepare breakfast for her father and herself, then immediately commence with the job hunt. Her dad and Jody had no work lined up until the following week, leaving Broderick to putter around the house the remainder of the day. Sheba refused the final offer of a ride while clearing the breakfast dishes and by eight thirty was on the road in search of gainful employment.

The nearest prospective employer on her methodically prepared list was the Maine Diner. Following an invigorating forty five minute walk she reached the restaurant's front door. The tiny diner sat on the ocean side of Route 1 but a good mile from the Atlantic. She walked into the building. The café consisted of a long counter supplemented by a short series of booths along the windows. A swinging door immediately in front of her led out to the kitchen. Sheba strode to the register and waited to be approached while two waitresses flitted between the booths and counter, refilling coffee cups and bantering with customers. Eventually, the older of the two waitresses, a tall, strikingly attractive woman in her mid to late thirties, walked in her direction and addressed her.

"If it's just you honey then why not just take a stool somewhere away from the draft from the door." The woman motioned with the same hand that held a coffee carafe.

"No, I'm not here for breakfast. I'd like to apply for a job."

"And you'd want to speak to the *man* who owns the place."

"If it wouldn't be too much trouble."

"You certainly don't want to waste your time speaking with the

35

lowly, female help."

"No, I didn't say that. Don't go and put words in my mouth."

"Well, right now I'm the only one you can speak to. What are your qualifications, if I'm not being too bold to ask?"

"I learn fast and I'm not afraid to work," replied Sheba.

"Oh, you aren't. Well, if you don't mind, why don't we let me be the judge of that." The woman beckoned to her and they moved behind the counter to the heavy swinging door. Pushing it open, the two were confronted with a room scattered with dirty utensils, and a back sink piled high with unwashed pots, pans, dishes, trays and assorted other items that Sheba could not even attach a name to.

"Our combination busboy and dishwasher quit on us Christmas eve. And a merry Christmas to you Linda Lee. That means a lot of this mess has been sitting here since Wednesday night."

"Does this mean I'm hired?"

"Let's say it's the start of your trial period."

"And when do I find out if I'm hired or not?"

"Now you do know you can't expect to start out with one of the glamorous jobs like mine. You do know that, right?

The woman blew back a strand of hair from over one eye and smiled for the first time. The two females turned and walked back to the main room and the diner's customers. Sheba noticed the heads of more than one male turn as they re-entered the room.

"I get it! I get it! The pans and dishes are mine—and if I pay my dues out back—slaving away—some day, some wonderful day in the distant future, I too, will ascend to waitress."

The woman stared at Sheba for a moment, seeming to be sizing her up, then spoke. "Oh, and in case you have to actually hear it, you're hired. There it is, straight from the owner's mouth. From now on it's yes Linda Lee, and no Linda Lee, and you don't look a day over twenty-five Linda Lee. And remember, it's not Linda—or Lynn—or Ms. Tuttle, it's Linda Lee." The tall, blond woman's voice carried across the room, drawing hoots from two or three male patrons.

"Well Linda Lee, my name is Sheba—not Sheena—or Sheila—or Ms. Smith, it's Sheba." The teenager extended her hand to her new boss. Sheba already felt an emotional bond forming with this woman who, ten minutes earlier, was a complete stranger to her.

Following her 'open to the public' hiring on the floor of the restaurant, Sheba disappeared behind the swinging door. She was not heard from for the rest of the morning, her only contact with the outside world coming when she quizzed the short-order cook, Ernie

Nason, on the operation of the dishwashing equipment. Linda Lee glanced in on her from time to time but did not disturb her progress as she attacked her mountain of work. It was nearly two o'clock when her boss retreated to the back wall of the building and joined Sheba as she finished up the last of the stockpile of dirty pots.

"Have you taken your lunch yet, Sheba?"

"No lunch, no break, no rest boss lady."

"I think we've found a real jewel here Ernie," called out Linda Lee, her arm wrapped around her newest employee. "Tell Ernie what you want for lunch and we'll deduct it from your profit-sharing check next year."

"Cheeseburger and fries," she answered.

"Come on Sheba, live a little."

"Cheeseburger and fries—and a vanilla frappe."

"You heard her, Ernie—and I'll handle the frappe out front."

While waiting on her lunch, the teenager had an assortment of employment forms thrust upon her. She sped through the paperwork and actually had the bulk of it completed before her burger arrived.

"Sweet sixteen and a day," commented Linda Lee as she reviewed the application. "Jesus, I wonder how many employment laws I've already broken today? Well, screw 'em if they can't take a joke."

Later in the afternoon, Sheba had her schedule worked out for the rest of the Christmas vacation and into the winter months. Her work was limited to weekends, except during school vacations. She volunteered to work long hours over the upcoming weekend while Linda Lee searched for a full-time dishwasher and busboy. Later that evening, it was a tired but elated sixteen-year-old who burst through the front door and informed her father of her new job and the financial assistance he could expect from her over the coming months.

6

December 28, 1969

IT WAS LATE SUNDAY AFTERNOON and Sheba was in the midst of riding out a tiring weekend when she was called out front to assist with
waitress duties. It was the restaurant's policy not to seat customers
after six-thirty on Sunday nights, and after already toiling over a hot
sink for six hours, it was a policy she enthusiastically embraced.
Arriving out front, she was assigned to service the booths. To date, her
work had been limited to the back room and, for short periods, assist-
ing Ernie at the grill. Just before five o'clock a jovial fellow rushed
through the door, immediately calling out to Linda Lee. Busy at the
end of the counter, she waved him off. Sheba was quick to approach
the man, presenting to him a menu and asking him if he wanted coffee or any other beverage. He expressed a desire for coffee just as Linda
Lee arrived at the booth, resting her arm on his shoulder.

"Sheba, this is Irv Rosen, one of our semi-regulars and a threat to
the chastity and virtue of everyone on our staff, except maybe Ernie."

"Don't listen to her, young lady. If I'm such a threat like she says,
how come I can't get so much as to first base with this one—and God
knows I've tried," confessed the man. Rosen was a slightly overweight
gentleman, approximately fifty years of age, with a bright, outgoing
personality.

"I've told you, Irv, I like my men young—very, very young. I don't
have the time or the patience to work with fellows of the middle-age
variety. The boys keep me young, and that's the way I like it. But, tell
you what, if the day ever comes and I feel like I'm slowing down—
really slowing down, to a crawl, I promise, you're the first old buck I'll
come looking for. Fair enough?" The woman affectionately ran her
hand over his shoulder before circling behind the counter. "Where
you been lately, anyway? It has to have been at least a week since you've
been in."

"California—remember I was telling you how I'd been cornered into visiting my sister out there?"

"That's right! And you not liking to fly and all. How did that work out?"

"That's a story in itself. Got a minute?"

The tall blonde gestured yes as she made her way across the room to make a fresh pot of coffee.

"Well, it's a little over a week ago that I go down to Logan for the flight out to Los Angeles. Already on the way down I have a knot in my stomach, you know, the nervous knot you get. So I'm sitting there in the waiting area trying to get myself relaxed when I see Rabbi Silverman standing around, and I notice he's with his daughter. A couple of minutes pass and then I can clearly see he's there to send her off and she's going to be on my flight. That's when my nervous stomach begins to show some improvement. So I'm thinking, you know, the rabbi has probably said a prayer or two for his daughter's safe flight. Yeah—I'm feeling quite a bit better about my seven-hour flight. But it gets better. No more than a minute later I look up and in walks three nuns—three, mind you—and based on where they check in and seat themselves, it becomes evident that they're on my flight too. So, here I am, sharing a flight with the rabbi's daughter and three brides of Jesus! I think to myself; am I covered, or am I covered? Every ounce of nervousness inside of me is gone and, I swear, I grow a pair of brass balls! Now I'm sitting there cursing myself for buying flight insurance. Hell, I figure the Russians can send a squadron of MIGs after our plane and they couldn't bring it down—not with a rabbi's daughter and three nuns on board. In short, the flight was a walk in the park. I actually enjoyed it."

"So Irv, does this mean you're finally over your ridiculous fear of flying?" asked Linda Lee.

"I wish. On the way home—no nuns, no rabbi's daughter—we hit turbulence over the Rockies and I'm shitting bullets the rest of the way."

The story brought a round of laughs from the surrounding customers while Sheba brought the man his coffee. Amid a chorus of social banter, Linda Lee gestured her young employee toward one of her assigned booths where two men dressed in suits had taken seats. While Irv Rosen continued to hold court at his booth, Sheba poured two glasses of ice water and made her way toward the men. Halfway across the floor she recognized one of the gentlemen. It was Attorney Bradford Blackburn, father of Felicia Blackburn. The lawyer sat with a blank expression, staring at the other man whose face was buried in the menu.

"I can't believe you've dragged me into this place considering we're only a few miles from the upper village," chided Blackburn.

"Lighten up, Brad, I'm just in the mood for a burger and some fries. Hey, it was your idea to schedule that damn meeting on a Sunday—and I was forced to sit through two and a half hours of oral diarrhea. Now it's your turn to humor me." The lawyer shook his head in disgust, holding back a response.

"Would you like me to run down our specials?" Sheba asked, in her best, sweet and innocent voice.

"Spare us," sniped Blackburn without raising his eyes from the table.

"For God's sake, Brad, live a little!"

"I'm discriminating about what I eat," the attorney answered, still making no eye contact with his waitress.

"Are you saying you're too good to eat anything we serve here?" Sheba came back. The question and tone from the teenager took the lawyer by surprise, causing him to glance up and make eye contact with his waitress for the first time.

"Cheeseburger and fries, with a side of brown gravy to dunk my fries in," called out the gentleman.

Meanwhile, Attorney Bradford Blackburn and Sheba Smith were locked in a prolonged period of eye contact, neither willing to look away.

"Brad—relax," injected the other man, causing the lawyer to drop his eyes.

"Water only for me—and I think we know what size gratuity is in store for our insolent waitress."

Sheba smiled down sweetly at the attorney's companion, collected the menus, and walked away from the booth. The sixteen-year-old visited them several times over the course of the meal and made a point to be gracious to the lawyer's associate while ignoring him completely. Before the two men departed, Blackburn approached Linda Lee and conveyed a message. She listened politely. Halfway through his lecture, the man looked back at Sheba as if to underscore his opinion. After speaking his piece, the lawyer stood by and heard Linda Lee's response. Following it, Blackburn glanced back at Sheba a final time and disappeared out the door.

It was seven thirty when Linda Lee, Ernie, and Sheba began flicking out the lights and preparing to head home. Her two employees stood by as the woman locked the front door.

"Where's your ride, Sheba?" asked her boss while looking about the parking lot.

"Oh, I just hoof it home at night. I don't have a ride."

"You live that close?"

"Kind of—Burnt Mill Road."

"What! You can't walk all the way up there in the dark! Are you crazy?"

"I've been doing it all week. It's no big deal."

"You'll be riding with me tonight, okay?" She did not wait for a reply to her question. She waived goodnight to her cook and ushered the teenager to the car. Hopping inside, they both let out with an audible shiver as they slid into the front seat and onto the cold upholstery.

"So, let me get this straight. You're telling me you walked home the last couple of nights in the freezing cold—and all alone—in the dark!"

"That's right. It isn't that dark in the winter with the snow on the ground and the moon shining off of it."

"Why didn't your father come and get you?"

"I didn't ask him—and—our family car isn't supposed to be on the road and he knows I don't like driving in it in that condition."

The attractive blonde looked across at her passenger. Sheba thought she detected a trace of admiration in her eyes.

"You know, I didn't know you were Broderick's daughter till this morning when I looked over your job application more closely."

"You know my father?"

"Just well enough to say hello. The truth is—I knew your mother growing up. We were in school together. Your dad was a grade or two ahead of us. Your mother and I were never friends or anything, but I was in school with her from first grade right through high school."

Sheba's eyes grew wide, learning of Linda Lee's common experience with her mother.

"When I try to remember Mama, it's almost like her face and my memories are in a dark room. Everything seems to be growing more and more blurry and vague as I get older. The truth is, I can barely picture her face anymore without staring at a picture."

"Your mother was very, very pretty—and very feminine. She was delicate—sort of like Audrey Hepburn. Not that she looked like Audrey, but she was what I call delicate like her. A lot of the boys in school really had a thing for your mother."

Sheba directed the woman up Burnt Mill Road, over the railroad tracks, and before long onto the driveway in front of the house.

"I'm afraid this is where I live."

"I don't want to hear anything like that out of you, young lady. Never apologize for who you are or where you come from," the woman scolded.

"Would you like to come in and say hello to Daddy? You wouldn't know it from the road, but I keep the house pretty clean."

"There you go again, talking yourself and your house down."

"I'm sorry, Linda Lee, but would you?" Already in the girl's mind, she imagined a connection between her father and this attractive, composed woman who happened to be her mother's age.

"Another time, maybe. I've got a kitty at home who is probably pacing the floor as we speak, wondering where his mommy is. But, there is something I wanted to leave you with. I got an earful from the delightful Attorney Blackburn—yes, he made a point of letting me know he's a lawyer, like I give a flying 'f'. Sheba, you do know you don't talk to customers that way, right?"

"I know," she replied, her head shifting downward from embarrassment. "What did you tell him?"

"I told him I put a lot more stock in what paying customers tell me than non-paying ones. Then I asked him if he found his ice water satisfactory."

Sheba broke out laughing, slamming the car door shut. She gave her boss a wave before following one of the driveway ruts to the house. Pushing open the door, she called out to her father. She heard him respond from the kitchen and walked toward his voice. Reaching him, it only took a moment to see he was troubled. He sat at the table with his hands around a coffee cup. When Sheba's concern registered on her face, her father rose from his chair, crossed the room, and embraced his daughter.

"I received a call late this afternoon from Mrs. Bibber. She called to tell me she found your grandmother—your grandmother apparently died in her sleep overnight and Mrs. Bibber happened in on her this afternoon. I'm sorry, sweetheart."

The teenager burst into tears as her father squeezed her tightly. She let out a long wail, a sound that sent a chill through the man. Following a prolonged embrace, she broke away from him and ran up the stairs in tears. Sheba did not leave her room for the rest of the night.

7

March 28, 1970

THREE MONTHS HAD PASSED since the passing of her grandmother, but her words from their last Christmas together continued to haunt Sheba. The old woman's story of their Indian ancestry and the existence of a sacred rock hidden in the forest stayed with her. From day one, Sheba had discounted her grandmother's story, but she was now troubled by the coincidental death of her elderly grandparent, an event prophesized by the woman in her account of their blood link to a holy man with great, mystical powers. For this reason, and to put the matter to rest in her own mind, Sheba asked for and received a Saturday off from work. Instead of going to the diner this day, she would venture over to Kennebunkport and follow the road as her grandmother directed. It was late March and the woods were largely free from deep snow. To satisfy the gnawing question, she would scour the woods in an attempt to find the holy rock, the rock where one of her ancestors supposedly not only spoke to the Great Spirit—but carried on direct, two-way communication with Him. If she could not locate this holy place from the directions given to her, it would go a long way toward ridding herself of the insane notion of somehow traveling back in time and going to the aid of her mother. The area around Cozy Corner in Wells was going through a thorough facelift at this time, and it was there Sheba caught a lift from an elderly gentleman who brought her eastward on Route 9. As luck would have it, the man drove her as far as Four Corners, the very intersection where she had been robbed of her happy childhood nearly a decade before. She piled out of the vehicle and stood by the edge of the roadway as the man's car turned onto Sea Road and drove out of sight. Standing alone and still for the next minute, she relived the most terrible moment of her life. *"Someone send for an ambulance—to Four Corners—there's been an accident! There's three people trapped inside a*

43

car—hurry!! Jesus, hurry!" With a sense of melancholy taking possession of her, Sheba crossed the road and continued, on foot, toward
Kennebunkport.

On this particular morning, Sheba would not be blessed with
another good Samaritan, meaning it would be almost an hour before
the sixteen-year-old would cross the bridge over the Kennebunk River
and arrive in Dock Square, the hub of Kennebunkport. Once in the
square, she decided to stop and rest for a few minutes before heading
out toward the open ocean. She had five dollars in her pocket, emergency spending money, and a paper bag containing a couple of egg
salad sandwiches wrapped in wax paper. She was not hungry at the
moment, but the morning walk had brought on a powerful thirst. She
ducked inside Smith's Market, no relation, where a number of middle-
aged and elderly men stood, exchanging guarded comments and one-
liners. They fell silent when she cleared the front door. The girl
grabbed a Royal Crown Cola, paid for it, and was out of the store in
under a minute. It only took the sound of the door banging shut
behind her to cue the men back to their storytelling. Sheba rested and
drank her soda a few feet away at a stone fountain in the center of the
square, watching the townspeople come and go while a few cast a sus-
picious eye toward the unfamiliar girl in their midst.

The road on her route toward the open ocean ran parallel to the
river. As she walked, Sheba's thoughts were swirling around her social
situation at school and not with the details of her grandmother's stories from Christmas. Since her skirmish with Felicia Blackburn on the
day before Christmas vacation, there had been an eerie truce between
the two young women but no open hostilities. Sheba had no problem
with things the way they were, limited to icy glares and chilly silences.
Since landing her job at the Maine Diner, she had acquired a few adult
friends. The best of these new friends was Linda Lee Tuttle, her
employer. At home, finances were still tight. The girl was now handing over three-quarters of her pay to her father to help with expenses
but, to date, she had not observed any real improvement in their living conditions.

The walk from Dock Square to the open Atlantic Ocean was a
pleasant one, even at this time of year. As the sea grew closer, the
sound of the crashing surf became more and more audible. Whitecaps
were visible atop the choppy sea just a hundred yards in front of her
when she walked in the shadow of the Grande Manse, a huge white
hotel sitting on a ridge above the ocean. Sheba stopped and peered up
at the magnificent building, the remnant of another era. She laughed

at herself, thinking she must look like a tourist as she stared hypnotically up at the structure. The stately building sat quiet and asleep this time of year. In two months, wealthy, out-of-state vacationers would flock here, when the weather was less harsh. Maine was not the destination of choice for these people in March, it was only for the struggling locals like herself. She, and people like her, would most likely never set foot inside the grand, old building, unless it was to make the beds or serve some uppity bluebloods their morning orange juice or sliced half grapefruit. Sheba imagined the people who frequented this place to be similar to Felicia Blackburn's father, too good to even look at a common waitress like herself. No, thought Sheba, if she was to visit the Grande Manse she would prefer to do so at a time like the present, when the hallways and rooms were void of people. Then, she would be free to wander the building at her leisure and, perhaps, hear the faint echoes left by visitors long since gone.

Sheba had reached the ocean and begun the walk northward by blowing cave and toward Walker's Point. Her grandmother's directions said to walk this way until the road pulled away from the sea. If her memory served her, that would be just beyond Walkers Point. She stepped farther off the side of the road after a car with Massachusetts plates roared by, missing her by only a few feet. She thought she heard the sound of laughter from inside the car.

It was turning into a nice day for her expedition. The temperature was moderate under a mostly sunny sky. After picking up her stride she was rewarded with the sight of the Herbert Walker house as it came into view. In the distance before her, she saw the point in the road where it turned away from the ocean. Replaying her grandmother's words in her head, she remembered the instructions: walk for about a quarter of a mile and enter the woods from the left side of the road. The holy rock, if it existed, would not be more than a hundred yards from the roadway.

When Sheba reached the section of the road where it veered away from the open ocean, she tried to visualize the quarter-mile distance as instructed. She remembered there were seventeen hundred and sixty yards in a mile. With that in mind, if she walked the approximate distance of four football fields, she would be near the closest point in the road to the sacred boulder. She had walked over the length of one football field when the car with Massachusetts plates approached her from the other direction. It slowed to a stop as a teenage boy rolled down the window.

"Hey, honey, care to join us for a ride?" asked a blond boy in a sickeningly sweet voice. He shared the car with two other youths.

"Maybe in your next lifetime," called back Sheba, continuing to walk.

"Where are you going?" asked the driver. Sheba stopped in her tracks and whirled around.

"I'll put this in words even you'll understand, okay? That house just up the road is where my four brothers and I live—and any one of them could kick the crap out of the sorry excuses for manhood inside that Ford of yours. So unless you want me to make a dash for the house and call them out, I'd back off."

"Oh, I'm shaking with fear," crowed the driver sarcastically. "Like we're afraid of a bunch of Maine hicks."

"So you'll stay right here till I go to the house and get them?"

"You're not worth it, you little sweathog," called out the boy before spinning his tires and roaring off.

Sheba walked another five minutes following her encounter with the boys before stopping by a group of fallen trees near the road. The confrontation with the punks had thrown her timing off in attempting to gauge where to enter the woodlands. Ahead of her was a tree stump just off the pavement. She walked to the stump and decided to enter the woods here. The nearest house was more than two hundred feet away, allowing her concealed access to the woods. The land in front of her sloped down, then inclined upward. Thick trees afforded Sheba protection from the road after only a dozen steps. She could hear the sound of the ocean at her back in the distance. The thought of getting lost in this woodland had already entered her mind, but she rationalized that she could follow the sound of the surf and find her way out in the event she got lost. For the next ninety minutes Sheba walked what she thought was parallel to the road, scouring the landscape, searching for the sight of an imposing rock. For the next hour and a half she would not set sight on any rock or boulder that even remotely fit the description of the sacred rock. She was beginning to entertain thoughts of abandoning the expedition when she observed a dark, shadowy section of forest ahead of her. She walked toward the formless patch of darkness, unable to distinguish the outline of any specific object. Finally, with the distance to the obscurity shortened to ten yards, it took shape. Before her stood a huge, gray boulder, rimmed by an uneven patch of pine and birch trees. The rock had a sheer face that rose to nearly fifteen feet.

Only the faintest sound of wind was heard through the treetops as Sheba deliberately walked around the boulder. The trunks of two fallen trees, one snapped into two pieces, draped over the enormous rock. It appeared to be three-sided with all sides nearly equal, forming an almost perfect triangle. Continuing to circle the boulder, she noticed that the height on the far side was lower, perhaps around ten feet. A crack also ran top to bottom on this, the lowest face of the rock. She could already see it was this far side that afforded her the easiest means to the top. There was a flutter of excitement within her. Her first order of business was to push the bough of the broken birch from the rock. She did this with relative ease. It crashed to the ground, breaking the near silence around her. The remaining piece of the white birch broke off and balanced above her head on top of the boulder. The second tree, a larger pine, leaned square against the glacial stone. Sheba was unable to even budge the tree despite several attempts. Circling around the rock, she initiated her ascent on the lowest side, placing her hands and feet in the perpendicular crack running from bottom to top. Following one unsuccessful attempt, the girl pulled herself upward, finally lifting her body onto the surface with a shout of triumph. Without a moment's hesitation, she assaulted the pine tree that leaned against one side of the great stone. Her height from the top of the boulder provided the leverage she needed and within seconds the pine tree was sent crashing down to the forest floor below her. She immediately lifted the last piece of the birch tree and tossed it down to the ground.

With the major portion of the cleanup behind her, Sheba walked to the edge of the boulder's point and sat, letting her legs dangle beneath her. She had managed to block most of the ongoing worries and concerns from her mind on this day, aided by the excitement of this incredible search. However, at this moment, the exhilaration of her find was being pushed from the forefront of her thoughts. Over the past few weeks her father's drinking had increased. Work was sparse right now, causing the Smiths to rely more on Sheba's part-time wages and tips. She was also concerned about a Father and Daughter Dance coming up at school. She had picked up on signs of the rift between her and Felicia Blackburn flaring up again, her concerns more intuitive than based on anything concrete. If this were not enough, there was a new problem waiting in the wings for her. Sheba had inherited the house in Wells upon the death of her grandmother. For the last half-dozen years, her grandmother had let the Smiths live there, for the most part, rent-free. Now, with ownership of the house came the responsibility for the payment of real estate taxes. Dorothy Lake's Kennebunkport house had been mortgaged to the hilt and was now the property of the bank. But she had managed to will her grand-daughter the dilapidated Wells house. Leaning backward, Sheba rest-ed the back of her head on the rock. She looked up at the white clouds racing across the sky, framed by the tops of the trees surrounding her. The moment and the location were too beautiful to allow her every-day concerns to weigh her down, she thought. She drove the unpleas-ant thoughts from her mind and concentrated on the rushing clouds far above her and the sound of the wind streaming around her.

In time, her grandmother's words came back to her and, once again, Sheba considered the enormity of their content. The unbeliev-able stories, accounts and predictions from that Christmas Eve, as incredible as they seemed at the time, continued to unfold before her as promised. She glanced around at the surface of the great boulder, the edges inclined toward the center, like the cupping of two hands, and intuitively knew she had found it. This was Mowalk's holy place.

8

May 8, 1970

SHEBA ARRIVED AT THE DINER on Friday in a bad state of mind. She sped by her fellow employees and the handful of customers in silence, proceeding to the back room and the mountain of dishes awaiting her. Linda Lee was out, using the slow midafternoon period to run personal errands and make a bank deposit. The staff picked up on the girl's sour mood and left her alone back at her work station. She had already made considerable progress on the dishes and silverware when Linda Lee paid her a visit at the sink.

"Someone's certainly keeping to themselves today," she observed, breaking the silence.

"It's been a really, really bad day."

"Well, I'm not someone to drag an employee from their work, but if you'd like a pair of interested ears, I'm here."

"It's Felicia Blackburn—who else?"

"Okay, let's have it."

Sheba leaned back against the sink, continuing to dry a dish she balanced in her hand. "After lunch when we got back to class, but before Miss Maitland showed up, Felicia went up to the front of the room and sat on Miss Maitland's desk, like she owned the school. She had this envelope in her hand and her friends signaled for everyone to be quiet. Everyone does, of course, cause it's Felicia Blackburn—don't you know. So she puts the envelope up to her head, like Johnny Carson does when he's doing the magician guy, and closes her eyes and pretends she's psychic. She says, 'And the answer is—*his next one*' and opens the envelope and blows inside like Carson does. All the boys in class are eating this up cause she's got her legs hanging down the front of the desk and she's wearing her usual short skirt. Then she takes the paper out. 'And the question is—*What is Broderick Smith's favorite alcoholic beverage?*' Well, a lot of people start laughing, especially the

49

boys. Some of the girls tell her to shut up and I jump up from my seat and go after her. One of the boys, Ronnie Reno, jumps in my way and stops me." Sheba paused as tears began to form in her eyes.

"She's quite the little bitch, isn't she?" observed Linda Lee, concern and sympathy showing on her face.

"Oh, she's a bitch, all right. But I'm the one who got the two-day suspension."

"You? For what?!"

"Miss Maitland came in just after Ronnie kept me from blackening the little bitch's eyes. And everyone just goes back and sits down. As you can imagine, I'm fuming 'cause I don't let no one talk about Daddy that way. Class starts and maybe goes for about fifteen minutes before an ambulance flies by the school with its siren blaring, and I see my chance. So I stand up in the middle of the class and say, 'Hey, Felicia, there goes the ambulance, so we should be seeing your ambulance-chasing, thief of a father pile-driving by any second now.' Felicia jumps up from her desk screaming and Miss Maitland calls me on the carpet. She ordered me to go down to the principal's office, and on the way out, well—"

"Jesus, Sheba, you weren't done?"

"On the way out the door I told the class that Felicia's old man wasn't just a crook, he was a cheap bastard who didn't even tip waitresses." Linda Lee's hand was up to her open mouth, dumbfounded by her young employee's story. "And that was the straw that broke the camel's back. Miss Maitland tossed my ass out then, for sure."

Linda Lee was careful to keep Sheba from waitressing duties on this particular afternoon and evening. The girl was clearly still charged up from her confrontation at school and the owner reasoned there was no point in putting anyone else in harm's way. At nine-fifteen, the two friends left Ernie to lock up and drove away toward Sheba's house.

"I'm really starting to get nervous about next week," announced the girl.

"And what's next week again?"

"Next Friday there's a Father-Daughter Dance at school."

"Nervous? That should be a lot of fun!" Sheba did not respond.

The drive to the Smith residence along dark, unlit roads was now a familiar chore for Linda Lee. It took only a few minutes to pick up on Sheba's need to talk. She restrained herself from initiating any idle chatter, attempting to get her young friend to open up. The strategy worked.

"I'm really getting uptight about that dance," confided the teenager.

"What about?"

"Well, I want to look pretty and a little more feminine, that's all. I just wish I was a little better at it."

It was impossible not to recognize the girl's poorly camouflaged cry for help.

"I'm not going to pretend I'm some sort of fashion expert or anything, but if you want, I'll help you in any way I can." Sheba's eyes brightened and she reached across the front seat, touching her boss lightly on the shoulder. "How does this sound? If it's okay with your dad, you could stay with me next Thursday night. I'll plan to get out early and we'll make a night of it at my house." The suggestion seemed to lift Sheba's spirits. "It'll be fun," added the woman, glancing over at her passenger. "I've got a few ideas about what we could do with your makeup and hair. Bring over what you want to wear and we'll work around that."

"I don't have much in the closet to choose from. But I've saved some money and I can find something better between now and then."

"No, no, save your money. I've got twenty things at home that I've hardly worn and that'll fit you. That's the good thing about having kept my girlish figure," she added with a laugh.

"You've taken a lot of pressure off me, Linda Lee—thank you."

The car turned quiet for a few seconds before Sheba spoke again. "I need to ask you about something—but before I do I want you to know that I won't be mad if you say no—and you don't have to give me an answer right now. See, my dad's been drinking really bad— worse than usual, anyway—and he's been getting sick a lot, not that he'll see a doctor. What I need to know is, if something happened to Daddy and I was left on my own, would you let me move in with you? I'd work for nothing for you at the diner, and I'd move out as soon as I graduated. I wouldn't be any bother. I'd be real quiet—and when guys came to visit you, they wouldn't even know I was there."

"Wow! You make me into quite the Mae West, don't you?" responded Linda Lee before breaking into a roar of laughter at the girl's declarations. "Hey," she continued more gently, "I'm sure your father's going to be just fine. But you might talk to him—tell him his heavy drinking is scaring you."

Sheba nodded her head. The vehicle turned into the Smith's driveway and she hurried to get out of the car.

"Thanks again, Linda Lee, for the ride."

"And in the highly unlikely event that something did happen to your father—and I stress highly unlikely—then you may come to live with me for as long as you want. Is that clear enough for you, young lady?"

The teenager flashed her friend a wide grin, then waved good-bye and darted for the house.

9

May 15, 1970

SHEBA STOOD BEFORE THE MIRROR in her room. In front of her was the image of a stranger who was every inch a young lady. The sixteen-year-old stared in disbelief at the sophisticated and beautiful creature before her. The night before she had been the guest of Linda Lee, as planned. The woman had performed a makeover on her young employee that had produced a desirable young woman. With her brown hair washed, conditioned and curled to set off her feminine, catlike features, her eyebrows plucked, her face made up, Sheba suddenly realized she was in fact a pretty girl. Draped in a form-fitting black dress that Linda Lee said was the second favorite of her entire wardrobe, Sheba felt an incredible confidence in her appearance. A pair of black, two-inch heels completed the transformation, giving her solidly athletic legs definition in the calves and ankles, and the additional height to stand out in the company of any female. Tucked away in her bedroom, she took in this foreign image of herself for over half an hour until the still in the house was broken when her father and Jody Pease's voices exploded on the floor below.

"You home, sweetheart?" hollered Broderick from the kitchen.

"In my room, Daddy," she called back.

"Come on down, Sheba, got some good news."

The girl looked in the mirror, considered a quick change back into jeans, then dismissed the notion. She descended the stairs and stepped into the kitchen. Broderick's back was to the doorway as he pulled out two cold beers from the refrigerator.

"Honey, Jody's gone and gotten us a signed contract…" The man stopped in midsentence as his eyes beheld his daughter from across the room. "Sweet Jesus," he exhaled. "You look beautiful, Sheba! Don't she look beautiful, Jody?"

The teenager glanced over to Pease, whose eyes were trawling up and down her long frame, with only the most momentary pause on her face.

"She's a real doll, all right," added Pease.

"I wanted to look good for you, Daddy—at the dance."

"Oh, you will, sweetheart, you will. I just brought Jody over for a celebration beer. One beer and then I'll start getting ready for the dance. Damn! This is turning into a good day! You see, Sheba, less than an hour ago, me and Jody got a signed agreement to put an addition on a house over at Cape Porpoise—a summer resident and no skimping on anything—five to six weeks of work, minimum. Jody's been working on this guy for almost a year. We'll finally have some money comin' into the house." Her father's exuberation appeared to be fueled by a combination of joy and relief. "They'll be cutting us our first check Monday and I want you to take a few weeks off from putting anything into the house. Okay?" Sheba nodded yes. "Listen, kid, if you'll stay here and entertain my brilliant partner, I want to run upstairs and check something out."

Before Sheba could find an excuse to leave the room, Broderick bounded up the stairs. There was a short, uncomfortable silence in the kitchen as the two heard the man crossing overhead to the far side of the house.

"God, you don't look like a sixteen-year-old high school kid in that dress, that's for sure." Jody's eyes continued to pour over her frame, forcing the girl to look away from him.

"Congratulations on finding the work, Jody. It comes at a good time for us." Sheba's attempt at civil conversation drew no immediate response from Pease. He took a long swig from his bottle, never taking his eyes from her.

"Your daddy talks about you a lot. About how you have a talent for saving money. Is that true?" Sheba shrugged her shoulders. "I'm just throwin' something out there, right now—knowin' you're a smart girl and wouldn't take this the wrong way. Between now and July, your father and me, we'll have some decent money at our disposal. Now, I'm sayin', think of an amount of money you'd like to earn real easy—and let me know how much we're talkin' about. It'd be our secret and I swear I'd take it to the grave." His voice was low and barely audible.

"There is no amount, and what's more—you make me sick. Stay away from me, I'm warning you," she threatened, pointing a finger at him. Her threat was followed by the sound of creaking floorboards above, signaling Broderick's return. Father and daughter passed each other on the stairwell. Sheba flashed him a smile. There was nothing in her manner to tip him off to the anger and revulsion she harbored inside her.

The girl barricaded herself in the bedroom, allowing her father and Pease to enjoy the moment downstairs. Following a twenty-minute interlude of celebration and informal planning between the men, Sheba heard her father escort Pease to the front door. She could feel a nervous knot building in her stomach. She was not deceiving herself into believing that the dance did not carry the risk of an embarrassing confrontation or incident. Up until now, she had been able to hold her own with Felicia Blackburn and her crowd. However, tonight her father would be added to the mix and she did not want to see his feelings hurt by anything Felicia or her pompous father could throw at him. As the minutes passed, she felt the excitement and exuberance of her feminine transformation replaced with a foreboding anxiety about the affair. She descended the stairs after hearing Broderick milling around the kitchen. Arriving downstairs, she saw him slouched dejectedly at the table.

"What's the matter, Daddy?"

"I'd totally forgotten the state of affairs my suit was in last winter at that luncheon Mrs. Bibber had after your grandmother's funeral." The man stood up, displaying a worn, brown suit badly in need of a visit to the dry cleaner. In addition, his mismatched shirt and stained tie seemed a fitting, final blow to her spirits.

"God, I'd meant to have that suit cleaned and pressed right away after the funeral, but then other things came up and it just slipped my mind." Sheba walked slowly across the room to her father, unable to mask the horror she felt coming upon her. She examined his wardrobe at close range, her eyes widening as if beholding a ghost.

"Is there something else you could wear, Daddy? Anything!"

"Let me check again, honey." He raced upstairs to recheck his closet as Sheba slumped down onto a kitchen chair. The stress of the situation took hold of her as she waited for her father to return from upstairs. She began to consider and weigh her options, should her father be unable to come up with suitable clothing. The thought of Felicia Blackburn's response to her father's appearance at the dance caused a stabbing pain of nervous energy to shoot through her stomach. She hated herself. The thought of being seen socially with her father embarrassed her, and she hated herself for it. At best, Felicia would sprinkle conversations with catty, insulting barbs about the Smiths, father and daughter. Sheba saw the worst-case scenario containing a direct insult on her dad, probably from Felicia. She sat alone, the anxiety of the moment beginning to make her physically ill.

Following a ten-minute disappearance, Broderick rejoined Sheba in the kitchen. His body language spoke volumes. He had not found any suitable clothing for the dance. He fell into the chair beside her, and quickly picked up on his daughter's shattered mental state and disappointment.

"I am so sorry, sweetheart."

"It's not you, Daddy, it's me. It's just that there are people at school who I just can't face—not like this. Please forgive me, Daddy." Sheba fell forward and wept on the table. The man stroked his daughter's hair as she sobbed uncontrollably. He waited for her crying to let up before he spoke.

"You know, it's a shame to waste the evening, not with you looking like you do." He pushed himself away from the table and crossed the room. Seconds later, he was digging through a collection of bottles beneath the sink. When he returned to her side, he produced a twenty-dollar bill.

"This is supposed to be for food bill emergencies. But I don't suppose we'll be needing this too soon with the work Jody and I have lined up. What do you say we head up to Portland instead of going to the dance? We'll find a nice quiet restaurant for dinner, then we'll find somewhere there's some music—nice music, not rock 'n' roll. Let's see how far twenty bucks can take us."

Sheba looked up from the table to eye her father, a hopeful expression etched on his face. Taking a deep breath, she held up one index finger and ran for her bedroom. She galloped downstairs a few seconds later, waving her own twenty-dollar bill.

"I'll do you one better, Daddy. What do you say we head up to Portland and see how far *forty* bucks takes us?"

At seven o'clock, the Smiths climbed into the family car and began the trip to Portland. Broderick had changed into casual attire. However, Sheba remained in her black dress, hoping to turn a few heads in the city. They had barely reached Route 1 when the girl let out a whoop.

"You've got an inspection sticker!" she exclaimed excitedly.

Broderick flashed her a foolish grin.

"Not exactly." Sheba stared at her father, then back at the sticker. "Look closer—much closer. It's just a piece of construction paper cut in the exact design of Maine's inspection sticker—with the number ten on it on account of I was born in October. Now, unless a cop stops me and stares dead at the damn thing, I've got me an inspection sticker, 'cept it's a Broderick Smith inspection sticker.

"Daddy!"

10

June 19, 1970

SUMMER WAS APPROACHING. For Sheba, the end of the school year could not have come too soon. Two days earlier she had taken her last final exam and turned in her textbooks. For her, there were no summer send-off parties, while for most of her classmates the last day of school meant a party down at Wells Beach on the sand in front of the Casino. For Sheba, the end of the Wells High school year meant the expansion of her working hours at the Maine Diner. However, on this morning she was back on the roadside hitchhiking in the direction of Kennebunkport. This marked her fourth visit to the sacred rock, and for the first time she was lugging supplies. A kerosene lantern was the most important of the objects she would leave this day before her scheduled overnight stay the following night. She also carried along her baseball bat. There was a lingering question in her mind whether the night before or the night after the longest day was the exact time for the miracle, so she decided to stay both nights and eliminate any chance of error. Summer would arrive at two forty-three in the afternoon on June 21st, or so said the Old Farmer's Almanac. This did not mean she positively believed the tale told to her by her grandmother the previous winter. She still harbored great doubt in the story of Mowalk.

She completed the eight-mile trip from her house to Kennebunkport on the back of two rides and entered the forest shortly before eleven o'clock. The day was overcast, warm and humid, not the weather she she wanted for her overnight stay. This was mosquito weather. Sheba hoped for cool, clear and breezy weather, weather allowing her to bury herself in her sleeping bag and away from insects. Arriving at the giant boulder, she dropped most of her gear at its base and climbed to the top, an extension of rope draped over her back. The climb up was somewhat dangerous, requiring two hands to grip the cracks and crevices in the stone. A tumble backward meant landing on a number of protruding tree roots and certain injury. A single, small tree grew near the top edge of the boulder. Sheba tied one end of the rope to the bottom of the tree and tossed the rest to the ground. She planned to tie the bottom end of the rope to the objects below and pull them up individually, climbing up and down until everything was on the top surface of the rock. She worked feverishly and had all her supplies above on the rock in thirty minutes. The last two times she scaled the boulder, Sheba filled her pockets with stones large enough to throw at any would-be assailant.

With her belongings now all high above the forest floor and organized on the surface of the rock, Sheba began to seriously consider her circumstances. Whenever she had contemplated her grandmother's tale, and the quest she was now acting on, she was unable to feel anything but disbelief and skepticism. But here she was. The adventure she was about to embark upon was requiring effort and considerable energy. As she had done many times before, she questioned herself on the rationality of this adventure. In approximately a day and a half, she would face the woods alone, absolutely alone.

In spite of the calm air and humid conditions, the mosquitoes were not a problem at the moment. Her gear spread out, Sheba laid back on the rock and looked up at the mostly cloudy sky. She had, of course, lied to her father about her plans. She had told him she would spend the next two nights at Linda Lee's. At present, Broderick and Jody's project was running behind schedule and over budget. Their optimism on the total profit to be realized from the work at Cape Porpoise had diminished over the last two weeks. The men's frustration led to an increase in their beer consumption, and the financial windfall predicted by Broderick only weeks before had now been downgraded substantially.

Sheba shifted her thoughts back to the details of her adventure, afraid she might have missed something. She went so far as to spend two days after school in the library, memorizing important facts to have at her fingertips should the improbable happen and she was catapulted back in time. Reaching into her back pocket for her wallet, she removed a picture of her mother taken when she was fourteen years old. In the photograph, Elaine Lake sat on a swing in the front yard of her home. There was a sad expression on her face. As her grandmother had suggested, she would use this picture and a photo taken at the Wells Beach Casino to establish the time period to be sent back to. She took great consolation knowing that after this whole matter at the holy rock was behind her and she walked out of the woods, no one would ever know what she had done or what she had allowed herself to hope could happen. She remained atop the great boulder well past three o'clock this day. She was comfortable in this place, surrounded by evergreen and birch trees. As she descended the rock and prepared for the eight-mile trip back to her house in Wells, she wondered if she would be this comfortable in thirty hours, when the forest grew dark around her and she faced the wooded outdoors alone.

11

June 20, 1970

SHEBA ROSE EARLY Saturday morning. She volunteered to open this day, requiring her to arrive at the diner by six. She was standing at the end of her driveway at five thirty when Linda Lee pulled up. The two had formed a close relationship over the past six months, but Sheba could not share even a hint of the adventure she was about to undertake. Her stomach churned with excitement, fear, trepidation and wonderment. The planning, the dreaming, the questioning, and the overwhelming doubts surrounding this whole obsession, these were about to be faced and acted upon. Linda Lee noticed the small knapsack her young employee tossed on the floor of the car, but did not question it. Ernie, who arrived an hour earlier than the women, had the coffee brewed and the diner ready to face its first customer when the two drove into the parking lot.

It was still the early stage of tourist season, but that did not keep Sheba from working nonstop throughout the morning. Out front at the counter, the number-one topic of discussion this day was The Sandpiper, an Ogunquit food and drink establishment, that had recently shocked York County by putting a topless mermaid on their new sign. For this reason, male customers inundated Linda Lee with requests to meet the challenge and pose for a similar sign, larger and more daring. "Wells must meet Ogunquit's challenge!" was the united cry from the male customers.

By now, Sheba was an all-purpose employee, and Linda Lee moved her from the back sink to waiting tables on a moment's notice. Today, she was even pressed into service helping Ernie at the grill. However, when the clock over the counter reached two, Sheba abruptly passed on her tables to Sue Lashua, another teenage employee, and punched her timecard out for the day. After changing out of her uniform, she waved good-bye to Linda Lee from the door, and started to walk north on Route 1, her knapsack flung over her shoulder. Although she made no effort to hitchhike, within minutes a car slowed down and Irv Rosen, a customer she knew well from the diner, offered her a ride to Dock Square. The drive from Wells to Kennebunkport proved to be pleasant with the middle-aged man sharing stories about the diner and his long friendship with Linda Lee Tuttle. Crossing the bridge over the Kennebunk River, she looked up at the marquee of the Lyric Theatre, which proclaimed June 26th as opening day. Grabbing her knapsack, she thanked Irv for the ride and stepped inside Smith's Market, where she purchased two packages of cupcakes to go with her sandwiches. With this accomplished, Sheba decided to walk the rest of the way. The day was beautiful with temperatures in the low seventies, thanks to an ocean breeze. It was the precise weather she had prayed for over the past month.

Sheba retraced her route back to the boulder, the trip now second-nature to her. She entered the forest at three thirty, careful to do so with no cars in sight and, therefore, undetected. An ocean breeze carried the sound of crashing surf inland. Arriving at the rock, she climbed to the summit with her supplies on her back. Her knapsack contained sandwiches, the cupcakes bought earlier, a book, wooden matches, and a canteen filled with water. The rest of her supplies had been left on the boulder the previous day. She lay back on the rock's flat surface, extending her arms and looking up at the magnificent sky. The clouds raced across the blue sky as the wind whooshed through the leaves only a few feet over her head. On those occasions when the wind subsided, the roar from the ocean filled the air. Nature was alive around her and Sheba thanked God for the perfect afternoon He provided her. For the next hour, she simply allowed her senses to take in the natural surroundings, uninterrupted. Finally, she rolled over and removed the book from her knapsack. It was *On the Road* by Jack Kerouac. She had chosen the book specifically for this occasion. If her experience turned out to be something less than predicted by her grandmother, she would, at minimum, share in someone else's travel adventures.

On into the afternoon, Sheba allowed herself to be swept up by Kerouac's storytelling, interrupted by brief periods of sky gazing. It was shortly after five o'clock when a small patch of dark clouds passed overhead, sending droplets onto the boulder for no more than a minute or two. Sheba was quick to cover the wood she had hauled up from the forest floor below, not allowing it to become dampened by the light rain. It was more than an hour later, with shadows lengthening in the woods around her, that the full realization struck the girl. Her time was at hand. Now she began to prepare the campfire in earnest. The euphoria accompanying the afternoon, and early evening sunlight began to fade along with the brightly lit forest around her. The night approached with the same subtlety as the shifting tide. Barring the arrival of a warm front, Sheba knew she would be facing an unseasonably cool night. Already the air was developing a measure of crispness. She struck a match and lit her lantern. Light would be important over the next eight hours. Her six-month wait was over.

With the setting sun came changes in the sounds within the forest. While the wind above her in the trees and the distant, muffled roar of the sea remained constant, the now familiar sounds from the birds and insects were gradually replaced by another set of calls, sounds more ambiguous and sinister. With a modest fire burning nearby and the woods a solid wall of black around her, Sheba glanced down at her watch. It was after nine o'clock. To reassure herself, she went over important facts she would need to draw upon in the unlikely event the rock she rested on carried the powers her great-grandfather swore it did. Her mother, Elaine, lived in a small cape on Tatnic Road in Wells. If Sheba's power of concentration on the photograph of the young Elaine Lake held up, she would be sent back to 1943 or 1944. She pulled out the photograph of her mother seated on a swing and studied it at length, along with a photo taken at roughly the same time in front of the Wells Beach Casino.

By eleven, the sixteen-year-old was settled inside her sleeping bag and keeping vigil over the campfire. The modest flame possessed a hypnotic quality, grabbing and holding Sheba's attention. She tried to push the matter of her complete solitude from her mind but found it creeping back nonetheless. She bolstered her confidence by counting down the weapons at her disposal: a Louisville Slugger, a fishing knife from her father's tackle box, and a pile of fist-size stones. Besides, she thought, most people or animals would be hard-pressed just climbing up onto the peak of the great boulder. Next, her rational side began to undermine her fragile confidence in this undertaking. She asked herself what she was doing out alone in the forest. Did she really believe in this incredible story about a holy man from an obscure tribe of Indians? Out here, away from the distraction of her dreary, everyday existence, her logical mind took hold. This adventure was nothing more than a childhood fantasy, acted upon. From the forest floor below came the sound of moving brush, reaching her above the crackle of the fire. She slid from the sleeping bag and jumped to her feet.

Running to the pointed end of the great rock, she looked down and spied two sets of eyes, illuminated by the campfire, looking up at her. The darkened woods hid the outline of the animals.

"Get the frig out of here—now!" Sheba ordered. There was neither movement nor sound from below. She knew, above all, to show no fear, although her heart pumped heavily inside her chest.

"Beat it!" The beasts responded by inching closer. She moved swiftly to the edge of the boulder and picked up three stones. She made a throwing motion, causing the creatures to stir but not retreat.

"You asked for it," she called out, then fired her first stone intentionally over the heads of the critters below. The rock struck a tree behind the beasts, causing a cracking sound. Within seconds the eyes below disappeared and the sound of scurrying was heard, eventually fading away in the distance. The teenager spent the next few minutes walking the perimeter of the boulder, searching out any other potential visitors. Eventually, she returned to the warmth of her sleeping bag as her heartbeat returned to normal. In the following minutes Sheba decided there was no need to spend a second night on the rock. The isolation here had provided her with the clarity of thought her everyday surroundings could not give her. It was decided, she would return home tomorrow with a clear conscience, knowing she had followed her grandmother's directions. With her head resting on the cold surface of the boulder, Sheba wondered why her great grandfather had conjured up the tale of the sacred rock, Mowalk and the Quintanoks. For her part, she had seen and heard enough. There was nothing here. She walked the perimeter a final time, reassuring herself of her relative safety, then burrowed back inside the sleeping bag a final time.

12

A SHIVER RAN THE LENGTH of Sheba's body as she lay in the fetal position. A rush of cold air blew over the surface on the boulder, causing her to grasp for the edge of the sleeping bag. When her hand came up empty she opened her eyes to find herself lying naked atop the rock. She scrambled to a sitting position and found no sign of sleeping gear, clothing or supplies around her. It was early morning, probably just after sunrise, with the sunlight striking only the tops of the trees. In seconds, she became very aware of the cold surface of the rock against her bare skin. She scrambled to her feet. "I've survived the night," she thought. Her mind raced out of control, unable to grasp her circumstances. Walking to the edge of the great rock, she peered down to the ground, trying to find her clothes, or sleeping bag, or supplies. Her body trembled violently from the cold air. Sheba folded her arms over her breasts and walked in place, hoping to create some warmth. Nothing made sense—none of this! She considered whether she might still be sleeping. She rubbed her hands along her cold skin, hoping to eradicate the cold through friction. The girl thought she saw a change in the forest around her, different from just eight hours earlier. She detected a change in color on some of the trees, particularly the birches. She paced the top of the rock, waiting for her rational side to produce an explanation for her circumstances. Only hours earlier, in the darkened woods, her rational side triumphed over the notion of anything like a sacred place, ending all debate on the validity of her grandmother's claim. It could not exist. Now, naked and shivering, the clear thinking from hours before seemed as lost and misplaced as her clothing.

Crossing to the back of the boulder, the girl began her descent to the forest floor. The crags in the rock pinched the bottoms of her feet as she cautiously maneuvered downward. Finally, she jumped onto the soft earth below and started toward the roadway. She moved cautiously toward the road, her eyes darting back and forth, fearing someone might happen upon her. She found herself actually considering the legitimacy of her grandmother's incredible story. Reaching the road, she stopped a few yards from the edge of the vegetation and waited. She remained in place for over five minutes, her arms wrapped around herself, until a vehicle approached. Her eyes widened in disbelief as a black Packard sedan roared by and disappeared around a bend in the road. Her nudity, the coloration on the leaves in the trees, the Packard, it all added up to one thing: The fantasy she had nurtured for nearly six months, that her rational self had downplayed in the face of mounting evidence to the contrary, was in the here and now. It was true. She had somehow tumbled back in time where her surroundings were shadows of the past, a parallel reality. It had been nearly a hundred years since her great-grandfather had journeyed back, acting on his birthright. By his own account, he merely explored the past. Now, his great-granddaughter would be the first female to go back. But, unlike him, she had plotted a specific course with absolute objectives. She hoped the calendar would give her sufficient time to accomplish her goals. Sheba turned and retreated back into the forest.

Following a fifteen-minute rest back at the holy rock where she collected her thoughts and planned a strategy, Sheba walked back toward the roadway. Her plan was to remain in the woods, out of sight, and walk parallel to the road. She had studied maps in the six months since Christmas and knew the shortest distance to town was overland, but she trusted neither her hiking skills nor instincts. Therefore, she would take the safest route and follow the line of the coast. She remembered her great-grandfather's account of his journey and how he had taken clothing from wash hung out to dry. She would do the same, if possible, or break into a summer home if necessary. She estimated it was about seven o'clock when she stepped off for Cape Arundel. A number of elegant ocean homes stood in her path, forcing her to retreat farther from the roadway. She was extremely cautious early on, afraid to be seen in the nude.

Sheba followed the tree line along the gently sloping ridge, keeping houses at a distance of thirty yards or so. Approaching a magnificent residence constructed mostly of large stones, probably brought up from the nearby shore, her eye caught sight of four lines of drying laundry at the back of the property. On closer inspection, she picked up on a second, more humble residence, behind the main house. It appeared the drying clothes belonged to the people in the smaller home. She crept closer, camouflaged by the shaded woods and vegetation, until she closed the distance between her and the clothesline to forty feet. Neither house showed any sign of movement or life. Her eyes reviewed the articles of clothing as they blew listlessly in front of her, and she considered which might best suit her purpose. She wanted her theft to come off quickly and efficiently. This meant knowing what she wanted in advance. After studying the four lines carefully, she sprang from the woods. The sprint from the tree line took only seconds. Without hesitation, she yanked down a pair of denim jeans, a checkered, black and red flannel shirt, and a man's undershirt. Once safely in her grasp, Sheba whirled and dashed back into the woods. The entire exercise took less than twenty seconds, start to finish. Back in the forest, she slipped behind a large, pine tree and waited for any sound or activity from the houses. There was none. Assured of a perfectly executed theft, the girl withdrew farther into the woods and slipped into her new wardrobe. When her freshly stolen pants proved to be much too large, she returned to the yard and picked up a length of loose clothesline rope she had noticed minutes before. After converting the rope to a belt, the exercise was complete. She could now push onward in full view of the world, if need be.

Relieved to be clothed, Sheba set off for Wells. For the time being, she remained off the main road, choosing the privacy of the forest. Eventually, she came upon a lightly traveled avenue. Appearing to lead in the right, general direction, she followed it. Soon, it took her past the entrance to the Grande Manse Hotel. The soles of her feet were beginning to pick up the sharp edges of some small rocks by the side of the road. As Sheba walked by the hotel, passengers in a Cadillac stared out at her as they cruised up the driveway. She may have been clothed, but the sight of a young woman, her hair disheveled and her feet bare, dressed in a loose pair of jeans and a man's shirt, must have struck the arriving guests at the hotel as odd. The teenager shot the car an unfriendly glance and continued on. Now retracing her steps from her route the day before, she walked along cautiously, trying to avoid road pebbles as she made her way back toward Dock Square. A steady stream of vehicles passed by, all appearing antiquated. The waterfront on her left along the Kennebunk River was largely void of pleasure craft while the shoreline, in general, appeared less developed. In time she caught sight of a two-masted schooner docked across the river. She remembered her father's stories of the *Regina*, a vessel belonging to the legendary Booth Tarkington that for years was moored somewhere in this vicinity. A few years after the author's death in 1946, Broderick had assisted in taking the deteriorating ship out to sea and sinking it. As much as the prospect of viewing this small piece of local history intrigued her, she knew she must not linger. As she tentatively plodded forward, she wracked her brain in the hope of coming up with a substitute for a pair of shoes. Sheba knew, if the opportunity arose, she would steal shoes, sneakers, sandals, anything, even if it meant snatching them right off a victim's feet.

When she finally limped into Dock Square, Sheba was immediately struck by the sight of an A&P grocery store standing where Colonial Pharmacy had been less than twenty-four hours earlier. She approached the building. A man with a handlebar mustache glared at her when she stepped through the door and glanced at the newspaper rack. The teenager scanned a paper for the date. It read: Friday, September 22, 1944.

"We ask our customers to kindly wear shoes," called out the man with the long mustache. Sheba gestured she was sorry and ducked back onto the sidewalk. Through the window she saw a display of produce. Her hunger was growing and even the prospect of tomatoes, lettuce, cucumbers and celery seemed appealing. However, the lack of money for purchasing or shoes for escaping with stolen goods left her with a single alternative. She turned from the market and began the long walk toward Wells.

Sheba played with the idea of hitchhiking as she passed over the Kennebunk River and into the town of Kennebunk. However, her circumstances, traveling with no identification and an absolute need to keep the specifics of her mission secret, required her to keep a low profile. She could not risk having some well-intentioned adult bringing her to the authorities where she could be detained and questioned. As she saw it, she needed to reach her mother and grandparents directly, without the complication of the outside world. There was the additional factor of not knowing how much time she had to make contact with the Lakes. She would need ample time to warn her mother of coming events. If, by some chance, the new moon came this very night, she would only have this one day to counsel Elaine. Sheba picked up Western Avenue, or as some called it, Wells Road, the most direct route to Wells, and forged ahead. Where possible, the girl walked off to the side of the road, on lawns or in grassy fields. In spite of these efforts, her feet were now in pain. It took over an hour for the sixteen-year-old to forge her way from Dock Square to Four Corners. Reaching the site of her mother and brother's fatal accident, she continued on without even a moment's hesitation, already concerned about a possible time constraint. As Sheba plodded forward, she attempted to distract herself from the pain in her feet by pondering her situation. It was 1944 and, incredibly, the accident at Four Corners was some sixteen years away in 1960. After traveling another half-mile she came upon the Mousam River and decided a rest period was necessary.

Making her way down the embankment from the road, she carefully stepped over to the water's edge. The tide was in, meaning the salt water from the nearby Atlantic filled the river basin. The soft mud felt wonderful on the soles of her feet but she cried out in pain when the ocean water made contact with two open wounds on one foot. The jolt of pain passed in a few seconds and the teenager extended herself the luxury of a full ten-minute rest. The sun was high in the sky, giving her the impression it was about noontime. She was now experiencing full-fledged hunger pains.

It was a reluctant Sheba Smith who climbed up onto the roadway and continued her journey toward Wells. She had hardly taken her first step when a truck slowed to a stop on the road ahead of her. A woman's head popped out from the passenger side of the vehicle and called back.

"We're heading down to Wells. If you're going in that direction and you don't mind sitting in back with the boxes—you're welcome to it." The presence of a woman in the cab and the isolation of traveling in the back of the truck seemed too good to pass up. Sheba waived her hand in acceptance and gingerly ran forward while the vehicle slowly rolled back to her. She climbed up onto the truck's wooden carriage and held on as the old workhorse of a Chevrolet pulled off.

"Where's your shoes?" hollered the woman out the window.

"Lost in the mud back in the Mousam," she yelled back. The woman nodded her head, accepting the explanation. Sheba rested her back against the cab of the truck as the vehicle sped off. For the next few miles, the teenager's eyes darted from side to side, taking in the foreign appearance of so many spots along the route. When she left her world the day before, the Cozy Corner Restaurant was soon to be torn down with a promise from the state of Maine of a streamlined intersection where Routes 1 and 9 fork. From her seat in the rear of the Chevy, Sheba looked out on the fork in the road she was born to and a restaurant where locals as well as tourists frequented. With the truck already on Route 1 and moving south at a healthy clip, she pulled herself to her feet and observed her world before it was her world. The sight of unfamiliar establishments like the Lynn Ideal Café were offset by places recognizable to her. The truck roared by a sign heralding Sleepytown Modern Cabins and Cottages, a resort Sheba had considered calling on for work the following summer, a summer now incredibly separated from her by twenty-six years. The wind blew her hair wildly around her face as she gripped the front panel of the Chevy and the pickup rolled past Wells Corner, all the while moving her closer to Tatnic Road and the family's home. A knot rose in her stomach when the vehicle reached the high school. Surprisingly, the building did not appear too different from the one she knew. A minute or two later, the truck began to decelerate. It was rolling to a stop in front of Howard Johnson's Restaurant when the woman called out to Sheba from the passenger side window.

"We'll be heading down Mile Road—so unless you're going that way, you might want to be hoppin' off now."

Sheba jumped from the back of the truck before responding. "No, this'll be fine. And thank you very much."

The man checked the road for traffic, then pulled a sharp left onto Mile Road. Sheba stood in amazement, watching the Chevy rumble east toward the Atlantic Ocean, approximately a mile from where she stood. The experience of traveling these familiar roads in unfamiliar times was already filling her with awe. Most of the past two hours had been spent in sparsely populated country in the Kennebunks with primarily nature surrounding her. Now she was home in Wells, where she could observe the changes twenty-six years could etch on the landscape. There were definitely more open spaces along Route 1 than she remembered. Sheba quickly wrote off her chances of being offered another ride under similar, cloistered conditions and made her mind up to walk the rest of the way. She crossed to the far side of the road, facing the traffic, and headed south. The ride from the couple had lifted her spirits. She hoped to arrive on Tatnic Road and intercept her mother before the young Elaine could reach home. In her mind, that meant waiting somewhere near the Lake residence and keeping vigil.

Sheba counted on a minimum of two hours before the school bus would drop off her teenage mother, allowing her to walk at a more leisurely pace and guard against any further damage to the bottom of her feet. She plodded on, taking in the dated vehicles as they passed her, and searching out any properties that appeared unchanged from 1970. Reaching Littlefield Road, she convinced herself that Tatnic Road came less than a mile ahead, all the while marveling at the abundance of open land on each side of U.S.Route 1.

By now Sheba had also observed a significant number of front windows displaying flags with stars, most blue but some gold. One house she passed had three of these flags in the window. It was a full hour later before Sheba staggered up to her mother's road, depleted of energy and extremely hungry. She turned onto Tatnic Road and began the hunt for the small, white house with the swing on the side. Tatnic Road, she learned, was not a densely populated roadway. The day was warm but not oppressive. The whisper of an ocean breeze played on her back as she trudged up the country road and away from Route 1. She had been walking for nearly twenty minutes when she passed a home in disrepair, its front lawn in need of mowing. In its front window hung another of the flags, this one bearing a gold star.

By now, Sheba had come up with the theory that gold stars stood for sons in the service who were officers, while the blue stars signified everyone else. Reaching the far end of the property, she spotted a modest garden with a number of ripened tomatoes. The sight of garden tomatoes sent a shockwave of hunger through her. The temptation just seemed too strong to resist. Beyond the property, she left the road, dropping down in deep grass a few feet off the pavement, and crawled on her stomach, edging back toward the garden. With no sound or movement from inside the house, she crawled into the garden area, only far enough to procure one, large tomato, then pulled herself out and back into the deep grass. Sheba consumed the tomato in less than a minute, but did not go back for a second, given the condition of the house and the son away fighting for his country. A few minutes later, following another rest period, she returned to the road and continued her trek. There was little traffic coming or going as she continued forward on bruised and bleeding feet. At one point, she stopped and questioned why she had not even reached the turnpike yet, then realized it was 1944 and Maine had not built one. Finally, the first sign for optimism came into view.

Just ahead, maybe two hundred yards or so, the road came to a fork. She walked to the intersection and began running her current circumstances over in her mind. Sheba had yet to come upon the house in the picture and she now expected the school bus to come along the road at any minute. Her best guess told her that Tatnic Road continued along the left branch of the fork. Without hesitating, she entered the deep grass within the fork and positioned herself out of the sight in the brush. She would wait out the arrival of the bus and take action at that time. She lay down on her stomach, invisible to any vehicle or pedestrian that might happen by.

13

THE WAIT FOR THE BUS was not unpleasant. She was where she needed to be. Sheba reasoned the school bus would have to come this way, unless Elaine Lake was absent from school today and she was the only student living in this neighborhood. She was beginning to work on a new contingency plan when the sound of an approaching vehicle caught her ear. She peered through the brush as a bus appeared, stopped, and four figures disembarked, waving good-bye to the driver. As it pulled away, three young boys splintered off and headed up one fork in the road, oblivious to the figure hiding just yards away from them. The fourth passenger, a slim female bearing a strong resemblance to the girl on the swing, began walking alone up the other road. Sheba's heart pounded as her eyes took in the teenage girl. She waited a few seconds, allowing the boys to continue home and out of earshot. Then, she quietly stepped from her grassy hiding place and out onto the road. In front of her, carrying her schoolbooks and walking leisurely, was most certainly her mother. After some difficulty, she forced the words from her mouth.

"Elaine Lake," she called out, prompting the girl to whirl around in surprise. Elaine's eyes widened in fear as she beheld the stranger less than twenty feet from her, a wild-looking creature in clothing not suited for a civilized person, her head encircled in tangled hair. Elaine's heart fluttered as this stranger, appearing far bigger and stronger than she, stared her down in a manner that made her think of a lioness who has selected her prey and was now moving in for the kill. The sight of Sheba, her wild, feline features emphasized by hours of perspiring, standing in bare feet and calling her name, terrified the delicate teenager.

"I don't have anything you'd want," Elaine said meekly. Sheba, choking with emotion, began walking toward the girl.

"I don't know who—." Dropping her books, her mother raced frantically into the adjacent field, hollering as she ran.

"Wait!" Sheba sprinted into the deep grass behind her, closing the gap between them easily and ignoring the pain from the soles of her feet. Elaine continued to scream as she ran, her cries becoming more and more hysterical. Sheba caught her within seconds and wrestled her to the ground. The girl continued to scream, but put up only token resistance. With her mother on the ground beside her, Sheba rolled her over, sat on her chest and pinned her shoulders against the deep, flat grass. Her mother's screams were replaced by sobbing.

"Elaine, listen to me! I'm not going to hurt you. I'm your cousin—I'm Cousin Sheba and I've come a long way to see you and your folks!" Sheba's reassuring tone of voice, probably more than her words, produced a calming effect on the hysterical teenager.

"You're my cousin?"

"That's right, your cousin. I know I should've written but I sort of made plans at the last minute. Now, if I get off of you, promise me you won't run away again or yell like that." The fragile girl nodded in the affirmative and began to exhibit signs of calming down. Sheba rolled sideways, relieving the weight from her mother's chest. Both girls scrambled to their feet and Elaine's eyes fastened on the larger-than-life stranger standing before her.

"Why haven't you got any shoes?"

"I lost them in the mud back in the river bed," answered Sheba, now comfortable with the lie.

"I actually thought you might be here to kill me."

Sheba laughed, brushing grass from her shirt and pants. Seeing Elaine Lake's face in close proximity for the first time, she was surprised by how pretty her mother was. Her features were delicate and appealing, with deep brown eyes set in a flawless complexion.

"I'd give my cousin a big hug, except I've been walking most of the morning and afternoon and I probably smell to high heaven," Sheba added.

"Will you be staying with us for a while?" asked Elaine, sounding simultaneously excited and dazed.

"If your mom and dad will have me."

The girls walked back to the road where books were strewn across the pavement. Now it was the young Elaine who provided the chatter, with Sheba content to take in every detail of her mother's face, manner, and inflection of voice.

"Why do you keep looking at me that way?"

The question caused Sheba some embarrassment. "I don't know, it's just that I've heard so much about you, and now that I've finally met you—well, it feels strange."

"Who exactly have you heard so much about me from?"

"My grandmother, and—." Sheba sensed herself being cornered in her own half-truths, and set out to change the subject. "How much farther up the road is your house?"

"Just a short way."

The girls collected the last of the books and papers.

"God, it felt like I was walking forever on Route 1, and having no shoes didn't help."

"It's over two miles from Route 1 to the house," added Elaine.

The girls strolled side by side up the road for a short time before a white house began to emerge from behind the trees.

"That's it, isn't it?"

Her mother nodded yes.

Sheba was close enough to make out a figure seated on the porch. In the next instant, her eyes shifted to the swing hanging from the tree beside the house. The individual on the porch, a woman, caught sight of the girls' approach, causing her head to arch upward slightly. Elaine excitedly pulled her cousin up the walkway to where the woman sat. The middle-aged woman was snapping green beans into a bowl balanced on her lap. Through an open window, the radio was audible all the way to the road. *"And now, Young Doctor Malone,"* crowed the radio announcer.

"Mama, you'll never guess who I met on the road! It's Cousin Sheba, and she's come to visit us!"

"Who?" The woman rose to her feet, suspiciously eyeing the stranger who approached with her daughter. Sheba's heart was racing at the sight of her grandmother. Dorothy strode to the top of the porch steps, her body language reflecting a degree of cynicism. Sheba locked eyes with the handsome, middle-aged woman. This was not the feeble, stooped Dorothy Lake with whom she had shared Christmas Day, 1970.

"I'm sorry, but I don't recall any relations by the name of Sheba. Who's your momma, child?" Sheba froze. The question left her fumbling for a reply. "You related on my side, or Alfred's side of the family?"

Her questions brought an uncomfortable silence.

"I'm related to Mowalk," she finally said.

Dorothy's mouth dropped open, not instantly, but slowly, like a drawbridge lowered after a passing ship. The words left Elaine confused, her eyes shifting from her mother to Sheba and back.

"I've come from the sacred rock."

Her words caused Dorothy to drop the bowl of green beans and reach for the post on the porch.

"Sacred rock? Sheba, stop talking nonsense," commanded Elaine. She scampered onto the porch to assist her mother. Dorothy and Sheba gazed at one another, each considering their common secret. With the woman's mind reeling, nothing was said while Elaine assisted her back to her chair.

"Darling, your cousin and I need a little time to ourselves, to discuss some sensitive family matters. She's kin, all right, but we'll need a few minutes to clear up some old family affairs. Why don't you make yourself a snack while we talk out here? There's some Jell-O in the icebox. We won't be long."

Elaine stepped forward and gave Sheba a hug. "I'm so glad you're here," she said, her words sounding warm and sincere, despite her gleeful giddiness. "I'll just get some Jell-O and listen to Young Doctor Malone while you get Mama caught up on whatever she needs catchin' up on. We're going to have such fun this weekend!" Elaine turned and scampered into the house.

Sheba turned to a shaken Dorothy. The woman took hold of her teenage visitor by the wrist and pulled her down into a chair beside her. Sheba stared intently into her grandmother's eyes. She felt Dorothy's hand shake as it clutched hers.

"Child, I swear, if my heart beats any faster inside my chest I'm afraid I'll keel over right here and now. I have so many questions to ask you and I'm afraid to ask even the first of them. Have you come here for play, or is it something you need to take care of, or make us aware of?" Sheba fidgeted in her chair momentarily, then jumped to her feet.

"I need to look at your calendar."

"On the door in the kitchen," answered her grandmother. She stormed into the house, heading straight for the kitchen.

"Done already?" Elaine was dishing herself a snack as her cousin stopped in the doorway. Sheba's eyes scanned the Sunbrite Cleanser calendar. It pictured an elderly man and woman standing in their garden, a basket of ripened tomatoes resting on the ground beside them. Sheba's mind flashed to the garden down the road where she had taken a single tomato, then refocused on the calendar. A new moon had passed on September 17th, meaning she would remain back in 1944 for the rest of the month. Flipping to October, she saw the new moon arriving on the 17th. She let out a sigh of relief. There would not have to be a mad rush to warn her mother of the car accident.

"No, Elaine, just starting. I have to get back to your mother." She hurried back to the porch, where a slightly more composed Dorothy had resumed snapping her green beans.

"I have plenty of time—Nana." The woman's hand flew to her mouth and her eyes filled with tears. She began to rock in her chair.

"I feel like this is a dream, and I'll be waking up any second."

"I felt the same way this morning," admitted Sheba, "but of course, I didn't. Everything that's happening is real, and you're the one who told me it would be real. And to get back to your question—I'm not here for play. I need to warn my mother about an accident—a car accident—that's going to happen if she's not told about it."

Dorothy stared at her granddaughter then, extending her hand, caressed the girl's cheek. "It's a little overwhelming sitting here next to my pretty, practically grown granddaughter—knowing she's also my angel of death. You couldn't be here if I wasn't gone."

"You'll live a long, full life, Nana—but my momma needs help."

"And you'll know everything else, won't you? You'll know about your grandfather—and the war?"

"I'll tell you as much or as little as you want. It's just that I must tell my mother what's in the future and how to avoid it."

"You're too young to have all of this on your shoulders."

"I don't mind, Nana. As long as I can get Momma to heed my words, it'll all be worth it."

The woman returned her attention to the bowl of beans in her lap, as though trying to focus on something familiar in the midst of this extraordinary circumstance thrust upon her. "In a couple of hours your grandfather will be getting home from work, and he'll be exploding when he hears there's an extra mouth to feed. He'll want to know who's getting to use your ration stamps while he's having to feed you. Let me handle him."

Sheba sat in silence. She barely remembered her grandfather. She had been less than three years old when the man passed away. If possible, she would not divulge that information to Dorothy, for obvious reasons.

"If I'm remembering everything clearly, you shouldn't be staying here too long—isn't that right?"

The girl's eyes dropped in acknowledgement. "I thought I could stay at least a couple of days before I have to head out. That wouldn't be too long, do you think?"

"I suppose not."

"But I won't leave until I'm sure Momma believes what I'm telling her."

The woman's eyes shifted to the porch floor, catching sight of her granddaughter's bleeding feet. "My word, child, your feet!" Jumping from her chair, Dorothy sped to the kitchen. In seconds, the sound of clanging pans reverberated throughout the house. "Don't you move, Sheba, not till we get some hot, soapy water to soak those feet in!" Elaine joined her mother in the kitchen.

"There'll be plenty of space in my room for Sheba to sleep," she announced.

"We'll start boiling some water so your cousin can take a good hot bath—after we get those nasty looking cuts on her feet taken care of." Elaine nodded to her mother and flashed Sheba a mischievous grin through the screen door, out of Dorothy's sight.

"Your cousin's not going to fit into anything of yours, Skinny Minnie, so I'll just have to give her something of mine to wear." Sheba was sitting only a few feet away from the mother and daughter, taking in their every word. For the first time this day, she felt a feeling of safety and contentment come over her. She was not alone for long. With Dorothy busily filling all available pots and pans with tap water for boiling, Elaine rejoined Sheba on the porch.

"Cousin Sheba, don't worry about having to sleep with me tonight, I only snore this loud: KKKKK-ZZZZZZ-KKKKKK," she roared, no more than three inches from Sheba's ear, then exploded into laughter.

"That's okay, cause my daddy tells me I pass gas from the minute I fall asleep till the second I wake up."

"I can't believe I'm hearing such nonsense from young ladies!" called out Dorothy, pretending to be agitated. The girls broke out in simultaneous laughter. Sheba paused to watch her mother laugh, her pretty face growing even prettier when it lit up in amusement. Laughter made Elaine's eyes sparkle and showcased her even, white teeth.

"What's your daddy like, Sheba?" Elaine asked with interest.

"He's a good man, Elaine—you'd like him."

Within minutes, Sheba's feet were soaking in an iron pail of water, with a well-worn bar of Swan soap provided for cleansing them. After fifteen minutes of soaking and washing, Dorothy applied iodine to the wounds, causing the girl to grimace in pain. Next, she was transported to the bathtub where no less than four pans of scalding hot water had been dumped and tempered with cold water from the tap. She took almost an hour to clean the dirt and grime from her body, allowing for a half-dozen or so periods of relaxation, when she simply allowed the warm, soapy water to wash over her. It was approaching suppertime when Sheba dashed from the bathroom to Elaine's bedroom wrapped only in a towel. After a short spell of giggling from the girls, Dorothy came through the door, handing her granddaughter a fluffy bathrobe.

"I'll muster you up something from my closet after supper. You being family, you can sit at the table dressed as you are. Your—your uncle should be home by six o'clock and we'll eat soon after that." The woman paused in the bedroom door for a brief moment, her eyes resting on the two young females. With the click of the closing door, Elaine catapulted from the bed and took a seat in front of her bureau mirror.

"Don't you think if I dyed my hair blond I'd look just like Veronica Lake?" She piled her hair in a stack atop her head as she spoke, her eyes on her own reflected image.

"I don't know who that is," responded Sheba, not knowing if her mother was speaking of a relative or a celebrity.

"You don't know who Veronica Lake is? Don't you ever go to the movies?"

"Not all that much."

"Isn't that wild? You know, her having the same last name as me? Once Daddy started kidding around and saying Veronica was the homely daughter the family gave away." Following a half-dozen poses or so, the girl grew bored and hurled herself back onto the bed.

"Cousin—I still don't know two things about you. Where do you live? And do you have a steady boyfriend?" Sheba looked over at her mother, spread out across the full-size bed, lying in a prone position.

"I came up from Massachusetts—by bus. I don't have a boyfriend—now, or probably ever. I've yet to meet a boy who I've ever wanted to get to know that well, if you know what I mean."

"What's your last name?" The question caused Sheba to pause, wondering if the release of that information could cause a problem.

"York—like the town." Sheba lied.

"Have you ever kissed a boy?" pried Elaine.

"No."

"I have—just once. It was dreamy."

"Really—what was his name?"

"Randy. He was a tourist, last summer at the beach in Ogunquit. My friend Lucille and I went to the beach for the day and this boy kept coming around our blanket and talking to us. He was pretty good-looking, so we let him put his towel and all with ours—on the blanket. He must have stayed with us for three hours or so." Elaine paused to remove a hair from the corner of her mouth.

"And you say you kissed him?"

"That's right. When Lucille and I began to get ready to leave, Randy got all sad and said how he'd be leaving Maine the next day with his parents and he'd have no good stories to bring home to Hartford with him. He was from Connecticut. Then he says to us, *'Now, if I could go home and tell the guys that I got to kiss two beautiful girls from Maine, that'd be a great story.'* At that moment, I knew what he really wanted was to kiss me—'cause Lucille is not a pretty girl, not at all. So Lucille starts to giggle and she looks at me, and I know she wants to kiss Randy. So we let Randy kiss us—and I must admit it was nice. Lucille, she still talks about Randy and her kiss."

"Elaine, maybe Randy really did want to kiss both of you. You know, it is possible."

Elaine shook her head, rejecting her cousin's suggestion. "Boys only want to kiss pretty girls, like us. They have no interest in girls like Lucille."

"Like us? You think I'm pretty?"

"Of course you are!"

"Do you think Randy would have wanted to kiss me?" Sheba asked through light laughter.

"If he was willing to kiss Lucille, he would have kissed a telephone pole."

Through the window came the sound of an automobile pulling into the driveway, then the front door slamming, heralding the arrival home of Alfred Lake.

"That you, Al? You're early," called his wife from the kitchen.

"Just a couple of minutes. There was a problem with two of the machines, so they closed down early."

"Just to let you know, we have a houseguest, for a couple of days anyway," announced Dorothy, greeting her husband in the living room. Alfred Lake was a man of modest stature, bald, and appearing to be in his late fifties.

"When did all this take place?"

"My niece turned up on the doorstep this afternoon."

"And which of your wacky family does she come from?"

"Shhh—keep your voice down. She's the daughter of my first cousin Edwina."

"Edwina?! How is it I never met or even heard of this cousin before?"

"They live down in Massachusetts—just outside of Boston."

"And how in hell did she find us way up here?" Alfred exploded, clearly not pleased to have his daily routine altered or invaded.

"I told you to keep your voice down. She's with Elaine in the next room! I've already told her she can stay." The man glared into his wife's eyes, then walked off in search of his newspaper. Sheba and Elaine maintained silence in the adjoining room, taking in every word of the adult conversation.

"Didn't you tell me we were getting low on ration stamps this month? That we had gone through too many?"

"Yes, Alfred, we are pretty low."

"And now there's another mouth to feed—for how long?"

"We'll give her plenty of vegetables from the garden," offered Dorothy, attempting to pacify her husband.

"What's for supper?"

"Treet," answered Dorothy.

"Sweet Jesus—again." Lying on her bed, Elaine gestured to her cousin, showing the same enthusiasm for the meal as her father had.

It was six-fifteen when the girls were called to supper, and Alfred Lake got his first look at the family's houseguest. Sheba walked wide-eyed to the table, eyeing her grandfather with a combined sense of fear and awe. Alfred sat quietly at the head of the table, peering over his newspaper at the girl he would never really know as his granddaughter. Sheba, her hair still wet from her bath, stepped gingerly in bare feet to her assigned chair, offering a weak smile in the direction of the stern-looking man.

"I hope you don't eat much," he blurted out.

"As a rule I don't—but tonight I'm famished, Uncle Alfred."

"Sheba can have all my Treet—I'll fill up on vegetables and bread," added Elaine.

The meal was spent in relative silence. Sheba, with only a tomato in her stomach after an arduous hike, devoured two helpings of Treet, a processed meat loaf derived largely from pork shoulders. Throughout the evening meal, she glanced up from her plate to catch Elaine staring at her across the table in amusement. Her mother's beautiful face was illuminated with the joy of having a teenage houseguest. She finished her meal before Sheba, but patiently stayed in her seat, ready to accompany her cousin back to behind closed doors in the bedroom. By seven o'clock the girls were lying side by side on the bed.

"Would you like to go bicycling down to the beach tomorrow?" Elaine asked. "We could put together a picnic lunch and start way down in Perkins Cove and follow the beach north."

"On the same bike?"

"No, I have two. One's a little small, but it runs okay. We can switch back and forth. We're sure to run into some boys down there."

"Oooh, maybe Randy's come back from Hartford!" Sheba dug an elbow into her mother, bringing on a spurt of giggling. Seconds later, Dorothy sailed into the room and up to Sheba, carrying a brown rectangular box.

"I couldn't help but notice that my niece was not blessed with tiny, little, dainty feet. I gave these moccasins to Alfred a few years back for Father's Day, and they've never been out of the box." The woman removed the cover and grabbed one of the moccasins. Sitting at the bottom of the bed, she slipped Sheba's left foot into the corresponding leather moccasin.

"And you've probably wondered all these years why God gave you such an ample foot!" crowed the woman.

Sheba sat up and slipped on the other shoe. "Thank you, Aunt Dorothy." Jumping to her feet, she pranced around the room, testing her new footwear for comfort under walking conditions. They seemed perfect.

It was just before eight o'clock when the girls were called from their bedroom. Sheba joined the Lakes in front of the radio to listen to *The Aldrich Family* on WGAN. *"Henreeeee—Henry Aldrich!"* squawked a woman's voice out of the radio. *"Coming, Mother."*

For Sheba, sitting in front of the radio with no images but those she produced in her mind seemed foreign. The Lakes sat back, absorbing every word, their enjoyment and entertainment reflected on their faces. How could they know that in ten years television would have nearly done away with this part of their world? As the program unfolded, Sheba's eyes shifted from one family member to the next. Her grandfather, who now puffed away on his pipe, spreading a wonderful aroma throughout the room, would be fast approaching his final breath. Nana, she would find herself robbed of a husband, forced to march into her golden years unescorted. Finally, in ten years, Elaine Smith would be anchored with two young children, one an infant girl named Sheba. The giddy Elaine Lake, the girl who boys from as far away as Hartford, Connecticut would do anything to get a kiss from, including embracing the not-so-glamorous Lucille—that Elaine Lake would have vanished from the sandy beaches of southern Maine. At some point in the program, Elaine glanced over and observed the serious mood now embracing her cousin. She pointed in the direction of the bedroom, and both girls excused themselves.

The teenagers retired early. Once nestled under the covers, Sheba was hard pressed to keep her eyes open. By nine-thirty, the physical demands of this day caught up with her. With the full cooperation of Elaine, she dropped into a deep sleep, her left arm and one leg entwining her mother.

14

September 23, 1944

THE SUNLIGHT GLOWED through the openings along green window shades as Sheba opened her eyes to a bright autumn morning. The house was peacefully quiet. Rolling her head to the right, she caught sight of her mother's brown hair cascading down the pillow beneath her head. Elaine's breathing was barely audible. There was a modest chill in the room, prompting Sheba to pull their partially discarded blankets upward to chin level. With her mother fast asleep, she took this opportunity to pull herself close against Elaine Lake, the vessel of her own birth. Reaching her arm around the girl, she wedged her fingers between her mother's, breathing in the fragrance of her shiny, brown hair. She had gone the better part of her life without the benefit of tender moments like this and she was not about to squander this miraculous opportunity. As Elaine slowly awakened, she rolled over squarely on her back. This allowed Sheba to methodically study her face. Elaine Lake was prettier than she, she thought. With their faces only inches apart, Sheba committed to memory every detail of her mother's profile, every feature. It was only a short time before Elaine's eyelids opened. Her first impulse was to roll her head toward her cousin. Her brown eyes, deep and hypnotic, squinted as she smiled.

"What are you thinking about?" Elaine asked.

"I was just thinking how wonderful it would be to be as pretty as you." The compliment brought no reaction. Instead, the fourteen-year-old leaned forward, resting her head on Sheba's shoulder, their faces touching.

"I think you're a lot prettier than you think you are. I wish there was some way you didn't have to go home—that you could stay here with us and go to school here."

"That'd be nice, but I know it can't be done." The words barely out of her mouth, Sheba realized she meant what she said. She was happy in this place. The small house on Tatnic Road was where she wanted to be—now—and a month from now—and a year from now. Sheba wanted to stay with these people. She wanted to grow up with Elaine, to adulthood. She wanted to remain under the watchful and caring eyes of her grandparents. Her thoughts were interrupted by the sound of activity from the kitchen.

"Mama's up," declared Elaine, with a yawn.

The teenagers were called to the table for breakfast by seven-thirty. For Sheba, a bowl of hot cereal and French toast came as a welcome change from her regular cold cereal routine. Elaine hurried their meal, anxious to roll the bicycles out from the shed for a quick inspection. Alfred came to the table just before Sheba finished her toast. The grownups were just lifting their forks when the girls sprang from their chairs, excusing themselves and racing for the back door.

"You'll both be brushing your teeth before you go out gallivanting," ordered Dorothy, as she lifted her teacup.

With their teeth brushed and the bicycles inspected and deemed roadworthy, the girls set off due east toward the Atlantic. Elaine strapped a modest picnic lunch to her Schwinn in anticipation of a long day at the edge of the ocean. Sheba, now wearing a blouse and undergarments provided by her grandmother, was comfortable in her new moccasins and stolen denim jeans, and rode behind her mother as they pedaled down Tatnic Road toward Route 1. When the two approached the property where Sheba had stolen the tomato, she closed the distance between the two bicycles.

"Who lives in this house here?"

"Mrs. Hines," answered her mother.

"Is her son a big shot or something?" Sheba called out. "I noticed that she has a gold star in the window—and most people have blue ones hanging in theirs. Is her son some kind of officer or something?" Elaine lowered her arm, signaling Sheba to stop. They steered their bicycles off the road, dragging them to a halt.

"Sheba, Billy Hines was killed in North Africa. The gold star is for Billy." The fourteen-year-old appeared astonished that her cousin did not understand the significance of these symbols.

"Oh—I didn't know," Sheba stammered, a sense of guilt taking hold of her. Following Elaine, she pedaled her bike back onto the road and continued on, but over the next mile her mind replayed her actions from the day before. She saw herself crawling into Mrs. Hines' victory garden to snatch a tomato. She tortured herself by imagining the woman seated inside the house, staring at a picture of her fallen son while Sheba slithered nearby, stealing the bounty of the woman's hard work.

When the two bicycles finally reached Route 1, they turned southward, heading for Ogunquit Village. 1944 had been another very quiet summer in Ogunquit. The war meant a temporary change in lifestyles. Even the summers during the Depression had seen more activity than the past three. The girls coasted in single file into the village, passing a Cities Service gas station and garage on the way in. Sheba could not recall having ever seen Ogunquit with this little activity, even in January or February. Also, for the first time, she was very much aware of the scarcity of young men. These were times unlike her own, she thought. Reaching the village's main intersection, Elaine asked her cousin to watch her bike, then ducked into the general store. Sheba looked on from the sidewalk as her mother disappeared into the back of the store, then reappeared with a pair of soda bottles in her hand. The proprietor, an obese man of indeterminate age with a puffy, red face and bushy, white eyebrows that almost obscured his vision, surveyed the teenager curiously for a few seconds before taking her coins. Emerging from the store, Elaine went straight for her bike, packing away her two bottles of Spur Cola in the saddlebags along with the other picnic items.

"I'll put the sandwiches and cookies between the bottles of soda to keep them from breaking." Finished securing her cargo, she turned back to Sheba. "Did you see how fat the man in the store was?"

"Actually, I was too busy checking out his eyebrows," Sheba replied. Her mother laughed, then mimicked the man by forcing her own eyebrows downward over her eyes. Following another round of clowning, the pair set off for Perkins Cove. They were diverted on the way, leaving the main road and climbing a steep roadway toward Israel Head, eventually reaching the pinnacle and a magnificent view of Ogunquit Beach down below them. The day was partly cloudy, giving the strands and patches of blue sky above a particular beauty. With few tourists around, and those few being of the elderly variety, the girls felt safe depositing the bikes in a clump of wild bushes, fully camouflaged, and walking through the neighborhood, which consisted of fine, proper summer homes, assuredly the property of rich out-of-staters, and weather-beaten camps. The girls separated for a short time, Sheba returning to the rocky shoreline while Elaine took a closer look at the area's opulent summer residences. As she wandered alone, Sheba thought about stealing the tomato from the Hines house, and a sense of shame rose within her. When not focused on the stolen tomato, her mind wrestled with her mission and the need to warn her mother of an event more than fifteen years in the future. She was still unsure how to introduce the whole subject of the accident at Four Corners.

"Sheba, come here and see this!" Her mother's voice came from an adjoining property. Sheba welcomed the distraction. Crawling up from among the jagged rocks, she walked toward Elaine's voice. "I'm on the porch!" called out Elaine. Sheba pushed her way through a hedge of wild bushes onto the lawn of an oversized Victorian home. The building was dark and brooding, giving off a sinister aura. Gray and austere, Sheba saw it as the perfect example of a country home from the nineteenth century. She approached the house to find her mother peeking through the window from the back porch.

"Look! See how this home is furnished? I'm sure it's Victorian! Can you imagine sitting in this room, with its red, velvet furniture? I picture myself here in the late autumn, with the fireplace burning and me sipping tea. Can't you picture something like that, Sheba?"

"No, not really, cousin dear."

"I swear—I'm pretty enough—I'm going to bag a man with lots of money and make him buy me a place like this," the girl continued.

Sheba looked down on her mother as she stared inside the grand house, laying bare her hopes and dreams. Her thoughts went back to the ramshackle house on Burnt Mill Road. Her mother's vision of the future was light years from the reality awaiting her and her family. What thoughts will run through the mind of Elaine Smith when she gazes out her front window into a front yard populated with rusting cars? Will she feel the same embarrassment as her daughter when she imagines what neighbors say behind her back about the dilapidated structure? Will she cringe when she meets classmates from school ten years after graduation, knowing her plight will be their topic of discussion over dinner that evening? Sheba caught herself sinking into a state of hopeless depression. She shook the grim hold of reality from her thoughts and resumed their conversation.

"Maybe Randy will come back and buy it for you," Sheba suggested, while pushing her face to within inches of her mother's.

"That sad sack's parents were up here renting last summer. I daresay the likes of Randy will never be in a position to own something like this." The pretty fourteen-year-old threw her arm over Sheba's, the two locked together at the shoulder.

"I'm so happy to have my darling cousin visiting me, you know that. Now, I just have to figure out a way to have my parents and your parents let you stay." She looked up at her cousin for some form of encouragement.

"I'm pretty sure that's not going to be possible," Sheba said.

"If it's my daddy you're worried about, well, don't be. Daddy'll do whatever I ask him to. Mama says that my daddy would celebrate Christmas in July if his Princess Elaine asked him to."

"It's not Uncle Alfred that's the problem. It's just really hard to explain. I just got to be heading back home soon."

Elaine searched her cousin's face for any sign of mediation or compromise. "Your parents haven't even called our house yet. They can't be missing you too much."

Sheba dropped her eyes, indicating the topic of discussion should be changed.

After closer inspection of the sprawling Victorian mansion, the girls retreated back to the heavy bushes where their bicycles were hidden. Elaine offered to exchange her larger bike for the smaller one, but Sheba declined. The morning was beginning to slip away as the two pedaled over the winding roads atop Israel Head. They eventually coasted into Perkins Cove, the brakes on their bikes squealing from the effort to slow their momentum. It was just before noon. The segments of the blue sky from earlier this morning were now gone. Wheeling their way along the finger of land that constituted the northern rim of the cove, they chose an unoccupied tarpaper shack as their designated lunch area. After leaning their bicycles against the side of the building, they sat together on the ground, their backs resting against the shack's northern wall. Twenty yards away, the Atlantic churned against the sea rocks, providing a pleasant, rhythmic cadence. Elaine emptied the contents of her saddlebag in front of them, then began dividing the provisions equally. Sheba grabbed her bottle of soda, suddenly noticing it did not have a twist-off cap.

"And how are we supposed to open this bottle, Einstein?" She poked her mother's ribs. Unflustered, the girl reached into the secret compartment of the bag and produced a bottle opener. For the next few minutes, the girls sat quietly, slowly nibbling away at their lunches as they listened to the calls from the men working the fishing and lobster boats nearby. Sheba finished the last of her lunch first, then was slightly taken aback when Elaine let her head fall sideways until it rested upon Sheba's shoulder.

"Cousin dear, if your beloved Randy were to show up about now, do you think he would be willing to kiss me for a chance to kiss his beloved Elaine again?" Sheba playfully poked fun at her mother's single romantic escapade.

"Oh, God, yes! I already told you, he hugged and kissed Lucille, she with the freckles and the horse face. Why wouldn't he kiss a beauty like my cousin Sheba? He'd be a fool not to!"

"Then you say this boy would go to almost any length to taste the lips of the beautiful Elaine Lake?" asked Sheba dramatically.

"Not almost any length—any length!"

"Would he kneel on the sidewalk in Ogunquit, his hands raised like paws, panting like a dog, for a single kiss from his Elaine?" asked Sheba.

"He would, most assuredly."

"Would he walk behind you on the beach, kissing each and every footprint you left in the sand?"

"If I required it of him—yes, he would," came back Elaine, trying to put on a snotty, British accent, and failing miserably.

"And would Randy kiss the flabby rear end of the fat man back at the market—the one with the bushy eyebrows?" The question brought a burst of uncontrollable laughter from Elaine, her head rolling into Sheba's lap.

"Well, would he?" Sheba asked, injecting a ring of insanity into her tone.

"Yes, yes—he would. But I wouldn't kiss him back after he'd done that," she blurted out, and both girls laughed with a giddy freedom that Sheba was unaccustomed to. She began to feel the joy that a relationship with a member of the same sex could offer, something missing from her other real life. With the outburst of laughter waning, Elaine lifted her head from her cousin's lap. Scrambling back to her bike, she searched within one of the smaller pockets for something.

"Call for Philip Mouuu-raaace!" Elaine sang out the slogan, imitating the catch phrase of the Philip Morris Company. She then produced a pair of cigarettes for her cousin's inspection.

"Where did these come from?"

"Daddy's jacket pocket, where do you think? You're not going to let me smoke alone, are you?" Her mother's question was in response to Sheba's surprised expression. She pulled a lighter from her pocket and lit both cigarettes. For the next few minutes the girls fumbled their way through the smoke, barely inhaling any of it, and largely posing with their symbol of wildness and independence.

By twelve forty-five, the two adventuresses were back on the roadway, pedaling their bikes up the rutted and potholed street back toward the village. This portion of their journey required more effort as they made their way up a modest incline, turning off just before the village center, where secondary roads and alleyways brought them back down to sea level and Ogunquit Beach. Reaching the sandy shore, they dismounted their bikes and pushed them onto the hard-packed sand. The exertion from pedaling from Perkins Cove temporarily stalled conversation, allowing Sheba to plan her words for her mother. She knew she would have to initiate a discussion about the future accident before returning to the house.

"I bet you can't guess who was a lifeguard here on this very beach, about twenty years ago," challenged Elaine.

"I don't know—who?"

"No—guess!"

"I don't know—uh, Cary Grant?"

"Not even close."

"I don't know!"

"Bette Davis! You do know who Bette Davis is, right?"

"Of course I do!"

"She was only a teenager. Her and her mother lived back near the cove. She was still only a kid—and I think she was performing at the Playhouse." They walked northward, their bikes' tires leaving twin lines in the sand behind them.

"You know, cousin—my coming to visit was not all for fun and games. I need to talk to you about something very, very important." Sheba's serious tone, as much as her words, prompted Elaine to look up and regard her soberly.

"Now, I'm telling you right in advance that when you hear what I have to say to you, you're liable to think I'm absolutely crazy." Sheba paused, stimulating her mother's curiosity. "I'm here to warn you about something that's going to happen to you years from now, unless you guard against it."

"If it's going to happen years from now, then how would you know about it now?" Elaine's voice expressed skepticism born of intelligence.

"The best way I have to explain it is that I can see things in the future. I know it sounds like hogwash, but you just have to trust me on this. Your mother knows about my powers, and she'll be the first to tell you that you have to listen to what I say."

"Why are you bringing up this craziness now, when we were having such a swell time together?"

"It isn't craziness—it's a gift. I have a gift, do you understand? Now listen to me. One day in the future—a long time from now—

you'll be driving your car and you'll stop at Four Corners in Kennebunk—do you know where that is?" Elaine nodded yes. "You will have your two children in the back seat and a big German shepherd in the front seat beside you. The dog is going to block your view or distract you in some way. Your car will be rammed by a truck when you pull out in front of it, and everyone in your car will be killed. Do you understand?" Sheba saw no harm in exaggerating on the death count.

"This isn't very funny," shot back Elaine.

"It's not a joke—don't you see?" Sheba shouted, already becoming frustrated.

"You sound like some loony, gypsy fortune-teller. I want you to stop talking like this! We were having such a good time, and now you've gone and ruined it! Cut this out, Sheba, I mean it!"

Sheba saw her warning going nowhere and backed off. The girls had reached a row of sand dunes at the northern end of Ogunquit Beach by now. Ahead of them, the long line of beachfront cottages at Moody Beach were coming into view. From the overcast sky came brief periods of sporadic rain. Reaching the unofficial dividing line between Ogunquit and Moody beaches, they pushed their bikes along an ocean access passageway and rejoined the road. Over the next fifteen minutes, they pedaled northward, the roadway hugging the coastline. When they reached Moody Point, Sheba waved her mother down. She stopped and gazed up at a cement bunker and watchtower sitting on the high ground overlooking the sea.

"What's that?"

"It's a security point. There's barracks over in the field. Sheba, the Germans have U-boats out there. They could be sending spies in here if we're not careful," said her mother, appearing shocked to have to explain something as obvious as this. The sight of this small installation, more than anything else Sheba had witnessed to date, brought the reality of the war into focus. However, their stop at Moody Point was brief. Soon they were back on their bicycles and moving ahead until Elaine signaled her cousin to pull over as the two coasted into Fisherman's Cove, a rocky coastal inlet and the only significant break in the town's miles of sandy beaches.

"There should be some seals around here somewhere," announced Elaine as she ran over small, loose rocks constituting the shoreline. Sheba leaned her bike against the seawall, and followed her mother. "The spring, and then the fall, those are the best times to see them," called out Elaine. She scrambled atop a large boulder. "They're there!"

she proclaimed, pointing to a ledge about fifty feet out to sea. Sheba joined her mother on the boulder. They sat side by side and observed the seals for a few minutes. Then Elaine reopened their conversation.

"There is just so much about your coming here that is hard to understand. The way you arrived—coming up behind me on the road—looking almost like a wild animal. Then, when Mama sees you she doesn't know who you are—until you talk about some sacred rock and a guy I've never heard of. Sheba, everything is so strange anyway—then you start talking about things that haven't happened and how you know they will. I just don't know what to think." She looked at her cousin with a bewildered expression, clearly asking for some form of explanation.

"I wish I could tell you more, but I can't. You're just going to have to trust me and your mother on this. I'm sorry." They stayed in the cove a short while longer, watching the seals flop around on the ledges offshore. Sheba returned to the bicycles first, followed shortly after by her mother. They were soon back on the road, continuing their journey northward along the coast. They were able to get back on the sand a half-mile ahead when they reached Crescent Beach, where they rolled down a boat access, and walked their bikes beside the advancing and retreating surf. The beach was practically empty, except for an elderly couple coming toward them and a solitary girl a hundred yards ahead looking out to sea.

"Did you ever think how wild it was, how you could come to the beach in August and be surrounded by hundreds, maybe thousands of people, and then you come back to the same beach and sit in the same exact spot, and you're alone, and there's no one around you. But you're sitting in the same spot—just at a different time, except no one else wants that spot except you when you go back. I like that feeling— being in a popular place when no one else wants to be there. That probably sounds kind of goofy, huh?" Sheba confessed.

"It's not goofy at all. Before the war, I remember going down to the beach alone the day after Labor Day and thinking how quiet it was compared to just the day before. Is that what you're talking about?"

"That's exactly what I'm talking about," answered Sheba, surprised by her mother's response. Now, Sheba too was feeling the frustration of having to leave this young woman with whom she shared insights as well as a common bloodline. The girls had just moved back from the wash of a particularly strong wave when Elaine stopped dead in her tracks.

"Oh, for God's sake! What's she doing down here?" she crowed.

Sheba looked up to see her mother glaring at the young woman ahead of them in the distance. The girl stood, oblivious to them, looking out to sea, her long, blond hair streaming down her back.

"It's not enough having to look at her pinched nose face in school all week—now she's invading my space away from school!"

"You really don't like this girl, do you?"

"God, I hate her! But seeing that she's here, and we're here—would you do me a big favor, cousin dear?"

"Go ahead," said Sheba, suspiciously.

"Would you go over and smash her in the face? Just slap her real good."

"Why? Has she ever hit you?"

"No, but don't let that stop you. It's just that she has every boy in school eating out of her hand—and she thinks she's so much better than the rest of us."

Her mother's words brought a smile to Sheba's face. "Yeah, I know the type," she sighed, thinking back to Wells High and Felicia Blackburn.

"Well, tell you what—I won't hit her, but I will see if I can shake her up."

The two proceeded forward toward the blonde girl who was unaware of their presence. She was Elaine's size. She stood frozen like a statue, facing directly out toward the Atlantic. When they were within hailing distance, Elaine called out.

"If you're thinking of drowning yourself, Tuttle, what's stopping you?" she hollered.

Startled, the blond girl turned abruptly.

"Tuttle," mumbled Sheba, while her eyes examined the girl's features, her pretty face, her blue eyes, the trace of freckles across her nose.

"Linda Lee Tuttle, meet my cousin, Sheba. It seems my cousin here has the same reaction to you as I do. We can't stand your face—and we want you off our beach."

The girl looked up at Sheba, her eyes reflecting more sadness than fear. Sheba stared at her, speechless, taking in the youthful appearance of her boss and friend.

"Come on, this is a bad idea," she said, throwing her arm around Elaine and pulling her away.

"No—I want the little bitch off my beach!" cried out her mother.

"It's a big beach—plenty of room for everyone," reasoned Sheba as she continued to guide her mother away from the Linda Lee. As they walked away, pushing their bicycles, Sheba turned back to survey her friend a final time. The young blonde stared back blankly as the cousins moved northward away from her.

"What's with you? I thought you said you'd help me shake her up. Why didn't you give her a hard time?"

Sheba, unable to come up with a logical answer and not in a position to tell the truth, shrugged her shoulders and withheld a response. Elaine gradually steered the two away from the crashing surf and toward the main entrance to Wells Beach. The dominant Casino building was in sight, as was the two sets of stairs within the cement seawall. Between the two staircases was the lettering 'Class of 44' and 'Kilroy was Here,' blunt reminders to Sheba of her place in time at the moment.

"Why don't we just head home by Mile Road?" suggested Elaine, still sounding cross from the averted confrontation.

While they directed their bicycles toward the nearer of the stairways, Sheba's attention was grabbed by something up the coast. Something about the terrain north of them seemed unfamiliar. She continued to stare until the cause of her curiosity crystallized in her mind. There was no jetty! The jetties constituting the entrance to Wells Harbor were not in place in 1944, she told herself. She vaguely remembered seeing the huge rocks being laid down, creating the north and south boundaries to the harbor entrance, but she was a young child at the time.

"Cousin, would you mind if we went on a ways more—down as far as the harbor?" Elaine raised her eyes in frustration but agreed.

"Let's bike it though—we'll take Atlantic Avenue up to the harbor."

Together, the girls pedaled the mile to the harbor and mouth of the Webhannet River. On arrival, Sheba abandoned her bicycle and walked out onto the grassy flatlands and dunes by the river's mouth. She had grown accustomed to the sight of dated cars and even the occasional horse-drawn wagon, but the absence of tons and tons of granite boulders lining the entrance to the harbor was a mild shock. She thought how the terrain here more resembled the landscape as Mowalk knew it than as she did. She was lost in thought when her mother's voice jolted her from a near meditative state.

"Are we ready to go yet?" she yelled out to her. By her tone and inflection, Elaine remained upset over the brief incident with Linda Lee. Sheba turned and walked slowly over to the girl. When they were finally face to face, she lunged at her mother.

"Oh, I'm ready all right!" In one, quick motion, daughter slipped mother into a head lock, bending the smaller girl forward. "I'm ready to introduce my cousin to a level of pain beyond her wildest dreams." Elaine's response was to let out a scream, followed by a burst of nervous laughter.

"Do you give up—and therefore agree to stop being such a crab?" snarled Sheba.

"I don't give in to threats."

"Fine!" Sheba released the girl's hand, only to bend at the waist and hoist the diminutive girl onto her shoulders. "It's called an airplane spin and it ends with a body slam to the ground." The moment she began to twirl her victim in a circular motion there came the call of surrender.

"I've had enough—I give up!" Following a brief pause, she lowered her defeated opponent to the ground. Winded, Elaine embraced her cousin.

"I'll stop being a brat—for now."

After rounding up their bicycles, they rejoined Atlantic Avenue and began the long trip home. Their journey was almost immediately greeted with isolated raindrops. Undeterred, they pedaled on, only to run into a wall of precipitation, propelled into their faces by a sudden wind off the ocean. As the two approached the junction at Mile Road, the rain's intensity caused them to break out in a fit of laughter. At Mile Road, they dismounted their bikes and took shelter beneath the overhang at the Beachcomber, a gift shop and Wells Beach landmark. The teenagers sat side by side, their backs pressed against the front of the building. Only a few feet away, rain poured down from the sky and the roof, flowing by them in a heavy stream at the edge of the sidewalk. Their clothes were saturated and strands of wet hair clung to their faces. A sideways glance at one another was cause for another round of hysterical laughter. The rain continued, unabated, for the next five minutes.

"We may have to spend the night here," joked Sheba, bringing a groan from her mother. With the onslaught from the sky still at full force, a weathered truck circled the nearby parking lot and pulled up in front of them. The driver leaned across the cab and rolled down the window.

"What do we have here—damsels in distress?" Sheba leaned forward to make out the figure whose voice sounded strangely familiar.

"How come in my dreams my knight in shining armor rides up on a white horse and not in a broken-down truck?" Elaine cried out, her voice indicating she knew the driver.

"A horse is not goin' to get you out of the rain, is it?" The young man behind the wheel backed the truck up slowly, allowing Sheba to finally take in his features. The face emerging from behind the vehicle's window caused her heart to speed up and her eyes to widen. Before her sat a young, virile Broderick Smith. With his sandy, blond hair worn long enough to touch the collar of his shirt and a disarming smile that came off as a hundred percent genuine, there was a great deal of charm to his appearance.

"Well, Princess Elaine, do you or do you not want a ride?" Elaine sought out her cousin's eyes for approval before responding.

"We'll take the ride—seeing that no one's going to see us in the company of one Broderick Smith or his jalopy."

The boy jumped from the cab of the truck and hurriedly tossed both bikes into the back of the vehicle while the rain continued. The girls made a dash for the front seat. They jockeyed for the window, with Elaine coming up short and forced to sit beside the driver. Seconds after settling in, they were joined by Broderick, soaking wet from his small chore at the rear of the truck.

"Well, look at me—personal driver to what are probably the two prettiest girls in Wells!" He stopped and looked at the young women, his eyes training particularly on Sheba. "Well, Miss Bad Manners, are you going to introduce us?"

"Broderick Smith, this is my cousin, Sheba, from Massachusetts. Sheba, this is Broderick Smith, one of the dumbest, if not the dumbest boy at Wells High."

Broderick reached across Elaine, extending his hand to Sheba. "Pleased to make your acquaintance, Sheba," he said, flashing her a grin while taking his eyes from the road. "By any chance, are you part Indian?"

Sheba's mouth dropped in astonishment. "How? How did you—."

The handsome seventeen-year-old gestured to the floor and her soaking wet moccasins.

"By the way, cousin, Mr. Smith here is laboring under the delusion that in a couple of years—when I'm a little older—I will actually date him. Have you ever heard of anything so ridiculous?"

Sheba laughed, holding back a response, content to stare out the front windshield as the wiper swished back and forth. With the truck motoring up Mile Road past the Lobster Landing, she spotted a lone person plodding on foot toward Route 1. Simultaneously, Broderick noticed the pedestrian, a female, and lifted his foot from the gas pedal.

"Isn't that Linda Lee?"

"So help me, Broderick—if you stop for that girl, then I'm getting out. It's that simple." There was neither playfulness nor compromise in Elaine's voice. Linda Lee, her clothing soaked and clinging to her body, turned to the sound of the truck's deceleration. The next second brought a roar from the vehicle's engine and it cruised by the girl. Instinctively, Sheba turned and stared into the fourteen-year-old's sad eyes as the truck sped by.

"Now that was downright mean. There was room enough for one more, particularly when you consider the weather," Broderick argued.

"I'm not sharing the front seat with that little trollop. And besides—I don't like her face. Her lips are too big. Don't you think she looks like a duck—with her big lips and all?" asked Elaine.

"That wasn't a nice thing to do," added Sheba.

"She looks like a duck! Why would you want to ride with a girl who looks like a duck?"

"Come on Elaine, Linda Lee's a pretty girl," injected the boy, albeit meekly.

"Pretty! She—looks—like—a—duck. She looks like Donald Duck!"

"Wouldn't she have to look more like Daisy, than Donald, Duck?" asked Sheba, her voice monotone and her eyes staring straight ahead.

"Then you agree—she looks like a duck."

Sheba, disappointed with her mother's childish behavior, chose to ignore the topic of conversation. "It just wasn't a nice thing to do," she added after a prolonged silence within the cab. Elaine finally picked up on her cousin's displeasure and retreated from the conversation.

Little was said inside the truck over the next few minutes as the three teenagers reached Route 1 and headed south toward Tatnic Road and the Lake residence. Broderick turned once, then a second time, as if to speak, but held back. His third gesture finally saw him pierce the quiet.

"I heard something yesterday from my grandmother but I'm sworn to keep it under my hat."

"Well, it's too late now, Broderick Smith—out with it," snapped Elaine.

The boy paused, as if this somehow minimized the offense against his grandmother's trust. "It's just that I heard the Tuttle family got word that Artie Tuttle's being sent home—that he's been seriously wounded and he'll be missing a leg when he gets here. That might explain why Linda Lee's walking down at the beach by herself—needing some time away from everything." The boy's story spread a further quiet over the threesome.

The rain had moderated by the time the pickup roared into the Lake family's driveway. The boy jumped from the vehicle without hesitation, pulling down the first of the two bicycles and wheeling it to beside the passenger door.

"Is there somewhere particular you want these to go?"

"Now—that's a very good question—let me think," came back Elaine, talking in slow motion while the rain washed down the young man's face. Sheba sat back, observing the antics of her youthful parents. What a tremendous gift this was, she thought, watching the budding relationship of the man and woman who would give her life. Her father, seventeen, strong and handsome, was already madly in love with this pretty, incredibly immature girl seated next to her. How could this boy even begin to imagine the pain fate was poised to deliver to his doorstep in the years ahead? She stared at his good looking face, then remembered the tired, middle-aged man who crumbled over the steering wheel on Christmas night, tears blinding his vision, expressing his love for the only woman he saw capable of bringing him happiness. The two images were almost irreconcilable.

"You may put the bikes out back in the shed, my good man," instructed the girl, an air of superiority carried playfully in her voice. Broderick rolled the bikes to the shed while the young women sat sheltered from the rain in the cabin of the truck. Returning to the passenger side of the truck, he opened the door, extending his hand to Sheba, who accepted it. He supported her step down onto the driveway, then ushered her to the porch. He returned to the vehicle, presumably to offer Elaine the same service. The girl had already slid to the edge of the seat. However, instead of repeating the service extended to her cousin, he swept Elaine up into his arms. She called out in surprise, kicking her legs frantically.

"You're as light as a feather," he commented through a wide grin.

The commotion brought Dorothy scampering onto the porch. The boy carried the young female up the stairs, placing her down by the front door. Back on her feet, Elaine played the role of the helpless, wronged female.

"I may never speak to you again, Broderick Smith."

Her threat only drew a fit of laughter from the boy. "We'll see," he said. He spun around and addressed Sheba, extending his hand. She followed suit.

"I hope to see you again, cousin Sheba," he said in a voice befitting a knight. Lifting her hand to his lips, he planted a gentle kiss on it.

"Trust me Mr. Smith, you will," she answered.

The teenage boy turned a final time, politely gesturing to Mrs. Lake and flashing Elaine a roguish smile, then made tracks for his truck. Moments later, the vehicle disappeared down the road, the sound of the truck's engine eventually drowned out by the noise from the rainwater cascading down from the roof.

Still wet from their time spent bicycling along the shore, Sheba and Elaine retreated to the bedroom and changed into dry clothes. For Sheba, this meant borrowing clothing from her grandmother. Once dry, they lay out side by side on the bed. Elaine yawned, showing the effect of the day's extended exercise.

"He seems like a nice boy," Sheba tossed out, curious to hear her mother's feelings for her father at this early stage in their relationship.

"Broderick's all right—I guess. You do know he comes from a broken family. His father ran away—and no one's seen him in years. His mother's a drunk—chases men too. Momma says he's from bad stock." Her mother's words were painful, but Sheba chose to pretend they were of little consequence to her and kept the conversation positive.

"He's cute—and he really seems to have a thing for you." Elaine glanced over, meeting Sheba's eyes.

"He's three years older than me. He's only two grades ahead of me because he stayed back when he was a little kid. I think it was in the second grade. I can't imagine staying back—it must be really awful." Sheba looked up from the bed, holding back a response.

"Cousin dear, have you given my words from this afternoon any thought?"

"If you're talking about that craziness about me getting killed in a car accident in Kennebunk, I don't want to hear any more of that." Frustrated, Sheba leaped from the bed and stormed out to the living room. Elaine did not follow, content to lie back and rest, her eyelids closed. Her cousin was not gone from the room long. Thirty seconds after rushing out, the door flew open and Sheba, joined by Dorothy, re-entered the room.

"Your cousin's been telling me that you've refused to pay her any mind about a matter she sees coming in the future—your future." The teenager's eyes popped open to see her mother and cousin standing over her. "Now see here, child, you know me and you know I'm not one to spin any crazy tales. Your cousin's come here for a reason—and that reason is your well-being. Your cousin Sheba's got a precious gift—a gift maybe you and me don't fully understand—but I'm telling you this: Sheba knows what's best for you and if she tells you to do this or do that—you're to listen to her. I tell you, she's got a gift—and I want you to follow her directions to the letter. Am I making myself completely understood?"

Her mother's orders, delivered in no-nonsense terms, appeared to penetrate Elaine's understandable skepticism. She nodded her head yes, a serious, almost fearful expression on her face. With that said, Dorothy turned and walked to the door. She stopped and turned before leaving.

"And not a word of this to your father," she commanded before making her way out into the living room.

The teenagers did not join the grownups by the radio on this night. Instead, Sheba spent the evening counseling Elaine on what conditions and situations to avoid. She, of course, did not divulge the circumstances by which she gained knowledge of her cousin's future, content to simply promote the notion that she possessed the power to see things before they happened. As the evening progressed, Sheba was encouraged to see a growing earnestness in her mother's attitude. It was just after ten o'clock when she pulled the chain on the table lamp beside the bed, casting darkness on the room and on her mother, already asleep beside her.

15

September 24, 1944

SHEBA OPENED HER EYES and felt the presence of another human being close by. Elaine, her arm draped across Sheba's body, was breathing in her face, her head resting on her daughter's shoulder. It had been a cool night and the warmth from her mother's body produced a cozy feeling between the covers. Elaine appeared to still be asleep. Sheba took this peaceful moment to savor the joy she felt from her journey back to 1944 and the wonderful gift her grandmother had passed on to her. To be here in her grandparent's house, developing a closeness to the woman who had been torn from her life at an early age, was beyond joyful. Sheba's period of quiet, meditative thought proved to be short-lived.

"I had a very romantic dream last night—and it involved you," whispered Elaine into her cousin's ear.

"Oh, really," answered Sheba.

"Yes—and in the dream you were running the length of Wells Beach."

"Is that right."

"But in the dream you weren't alone," continued Elaine.

"Well, that's a relief—seeing that it's a romantic dream and all."

"No—you were running along the beach—your eyes full of love—and running hand in hand with—with—the fat guy from the market in Ogunquit!" She burst into a gale of laughter, barely getting the last few words out of her mouth. Sheba, pretending to be angry, rolled over onto her, quickly pinning her down to the bed.

"Someone in this house is about to die. Someone every boy at Wells High will grieve for—especially a certain boy who drives around in a crappy truck and who stayed back in the second grade." She spoke while staring down into her mother's eyes, her hair dangling in the girl's face as a crazed expression distorted her own. Elaine cried out and laughed simultaneously. The bedroom door opened behind them.

"I'm glad you two see fit to keep holy the Lord's day," chastised Dorothy. "We'll be having breakfast in forty-five minutes or so. Your father's still catching a little more sleep. Sheba, you'll be joining us for service this morning."

"Aunt Dorothy, I'm afraid I don't have anything proper to wear."

"I've already taken care of that. There'll be no heathens under my roof."

Following breakfast, the family piled into the Lake's white 1938 Pontiac sedan and headed for church. Sheba's outfit came complements of one Elizabeth Littlefield, daughter of the church minister. On Saturday, Dorothy had the foresight to telephone the Reverend Littlefield and explain her houseguest's problem, namely, the lack of a proper dress to wear to church. The phone call was made to pose the following question: Would it be acceptable to bring a young Christian woman to Sunday service dressed in everyday clothes? After determining that Sheba and his own daughter were of similar height and stature, the good man offered one of his daughter Elizabeth's dresses as a gift to the Lake's visitor from out of town. Dorothy had Alfred drive her to the minister's house, where a dress was picked out and brought home to Tatnic Road. Dorothy wisely chose a full-length dress, one practically reaching the floor. This way, her granddaughter's moccasins would probably go undetected.

The family sat together during service at the Second Congregational Church of Wells. The church stood a hundred feet back from Route 1 a short ways north of the town center. Over the course of the service, Sheba glanced around at the faces in the building, thinking she might identify one or two individuals from her other life, the life she would return to in three weeks. She was disappointed to find no face resembling anyone she knew in 1970. With her curiosity on the makeup of the congregation, she lost much of the message contained in Reverend Littlefield's sermon, although she did know that much was made of the need for continued prayer on behalf of the men and women overseas, defending the country. In particular, she peered over the inside of the church, hoping to spot her father. However, he was not in attendance. With the service over and the final hymn sung, the family piled into the car. The teenage passengers grew restless on the drive home. Reaching Littlefield Road, they asked for permission to walk the rest of the way. Permission was granted with the stipulation that the two be home for Sunday dinner, tentatively scheduled for one o'clock.

* * *

Standing by Route 1, they waved good-bye to Alfred and Dorothy and watched the car motor away. They set off walking. With gas rationing in full effect, traffic was minimal. However, every minute or so, a car would pass. A few honked, these being people who knew Elaine. Ten minutes into their walk, a vehicle stopped and offered the girls a ride home in the rumble seat. It was two members of the congregation. Although tempted, they turned down the ride and continued on their way to Tatnic Road. Their conversation remained lighthearted, each telling the other about their experiences in school. Twenty minutes into their walk, they came upon a yard crowded with children playing. They were all boys and most were still in their church clothes. The group was noisy, energetic, and totally carefree, thanks to the absence of any adult supervision. The two young women stopped to watch the mayhem, leaning against a picket fence separating the children from the road. Sheba's attention was drawn to one boy in particular. He was slightly bigger than the others, and was putting his size advantage to use. He had singled out a smaller youngster and was tormenting him, removing the boy's cap and sailing it in the general direction of a large mud puddle in a corner of the yard. After protesting, the small lad would calmly retrieve his cap, only to have it pulled off and tossed back in the vicinity of the puddle again. After three repetitions of this, Elaine had seen enough.

"Jody, I want you to stop that right now," she ordered. The boy responded with a sneer. Then, after glancing back at the girl in defiance, he again grabbed the cap from the smaller child but, this time ran to the puddle and dangled it above the dirty water.

"Don't—you—dare, Jody Pease!"

"What did you say his name was?" blurted out Sheba.

"Oh, he's just a fresh, little boy I know from Bible Study at church."

"No—his name."

"Jody Pease."

Sheba looked over at the boy, immaculately clean and dressed in his church suit. She studied his young face, looking for similarities to the Jody she knew. Analyzing his features, she ran the math in her head. She had traveled back twenty-six years and figured the Jody she knew was in his early thirties. She was convinced this chubby, fresh, little boy was the Jody Pease she knew and despised.

Without saying a word to her mother, she swung open the creaky gate to the yard and strolled in the direction of Jody and his tormented playmate. Pease stared at the stranger with some degree of suspicion, following her with his eyes as she approached. However, when she was still twenty feet away from the boy, she veered off course and picked up an empty beach pail leaning on its side against the fence. After inspecting it for holes, Sheba walked back toward Jody and the puddle of water. Jody had not moved a muscle, content to torment the younger boy by dangling his cap above the puddle. Reaching the six-inch-deep pool, no doubt left from the prior day's downpour, Sheba trawled the bucket through the watery muck, filling it to near capacity. She stood up and addressed the young Jody, a warm smile masking her contempt for the boy.

"Don't you think that little sissy would look good wearing this?" Sheba asked, shifting her eyes to the younger child and back to Jody. She flashed the boy a mischievous smile, followed by a wink.

"What are you doing?" hollered Elaine from outside the fence.

Sheba extended the dripping pail and Jody reached for it. In the next second, the filthy contents were poured over his head. The muddy water cascaded over his shoulders and down onto his Sunday suit. Jody's mouth flew open in shock. He stood frozen in place, seemingly unable to force a sound through his vocal chords.

"Oh, dear—you seem to have splashed a few drops on me," commented Sheba in a matter-of-fact voice. Looking into the boy's face closely, she thought she detected the first trace of tears in the lad's eyes. Reaching down, she snatched the slightly soiled cap from Jody's hand, then nudged his rigid body hard enough to send it teetering backwards. He fell in the puddle on the seat of his pants, displacing a generous amount of water over its banks.

"Aaaaaaah!" Jody wailed, at last catching his breath.

"Sheba!" a stunned Elaine cried out.

Sheba calmly walked over to the smaller boy and handed him his cap while Jody bawled uncontrollably. She ran for the gate, noticing her mother was already sprinting away from the confrontation. She raced at full speed after Elaine, laughing heartily as she closed the distance, finally catching her a hundred yards up the road.

"Are you crazy?" Elaine asked, trying to catch her breath. "He's only a little boy!"

Sheba did not respond. She collared her mother in a playful headlock and led her off Route 1, through an open field and away from traffic. "Maybe we should stay out of sight for a while—in case Jody's mommy and daddy come looking for me."

"I don't understand you sometimes, cousin—I really don't."

Elaine's confession appeared to have no impact on Sheba, whose face reflected a look of immense satisfaction. The teenagers proceeded south, careful to stay fifty to a hundred yards back from the roadway and invisible to motorists. They were an odd sight to anyone who happened to look through their back windows, these girls dressed in their church clothes, traipsing through forest, brush and open field. Elaine and Sheba did not return to the main route until they reached Tatnic Road. Their conversation was stunted after the incident. It was Elaine who first spoke as they made their way back to the house.

"Wouldn't you love to be a fly on the wall when Jody gets home and walks through the door, wearing his Sunday best?"

The rhetorical question was followed by a burst of laughter from both girls.

"Just think—maybe when Jody gets home, his mother'll be in the bathroom—and she'll hear the door close and know it's him," said Sheba. "Now, Jody, I want you to take your suit off this minute and hang it up—so you can wear it again next Sunday. Knowing him, the little moron will probably do it!" blurted out Sheba, to another roar of laughter.

The girls were practically in front of Mrs. Hines' house when Sheba glanced over and noticed the property. A woman she assumed to be Mrs. Hines emerged from the side of the building as the young women walked past. The woman appeared older than Sheba had imagined. She was thin and tall with a crop of thick, white hair.

"Hello, Mrs. Hines," called out Elaine.

The woman waved back, but did not respond. There was a certain sadness in her manner, thought Sheba, a halting, stunted quality in her every movement. She wondered if the woman was thinking of her son at this very moment. Sheba thought back to the day she arrived home from the hospital after the car accident. The hospital had kept her overnight as a precaution. Arriving back home that day, she had been overcome by the silence and by the absence of half of her family. Her grandmother had taken charge of most of the duties surrounding the funeral and church service, leaving father and daughter to do battle with the silence and emptiness. As she felt her mood being swallowed up by the depression that came from remembering the accident, she forced it from her consciousness, an act of self- preservation. A few moments later she laughed out loud.

"What's so funny?" asked Elaine.

"I was just trying to imagine what it felt like when Jody's rear end hit the water. Think of it—the water from the puddle traveling up his pant leg—both pant legs—and grungy water soaking through his pants on impact—and all this cold, filthy, brown slop reaching his fat, little can at the same time."

"Oh, and don't forget the bucketful you dumped on his head."

Her mother's comment prompted Sheba to break into song. *"Well, I love that dirty water...love that dirty water...ooh, ooh, Boston, you're my home."*

Elaine pulled back and eyed her cousin curiously. Immediately, Sheba realized she had unwittingly given her mother a small preview of rock music, more than a decade before it would come into existence. Quickly, she changed the subject.

"I did good, cousin—I really did good," said Sheba. Her comment caused her mother to stop and survey her.

"My life was so boring before you came here. I don't want you to leave." There was no response from her cousin. Sheba looked away. "I won't let Mama send you back to Massachusetts. You'll see, I'll get my way."

"I'll have to go soon. I'm sorry, cousin, that's just how it is." The exchange of words transformed their walk home into a silent march.

The girls were called to the table for Sunday dinner at one o'clock. Sheba observed a certain ritual at this time. Alfred and Dorothy still wore their church clothes, lending formality to the meal. At the center of the table, a platter showcased a meat loaf. It was small by Smith family standards, hardly enough to satisfy her and her father back home. When Dorothy finished placing the bowls of vegetables, potatoes, yellow beans and squash, on the table, she served Alfred a generous portion of the loaf. Next, a smaller but reasonably substantial slice was carved off and placed on her plate. The woman approached Elaine next, where she sliced off half of the remaining meat. Approaching her granddaughter, she stopped in her tracks.

"What's that on your dress?"

Sheba glanced down at her sleeve and noticed a sprinkle of brown stains on the material.

"Is that mud?" The girls burst out in simultaneous laughter. "Quite the little tomboy, aren't you?" Alfred shook his head in disapproval but did not offer a comment. "Well, just be sure to eat all your dinner—you can fill up on vegetables and bread. We're only getting food rations for three," explained Dorothy, embarrassed by the small portion of meat extended to her guest. The meal was preceded by a prayer for victory and peace.

Following Sunday dinner, the girls returned to Elaine's bedroom, where Sheba changed back into her jeans and red checkered shirt.

"Do you think Uncle Alfred would mind if I borrowed his lawn mower?"

"Daddy wouldn't mind, but the lawn looks fine."

"I was thinking of going down to Mrs. Hines' house and mowing her lawn. It could really use it."

"Why? Do you think she'll pay you?"

"No, not for money. I just think it'd be a nice thing to do," answered Sheba. She was still troubled by the theft of the tomato two days earlier. She saw mowing the woman's lawn as a way of earning her ill-gotten vegetable. "I'd like to think that my beautiful and charming cousin would come with me, you know, keep me company while I cut the grass," hinted Sheba.

Elaine wrinkled her nose, then indicated with a nod she would. A short while later, the lawn mower was pushed out of the shed and wheeled down Tatnic Road. It was just under a mile to the Hines' house.

Arriving at the elderly woman's house, Sheba climbed the steps to the porch. There was no sound from inside the building. Three raps on the front door set off the sound of scurrying from inside, and footsteps approached the door. When it opened, Mrs. Hines appeared, looking younger to Sheba than she had earlier.

"Yes, girls?"

"With your permission, we'd like to cut your lawn for you—get it nice and neat before the leaves fall," said Sheba.

The woman smiled. "I'm afraid I'm not in a position to pay you for cutting the lawn," she confessed.

"No, we don't want any money. We just thought you might like your lawn to look good," explained Sheba.

"I'm afraid it is a sight," answered Mrs. Hines, sounding embarrassed.

"Oh, no, it's not that—I wasn't saying that." Sheba realized she had unwittingly made the woman uncomfortable. "The truth is—I offered to mow your lawn because on Friday, I stole a tomato from your garden—and I just wanted to pay you back in some way. My cousin Elaine had nothing to do with stealing the tomato." Elaine flashed the woman a minute smile but remained silent.

"I had already brought in everything from the garden I planned on taking, dear, so there was no harm done."

"Please, Mrs. Hines, let me cut your lawn."

"Go ahead, dear—go right ahead."

Sheba went straight to work on the front and back yards, pushing the manual mower over every square foot showing the slightest hint of grass or weed growth. Elaine borrowed a pair of shears from the barn and cut around the house, then raked up much of the cut grass on the front half of the property. When their work was done, Mrs. Hines invited the teenagers to join her for tea and homemade cookies. For Elaine, the cookies represented a genuine treat, thanks to the rationing of sugar. The girls stayed and chatted with the woman for an hour, careful to keep the conversation light while sitting in the shadow of a fireplace mantle lined with photographs of the fallen Jimmy Hines.

It was a quiet walk back to the house. This day, like the day before, had been physical and hectic. During the hour spent in the living room with Mrs. Hines, Sheba found herself further contemplating this place and time. She had left behind her own war, Vietnam. Hers was a troubled time, a noisy time, a painful time. However, her time was not as all-consuming as this period. Her parents' and grandparents' war was impossible to hide from. This war made you eat differently, travel differently, even talk differently. This war took so many young men from the general population that it became noticeable on the streets of every city and town. The radio called out to buy war bonds, prodding men and women to even invest differently.

Dorothy was seated on the porch when Sheba, pushing the lawn mower in front of her, and Elaine approached. There was something in her demeanor that communicated trouble was afoot.

"Your father would like to have a word with you, young lady—and I think he'd like your cousin to join you."

The girls shot each other apprehensive glances. Sheba leaned the mower against a tree and the two walked single file into the house. Alfred sat in the living room, smoking his pipe and listening to the Red Sox broadcast. With the girls' arrival, the radio was shut off. The man gestured for them to take a seat. They opted for the couch, sitting side by side and directly across from him.

"An hour ago, I had the misfortune of getting a call from Mrs. Pease, a woman I don't know and would have preferred never to know. She called to tell me about an incident that took place earlier today—an incident where her little boy was doused in mud and pushed into a puddle—while dressed in his best clothes. She went on to say that while she did not actually attack the little boy, my daughter was there and was a companion to the girl who did."

"Daddy, I think *attack* is a little too strong a word."

The man stared momentarily at his daughter, his expression showing no amusement from her comment.

"The woman was practically delirious—talking about trying to clean the little boy and having to wash parts of his body two and three times." It was here Alfred shifted his eyes toward his houseguest. "It seems we have quite the little Calamity Jane under our roof."

"I'm sorry, Uncle Alfred. I was the one who did everything to him—and I know this'll sound nuts, but—he had it coming to him."

"For God's sake, he's only six years old!"

"It'll never happen again—not while I'm under your roof."

Instinctively a man of few words, he nodded his head and returned to his chair. Within seconds, the radio volume was turned up and the air crackled again with the sound of the Red Sox broadcast.

As the teenagers rose from the couch, Dorothy beckoned to Sheba from the doorway to join her on the porch.

"Your mother wants me. Let me talk to her for a minute and I'll catch up with you in your room after," instructed Sheba. By the time the sixteen-year-old made her way out the front door, the woman had descended the porch steps, waiting on her granddaughter in the yard.

"I thought we could go for a short walk—and maybe have a talk—just us two."

Grandmother and granddaughter had only just begun their leisurely stroll when Dorothy reached down and took Sheba's hand.

"We have a lot to cover young lady, and so I might as well get right to it. Let me start by saying that the fact that you and Elaine have hit it off so well is not going to make things any easier. Then again, on the plus side, she's more likely to listen to what you have to say. We both know you can't be staying here too long—and I've already taken steps to find you somewhere to go."

"Nana, how soon are you thinking you want me to leave?"

"Child, I'll be having your grandfather bring you to Portland tomorrow morning. No one will know you or him there. That craziness you pulled with the Pease boy is probably all over Wells and half of Kennebunk by now. I think it's just best to get you as far away as possible as soon as possible—and if you think it's not so, consider this: While you girls were out, there was a phone call from none other than Broderick Smith, asking if he could speak to none other than Elaine's cousin Sheba. Now, Elaine may not give two hoots about the Smith boy, but she's grown accustomed to all the attention and flattery that comes with him. What we don't need is a rift between you two over some silly boy when her well-being is at stake."

The woman's words hung in the air around them while Sheba's

mind raced. The mere thought of receiving a flirtatious phone call from her father made her deeply uncomfortable. The wisdom of the directive from her ancestors, counseling her and those who went before her to separate themselves from those closest to them after completing the purpose of their journey, was now becoming clearer.

"I've spoken to a woman I know who lives down in Boston. She runs a nice, respectable boarding house where, occasionally, she takes in girls who might be in the family way. Now, she knows there's no baby here or anything, but she'll be able to look after you until next month when you go back. You know, you're the first to do this since my father—and he said he was only back a few days. Child—all of this is so hard to believe."

They reached the fork in the road where Sheba had surprised her mother two days earlier.

"Now this woman in Boston—she doesn't put young women up out of the goodness of her heart. It'll pretty much empty out our cash fund here at home. But, you're here for all the right reasons—even if you are a handful." The woman stopped and embraced her granddaughter. She was visibly shaking, holding back tears. "I know you'll be safe down there," she added, to reassure herself as much as Sheba.

"I'll be leaving a note for my mother—as a sign. I've already thought about this. I thought about this a long time before I came."

"Your grandfather will drive you to Portland tomorrow morning after Elaine leaves for school. We can't have you standing around down at the Moody Post Office waiting for the bus. There'll be hell to pay when people figure out, particularly that Pease woman, that the girl who made such a mess out of her little boy is none other than our houseguest. Not a word to Elaine about you leaving tomorrow."

Sheba reluctantly agreed and the two women turned and started back toward the house.

"Them moccasins must be almost worn through with all the walking you've been doing."

"They sure beat walking barefoot," answered Sheba, laughing.

The return walk to the house saw Dorothy again taking her granddaughter's hand. The clarification of her plan and her granddaughter's acceptance of it seemed to lift a weight from the woman's shoulders. For the last twenty-four hours she had wrestled with the prospect of sending Sheba out into a world and time so foreign to her. She began taking comfort with the knowledge that this teenager with wild, tangled hair and an adventurous spirit seemed emotionally equipped to take on anything the world decided to toss at her. Reaching the front porch steps, Dorothy hooked her arm around Sheba's waist.

"Child, I don't believe you've told us what your last name is—unless I've just happened to miss it."

Sheba gave pause to the question, giving the outward appearance of someone mulling over a delicate response.

"Nana, I honestly think that would be giving you more information than what is good for you—or anyone else."

"Wise you are—wise beyond your years."

Seconds after re-entering the house, Elaine welcomed the two back from their walk, providing growing evidence of her attachment to her cousin.

"Mama, you're not thinking of giving Sheba my room and throwing me out of the house, are you?" The girl added a comically pathetic quality to her voice, causing Dorothy and Sheba to laugh aloud.

"Wait a minute, cousin. Didn't you yourself tell me that your mom and dad tossed out another daughter named Veronica—just because she wasn't as pretty as you? Well, you can't win them all. Remember the old saying: Sometimes you eat the bear, and sometimes the bear eats you."

The petite fourteen-year-old let her head drop in mock surrender. "I'll have my bags packed and ready to go by morning," she said.

The evening meal was still more than an hour away. Sheba told Elaine she would need some time by herself to jot down some personal details. So, after borrowing a pencil, tablet of paper and an envelope, she retreated to the privacy of the porch. A full hour passed before she rejoined the family. She caught up with Elaine in the dining room where she was helping her mother set the table. The time on the porch spent jotting down instructions and expressing her deepest feelings dampened her spirits. The evening meal found little in the way of conversation. What little that was said came from Elaine and focused on her general lack of enthusiasm toward the upcoming week of school. With neither adult even halfway through their meal, the teenagers excused themselves and retreated to the bedroom.

With the bedroom door closed behind them, Elaine hurled herself onto her mattress. Sheba collapsed into a corner chair, allowing her long body to stretch forward, her legs straight and extended.

"You haven't forgotten everything I've told you about now—about being careful driving your car—especially anywhere near Four Corners?"

"I haven't, I promise. And how about you—have you asked Mama about how long you can stay?"

"In due time," she answered, her voice barely carrying across the room.

"I think you should be asking her about enrolling you at Wells High. You do want to stay, don't you?"

Sheba, now aware her quiet, serious frame of mind was raising suspicion, set out to masquerade her feelings.

"Nothing's going to keep us apart, cousin—you wait and see," she blurted out. Pulling herself up from the chair, she joined her mother on the bed. Elaine nestled up beside her, their arms in perfect alignment.

"I can't believe how much darker your skin is than mine. You must have spent a lot of time in the sun last summer," Elaine commented.

"That's because I have some Indian blood in me. Besides, I happen to know all you gorgeous—no—drop-dead gorgeous girls make a point of staying out of the sun, so your perfect skin won't dry up and wrinkle."

"Really—honestly—do you really think I'm gorgeous, Sheba?"

"Put it this way—I can practically hear it now: *And representing the state of Maine at this year's Miss America Pageant—from the town of Wells Beach*—that sounds more exotic than Wells—*from the town of Wells Beach, Miss Elaine Lake.*"

The teenager let her head drop onto Sheba's shoulder. "Before you came, I always loved being an only child. Now I want to have a big sister like you—even if you're only my cousin."

Spread out on the bed, the young women talked for two hours, their heads remaining side by side. They recounted stories and incidents heretofore shared with no one else. Sheba detailed the intrusion into her bedroom of a man and what she did to prevent him from taking sexual advantage of her. Naturally, the name Jody Pease was left out of the account. All the while the two traded personal experiences, the topic of Sheba's departure was never raised. By nine-thirty, both girls were asleep.

* * *

The bedroom was in near total darkness when Sheba awoke. The only light visible came from a faint ray protruding through the keyhole in the door. It took only seconds for her mind to begin to race with thoughts of her bus trip. It struck her: This incredible journey she found herself on had only just begun. Thus far, she reasoned, she had the comfort of close relatives and familiar places. On Monday, she would lose the protection of family members, particularly of her grandmother, and travel south to Boston. The prospect of hiding away in an unfamiliar boarding house for better than three weeks among strangers was not appealing. Originally, she was relieved to learn that the next new moon, and her return to 1970, was nearly a month away. Now it seemed troublesome. Beside her, her mother breathed easily through a deep sleep. Sheba slipped from beneath the bed covers and advanced carefully toward the speck of light visible from the keyhole. Pulling open the door, she spotted her grandmother seated at the kitchen table two rooms away. She stepped cautiously through the darkened living room, careful not to stub a toe on the furniture, and joined the woman at the table.

"Can I get you anything?" Dorothy asked, her finger looped through the handle of a tea cup.

Sheba nodded no.

"I swear, I've lost track of how many times I've used this same tea bag. God, how I hate this war. You know, I think everything's begun to catch up with me. Child, I mean—this whole business of you coming here—as if out of nowhere—and the truth being no sane person would believe us even if we told them."

Her granddaughter responded with nothing more than a sad expression.

"Child, I am truly wrestling with this decision to send you off somewhere."

"No, Nana, don't. It's probably best—I know it is. Oh, wait—I have something for you!" Sheba rose from the table and walked back to the bedroom. Thirty seconds passed before she returned carrying a tablet of paper. "I've written down some facts and information that you might put to good use." The girl handed the woman two pieces of paper. "At the top of the first sheet are some sports results you might wager on in the future. For example, a fighter named Cassius Clay will be a big underdog when he fights a man named Sonny Liston for the heavyweight championship of the world. Bet on Cassius Clay. Also, there's another fighter my dad told me about named Rocky Marciano who never loses a fight. He's a heavyweight champion too. Always bet on him if you can because he never loses. The Red Sox will win the pennant in 1967—and they'll be long shots. Bet on them to win the pennant, but they'll lose the World Series." Sheba pointed down to the notes on the page, explaining each of the facts to her grandmother. "Everything else besides the sports stuff are companies on the stock market. Before I came, I looked up companies that started in the 1950s and went way up in value into the 1960s. I memorized as many as I could."

Dorothy looked down at the papers in amazement. "I swear, child, you are one smart cookie," she exclaimed.

At that moment, a sleepy-eyed Alfred Lake appeared in the doorway.

"Did we wake you, Alfred?"

"No, I rolled over and you weren't there next to me—so I came looking for you, that's all."

"Can I make you some tea?"

The man waved off his wife's offer. "I did want you two to know that if the decision to send off Calamity Jane has anything to do with me or the food situation—we can make do with the stamps we got. The girl really doesn't have to go."

Dorothy rose from her chair and approached her husband. "The decision has nothing to do with food or you—but it's good to hear an old grouch soften up once in a while."

Sheba smiled up at her grandfather, this man she would never truly know in later life.

"Well, I've got a long day ahead of me tomorrow, so I better be getting to bed," said Sheba, pushing herself up from the table.

16

September 25, 1944

Three sharp raps on the bedroom door brought Sheba to a sitting position as she awakened from a night of restless sleep. Beside her, Elaine moaned and buried her head under her pillow. Rising from bed, Sheba stumbled to the bedroom door, a knot of nervous energy already building in the pit of her stomach. Entering the living room, she spotted her grandmother standing in front of the kitchen stove.

"Toast and Quaker Oats—how does that sound?"

"No complaints from me," she answered, her eyes still half closed.

"Now Sheba, no mention of your going to Elaine. Pretend you're planning on hanging around all day and helping me with chores."

Sheba was unresponsive, not knowing if she could flagrantly lie to her mother's face.

"I'm too sick to go to school," came a cry from the bedroom. "I'm too sick and too tired to go to school. That's it, I'm sick and tired *of* school and I'm too sick and too tired to go *to* school," hollered Elaine from two rooms away.

"You don't look sick to me," came back her mother without even turning from the stove.

The pretty brunette, her hair tumbled over her eyes, stumbled to the table and collapsed onto the chair beside her cousin.

"And if you are so sick, maybe we should have your father bring you to Doctor Ross for some tests—some uncomfortable tests. You know how much you hate it when he sticks that stick down on your tongue and looks down your throat. Shall we call Doctor Ross?"

"No, I don't want to see that butcher! Maybe cousin Sheba can take me into the forest and use Indian medicine on me. She's part Indian, you know."

Her daughter's words caused Dorothy to stop and eye her grand-daughter, wondering how much detail she might have shared over the past two days.

"Why don't you send Sheba to school with me—so she can register. The girl's suggestion brought no response.

Seconds later, Dorothy turned and served the teenagers their oatmeal without so much as a word.

"Has Daddy already left for the plant?" Elaine asked in the next breath.

"Your father's going to work a little later this morning. Right now he's sleeping."

Breakfast passed with minimum small talk before Elaine retreated to her room and dressed for school. Sheba lingered over her cereal and toast, keeping distance between her and her mother. It was a few minutes before seven o'clock when the fourteen-year-old emerged from the bedroom and made her way to the front door. Dorothy rose from the table and joined her daughter. Reaching her at the front door, she kissed the girl on the cheek.

"Hey cousin, aren't you going to wish me a good day in school?" she called.

Sheba pushed herself from the table and walked to the kitchen doorway. "Knock em' dead, kid," she said with an obvious lack of conviction.

"Now I expect you to be waiting for the bus down at the fork when I get home."

There was no response from Sheba.

"Sheba—say you'll be waiting for me when I get home." Elaine stared intently at her cousin, reading her face for any sign of a positive response. When her cousin's eyes unconsciously fell to the floor, the girl became alarmed. "Cousin, tell me you'll be here when I get home."

Sheba walked up to Elaine in silence, ultimately throwing her arms around the girl.

"I'll be back in your life sooner than you think," she whispered to her. "And remember everything I've told you."

"No, I don't want you to leave."

Dorothy stepped forward, grabbing her daughter by the wrist and directing her out onto the porch. "Off with you now. You heard your cousin—you'll be seeing her again."

The fourteen-year-old began to sob as she reluctantly made her way down the steps and toward the road. Sheba stood in the doorway, taking perhaps her last look at her mother.

"I promise you, cousin—I'll be back in your life sooner than you think, I promise," she called out.

Elaine took a few steps, stopped, and looked back at the house. Her sobbing was still audible. Then, frozen in her tracks, she raised her hand slowly and offered Sheba a resigned wave. She remained statue-like until her cousin returned the gesture, then turned and walked away. Sheba stood clutching her grandmother as the girl headed down Tatnic Road, finally disappearing behind a line of trees.

In the next instant, Sheba excused herself and rushed to the bedroom where she fell onto the bed, burying her face in her mother's pillow. She did not want her grandmother to see or hear her crying. She felt herself growing ill from grief and pain. Over the weekend, she had come to know her mother in a way no daughter could ever expect to know a parent. She had bonded with the woman who gave her life, as a peer, sharing two days in the teenage life of Elaine Lake. It was clear to her: The gift she had been given as a direct descendent of Mowalk came at a price. For ten minutes Dorothy respected the teenager's privacy, leaving her to purge some of her pain alone. Eventually, the woman knocked on the bedroom door, summoning Sheba back to the living room.

"I'm assuming you'll want to be traveling in your jeans and a comfortable blouse. We'll pack you the dress from the Littlefield's and some clean underwear and stockings. That should get you through the next three weeks."

Emerging from the bedroom to face her grandmother, she caught sight of Alfred in the kitchen, pouring his first coffee of the morning.

"Get the bathroom before your grandfather," whispered Dorothy. "I'll give you the money for the trip when he's in there shaving. I don't need for him to know about how much money I've given you until you're long gone."

Sheba stepped back into the bedroom, then emerged with an envelope.

"I want you to tape this up somewhere in my mother's bedroom—and make sure she obeys what's written on it."

The woman took the envelope, which contained the following message: To Elaine... Do not open under any conditions until August 5, 1945. Sheba

Dorothy tucked the envelope inside her apron pocket, then immediately returned the conversation to its original topic.

"Your grandfather can't be missing too much work, so I'd like to see you ready to leave by eight-thirty. As I told you last night, he'll be taking you to Portland. There's a bus scheduled to leave for Boston at ten minutes past two. You won't be in time for the earlier one. Do you have any questions, child?"

The girl shook her head no.

"Take this—it's a pouch with sixty-five dollars in it. That's enough to cover the bus fare plus room and board in Boston. It's all I could come up with. Your grandfather thinks you're just going home to your family—so don't mention the money and don't let him know about the boarding house." Dorothy glanced out to the kitchen, assuring herself they were not being scrutinized by Alfred, then handed Sheba the pouch.

The Pontiac was already idling in front of the house when Sheba pushed her way out the front door. Her grandmother stood at the top of the porch steps, the strain of this good-bye now reflected on her face. For Sheba, there was a certain finality at hand. Sheba, this child of the turbulent '60s, would never set eyes on her grandmother again. If grandmother and granddaughter's understanding of the rite from their Quintanok bloodline was correct, the teenager would return to the summer from whence she came. For the middle-aged woman, this was a strange farewell. Dorothy would now have to wait until she was blessed with a granddaughter before the two would meet again. Then, this grandchild would represent an hourglass of her own life, the sands spilling down with the passage of time until her granddaughter reached her sixteenth year.

Sheba approached Dorothy, one hand clutching a paper grocery bag with all her possessions. She reached around the middle-aged woman and squeezed tightly.

"I love you, Nana—I love you so much," she whispered, her tears already streaming down her face. "Be sure Momma never forgets what I warned her about—and that she reads my note next August—and that she is particularly careful on August 14, 1960."

"Child, God be with you—and don't you fret—I'm sure Mowalk's with you too." Their embrace went on for an extended time before Dorothy pulled herself free and fled inside the house. Sheba walked to the car and took her seat beside Alfred.

"You needn't be so sad, girl—we'll have you back for a visit next summer," consoled the man before pulling out onto the road. On the drive down Tatnic Road, Sheba struggled to keep her crying under control by burying her sobs within herself. By the time they reached Route 1 and turned northward, the only sound in the car came from the engine. For the next few miles, Sheba took in the sights of her hometown during wartime. In only three days she had gained an appreciation for the people who had come before her and the sacrifices made by them in the war effort.

Following a prolonged silence, and with the Pontiac just motoring by the high school, her grandfather spoke up.

"Your cousin's going to miss you terrible—you do know that?"

"And I'll miss her." As she spoke, her eyes were glued to the four-column building. Her mind hastened back to the mornings from her other life and time, mornings when she stepped down from the school bus and glanced over to the cemetery across the road where Elaine and Billy Smith lay buried beneath the ground. It was a chilling reminder of the purpose behind her journey back here and the justification for any hardship or inconvenience she was about to face. By the time the car cruised by Burnt Mill Road, her home from that other life, Sheba had pushed thoughts of death and cemeteries from her head.

As the Pontiac cruised northward on Route 1, through Kennebunk, Biddeford, Saco and Scarborough, Sheba stole glances across at her grandfather, hoping to imprint his image in her memory. Her grandparents had dipped into their reserve gasoline supply for this unscheduled trip to Portland. Even Alfred's A card did not provide him with enough gasoline necessary to support this overland journey. U.S. Route 1 was not in the same state of repair as the road she left in 1970. She was not uncomfortable with the lack of conversation between her and her grandfather. He was a quiet man who saw her as someone only related to her by marriage. Sheba wished there was some way she could let him know of their kinship.

They were already within the city limits of Portland when he spoke up. "Now, if I can just remember how to find the bus terminal, we should be in business. Once you're inside and you have your ticket—I suggest that you find yourself a nice, quiet corner out of everybody's way and keep your nose clean. You know what that means?"

Sheba looked across the car and nodded blankly.

"Well, Calamity Jane, it means to stay out of trouble." He drove down a series of streets, seeming to know his way. Finally, the Pontiac rolled toward a block where a half dozen buses lined both sides of the street.

"This looks promising—now, if I can find a parking space, we'll be all set," he added. They passed a neon sign reading "Bus Terminal" before locating a space to park. Sheba was surprised when he began to secure the car, evidently intending to accompany her inside.

"You don't have to go inside, Uncle Alfred, I know you're late for work as it is."

"I've come this far—so why not do it right?"

Sheba lifted her paper bag after checking the contents inside, then accompanied the man up the street and into the terminal building. He prodded her into a short line where she purchased a one-way ticket to Boston, Massachusetts. He was sitting alone on one of the wooden benches when she rejoined him and displayed her ticket.

"I guess all I have to do now is wait. The man at the window said they'd announce when and where to board the bus as the time approaches."

Her grandfather produced a dollar bill from his pocket. "Take this, Calamity Jane—you'll want to be getting something to read and chew on. It's going to be a long wait."

Sheba's eyes lit up with appreciation. "No, Uncle Alfred—I can't." She pushed the money back at him, then shocked the man by throwing her arms around his neck. "I'll miss you, Uncle Alfred— thank you for everything." Sheba kissed her grandfather on the cheek while inhaling the scent of his Aqua Velva, knowing instantly it would be a lasting reminder of her short, personal encounter with him. Pulling away after feeling his weak return of the embrace, she took a seat on the bench a few steps away.

"We'll have you back next summer—when school's out. Maybe your folks will let you stay for a month or so. I know Elaine would like that."

She smiled up at him, offering a feeble acceptance.

"Gotta go," he said, glancing down mechanically at his watch.

Sheba offered the man a final good-bye and watched as Alfred Lake, for all intents and purposes, walked out of her life.

17

THE TERMINAL WAS RELATIVELY QUIET as Sheba tried to make herself comfortable for the next few hours. A few discarded newspapers were scattered along the wooden benches, prompting her to review the selection of free reading material before selecting a Portland paper. She moved farther from the door where an aggravating draft blew over her every time it swung open. Eventually, she settled on a bench along the far wall, sitting at the extreme end with her bag resting beside her. Glancing down at her newspaper, she saw nearly every page dominated by news of the war. Flipping forward, she finally found the comic section. Largely to kill time, Sheba decided to read every comic strip, in full, even the serious ones of the serial variety. Oblivious to everything around her, she poured over the individual features, rereading some over and over if she did not understand the message or joke contained in the text.

"*Boston and Maine Trailways bus leaving for Bangor in ten minutes—now boarding at the front of the building,*" called out a disinterested sounding voice over the speaker. Her eyes came up from the newspaper and focused on a clock across the terminal. It was ten minutes past ten. If her memory served her correctly, she had been lost in the comics for nearly half an hour.

Sheba was surprised to see the waiting area within the terminal filling up with travelers. Nearly alone only thirty minutes earlier, there were now at least two dozen men and women scattered on the benches around her. The nearest person to her was a man seated off to the left on the bench facing hers. He was young, perhaps in his mid-twenties, with sandy hair and a sad face. She trained her eyes on him, studying his features momentarily. When he happened to glance up and catch her contemplating him, he responded with a dim smile, temporarily erasing the sad look that originally caught her attention.

His smile elicited a glare back from her. The young man quickly dropped his eyes and resumed reading his book.

Before returning to her newspaper, Sheba reached around, lifted the paper bag from the bench and balanced it on her lap. The teenager opened the bag and removed the pouch containing her money. Pulling it open by its drawstring, she removed the bills and counted out fifty six dollars. This is what would have to support her through her stay at the home of Miss Mary Gorman at 44 B Street in South Boston. Her instructions were to call a cab after arriving in Boston and be delivered to the doorstep of this Mary Gorman. This seemed simple enough. After returning her pouch full of money to the paper bag, she discreetly pulled the corners of her wardrobe up from the bag and examined each. She wondered if there would be an opportunity to wear the dress during her extended stay at the house. While running her fingers over the fabric of the dress given to her by the Littlefield family, she looked up, catching the young man with the sad face staring at her and her paper bag.

"What are you looking at?" she snapped.

"Nothing—I was just wondering if you had to pay a lot for that magnificent piece of luggage of yours?" There was playfulness in his voice.

"What's it to you—creep?" Sheba exploded, causing more than one person to turn their head in her direction.

Shock registered on his face. Sheba followed up with a hostile glare at the man who now fidgeted in his seat, uncomfortable with the attention this minor altercation was bringing him. Seconds later, he rose to his feet, lifted his single piece of luggage, and moved away. As he made his way to another set of benches, Sheba noticed a pronounced limp in his step. It made her wonder if he labored with a disability or if his foot was merely asleep from sitting in the same position too long. Finding a quiet, less crowded section of benches halfway across the room, the young man dropped himself and his things down.

Settling back on her bench and now rid of the man with the sad eyes, Sheba found herself an object of curiosity for no less than half the males in the terminal. When she tried to return to her paper, she was distracted by the peering, probing glances of men who, probably, waited on her next emotional eruption. Out of curiosity, she scanned the terminal in search of the fellow with the limp. She spotted him, the back of his head anyway, some distance away. Now, after checking her belongings no more than ten minutes earlier, she reached back into the shopping bag and removed the pouch containing her fifty six dollars. A few steps away, a red-headed gentleman with a protruding nose rose to his feet and stretched, letting out with a yawn, his arms stretched horizontally. She eyed him cautiously until he returned to his seat and opened a copy of *Look* magazine. She began to feel uneasy about leaving her pouch buried inside the paper bag and decided to remove it. She would hold it in her hand with the draw strings looped around her fingers. Her eyes gazed across at the clock on the back wall. It was ten twenty-three. She yawned and rubbed her eyes. It was going to be a long day, she thought. The man with the red hair was on his feet again. Why couldn't this guy just sit in one place? She half closed her eyes, no doubt from boredom, when a rush of footsteps sped toward her.

Without warning, there was a rush of activity surrounding her. She let out a cry when the red-headed man came crashing down on her. His impact sent her crashing to the floor. Sheba cried out, her mind trying to make sense of the bedlam breaking out on the floor nearby. The weight of the man was now resting on her, crushing her against the dirty, wooden floor. An instant later, her fingers felt a ripping sensation as the strings of the money pouch were torn from her hand.

"Give me back my money!" Sheba cried out, before slamming her fist against the side of the man's head and wrapping her legs around his waist. He tried to raise himself but was held back by the strength of Sheba's legs. She was already punishing his face and neck with one blow after another, all the while her legs preventing his escape.

"This man has my money—help me!" Around the two was an atmosphere of shock and confusion with most people looking down at the two in disbelief. Sheba continued flailing away, her knuckles catching the man on the bridge of the nose and sending him reeling onto his back. Like a cat, the teenager pounced on him, his nose now cascading blood. She was balanced on the red-headed man's chest.

"I want my money back," she screamed, striking him again on the side of the face. Then, she felt her arm restrained from behind.

"He doesn't have your money—it's someone else."

Sheba looked up to see the young man with the sad face speaking to her.

"This man was pushed into you as a diversion. I saw it all. The guy who's got your money ran out the front door and up the street. He's the one who grabbed your purse. I chased him a short way but there was no way I could keep up."

She scrambled to her feet and raced from the terminal. Clearing the front door and onto the sidewalk she frantically searched the street for signs of anyone fleeing from the building. She sprinted to the nearest corner and, again, looked for anyone in the process of running away. There was no sign of the thief. After frantically stopping two pedestrians and asking for help, she returned to the terminal, shaken and beside herself.

Walking back to the scene of the theft, she saw the red-headed man being assisted by the young man with the limp.

"I'm calling a cop. Don't let this little bitch go anywhere," ordered the man while holding a handkerchief to his nose.

"I thought you'd taken my money—it wasn't my fault."

"I want a cop. This was a case of assault and battery."

"No cops—I don't want to talk to any cops." Sheba was already imagining a question-and-answer period with the police.

"And what is your name, young lady? Give us your name and address. We'll have to be contacting your parents, you know." The girl knew she could not consent to a visit to the Portland police station.

"Never mind what you want," came back the man.

The young man with the limp spoke up. "You know, sir—I'm not so sure—if I was you, that is—I'm not so sure I'd want to be parading in front of the police, looking like you do—them knowing a teenage girl got you that way. You might be in for a terrible ribbing—maybe even wind up in the paper—terribly embarrassing. You and I know you purposely wouldn't strike a woman, no less a girl, and that's why everything came out this way—taken advantage of by this little tomboy. But the newspaper—they'd probably make it into some crazy thing about a man getting a thrashing by a little girl. There'd be no living it down." The soft-spoken young man dusted off the gentleman's coat a final time and handed him his hat. The man, crimson-faced from Sheba's punches, took the hat and walked quietly from the terminal.

Sheba walked back to the bench where her shopping bag, flattened and partially ripped, sat unattended. Turning back to the young man, she saw he had already returned to his own bench. Picking up her belongings, she slowly wandered over in his general direction. When he failed to lift his eyes on her approach, she sauntered up beside him, standing over him without uttering a word. She stood there, her moccasins practically touching his oxblood shoes. Neither said a word. Following better than a minute of silence, it was he who spoke.

"If it were me, I'd report the stolen money to the police. Maybe they have some fund where they could reimburse you for your loss."

"I can't go to the police—I told you that."

He still made no eye contact with her.

"I shouldn't have called you a creep—okay?"

"Oh—so I am still a creep—you just shouldn't have called me one. Is that it?"

"I don't know—if you are or aren't a creep. I'll know in two or three days when I know you better."

Now the young man's head was up, looking at her in amazement.

"Excuse me—excuse me—you're not going to know or see me two days from now. I just did you a small favor back there—a favor I was never thanked for, by the way. But, that's it! When I get on my bus in an hour from now, that's the end of me and the nuts-in-the-head girl from the bus terminal."

Sheba collapsed onto the bench beside him, prompting the young man to slide to his left, attempting to put some distance between the two.

"He got all my money—the money my grandmother gave me to live on," she said, trying to inject a degree of pathos in her voice.

"I'm sorry to hear that—I really am."

"You know, the more I think about it, the more I begin to wonder if you might not be in cahoots with the robber. Maybe you're just going to meet up with him later on—and share my money."

The man lifted his head and stared directly into the girl's eyes. He had brown eyes.

"So, let me get this straight. I team up with the robber and help him make off with your money. Then we meet up later in Lowell and split the money—all ten dollars of it. Is that how it is?"

"There was over fifty dollars in my pouch—money my grandmother and grandfather scrimped and saved for," snapped back Sheba.

"Sorry, fifty dollars."

"Where's Lowell? Is that where you're going?"

"It's in Massachusetts and it's none of your business." The young man's tone made it clear he wanted no part of her, but Sheba saw little in the way of options at the moment. But, even beyond her predicament, she felt an inexplicable fondness growing for this stranger. There was a trustworthy quality to him and evidence of basic goodness.

"Show me you ticket so I know you're not lying about going to Lowell," she ordered.

After pausing, then rolling his eyes, he produced a ticket from his pocket. It read: DESTINATION; LOWELL, MASS.

"Okay—okay, it sounds like you're not lying," she admitted. She picked up her bag and left the stranger to himself.

* * *

Ten minutes after being granted leave of her company, the young man with the brown eyes glanced up to see Sheba walking toward him, displaying a bus ticket in front of her face. Reaching him, she deposited herself onto the bench, directly to his right, actually brushing against his leg as she fell back.

"They were very understanding with me at the ticket counter. They let me exchange my Boston ticket for one to Lowell. Did you know we have a layover in Portsmouth?"

"Yes I did—and what's going on here?"

"I figured, well, I don't know a soul in Boston—and I do know someone in Lowell—so I traded tickets so I could go somewhere where I knew someone."

The man pulled back from her, showing annoyance.

"Wait a minute—wait a minute—I don't know you—and you have a hell of a nerve trying to palm yourself off on me. What's the matter with you?"

His words caused her to recoil, tears welling up instantly in her eyes.

"For God's sake, don't cry," he whispered, looking around to see if anyone was privy to their conversation. "You really should contact the police—they can help you."

"I told you—I can't. But don't worry yourself over me—I'll be just fine. I'll get by somehow with no money—and no place to go—and nothing to eat."

The man buried his face in his hands. "I'll buy you something to eat on the bus—when we stop. I can give you a few dollars when we get to Lowell, too—but that's it."

Sheba rubbed the tears from her eyes and looked over at him. Her expression remained a sad one.

"Thank you—whatever your name is."

"Kevin."

"Thank you, Kevin." She smiled at him for the first time. "Now that we have that settled, maybe I should let you get back to your reading."

He gestured yes with a nod of the head and returned to his book.

"I'm surprised you haven't bothered to ask me what my name is," she said. Her comment drew a weak chuckle from the man.

"All right—I can take a hint. And what would your name be, Miss?"

"My name is Sheba—like in the Bible—Sheba Smith."

"And if I may be so bold—how old are you, Sheba Smith?"

The question caught the teenager off guard. She asked herself what age she should be. What would be the best age to say she was as far as this fellow was concerned? She ran the question over in her head too long, causing an extended pause. "I'm eighteen," she blurted out. "I turned eighteen last Christmas. You see, I was born on Christmas day." Sheba's answer sat well with her. Granted, it was a lie, a white lie, but it was garnished with a pinch of truth.

"And in what year would that have been?"

She went to respond, then realized the follow-up lie required some math. She struggled with the calculation, causing her to become out-wardly flustered. "I won't be treated like a barefaced liar! How dare you question me on my age! Do you take me for a liar?" She raised her voice, causing others in the terminal to, again, take notice of them. Kevin returned his attention to his book, embarrassed by the stares from those seated nearby.

For the next few minutes Sheba sat quietly while Kevin deliberat-ed over the pages in his book. However, she was now experiencing hunger pains, made more unbearable by the boredom of sitting qui-etly next to the young man.

"Kevin," she said, waiting for him to look up.

He did not, choosing to ignore her.

"Kevin, I'm hungry," she muttered, kicking him in the leg to get his attention.

"I told you I'd get you something once we're on the bus—at one of the stops."

"There's a candy bar machine over in the corner of the building. Couldn't you give me some money for a candy bar? Pleeeeeeease? Pretty pleeeeease?"

"Sweet Jesus, you can be an aggravating pest," he complained, rifling his hand through his pocket. Finally, he dropped a nickel into the palm of her outstretched hand.

"Five cents? That's all I get?"

"I'm not buying you more than one candy bar." She remembered it was 1944 and relented. Scampering across the terminal, she deposited her buffalo head nickel into the machine and was rewarded with a Baby Ruth bar. She returned to the bench, seated herself next to Kevin, and slowly gnawed at the candy, drawing pleasure from every small bite she took from it. With the candy bar half gone, she offered her benefactor a bite, but he declined. With the Baby Ruth nearly gone, she glanced down at the cover of Kevin's book.

"Oh, my God! You're reading *Ulysses!*" Sheba exclaimed. "We talked about that book in school. One of my high school teachers said it was a masterpiece, but the women at the library, well, they said it was nothing but filthy trash—s-m-u-t, smut. Kevin, I am very disappointed in you, young man," she said, waving her finger in his face. "*Ulysses*, by James Joyce. Now, there's a terrible last name for a man—Joyce."

"What's so bad about it?"

"It's a girl's name, that's what's so bad about it."

"So what?"

"So what? Well, how would you like to have a girl's name for your last name? Okay, we'll call you Kevin Mary. Think of it. Here comes little Kevin Mary—who talks just like a girl. Oh, Kevin Mary, don't you go play football with the boys—they might rip your pretty dress. Oh, Kevin Mary, you look so cute in…"

"Are you always like this?" he interrupted.

"No, just around you, Kevin Mary."

The young man appeared more annoyed than amused by her bantering. Content to return to his novel, he refocused his attention on his reading material while Sheba licked her fingertips, savoring the last, precious traces of her candy bar.

A few seconds later came the sound of a man blowing into a microphone. *"Boarding in fifteen minutes—Trailways Bus number two-sixty-two for Portsmouth, with stops in South Portland, Scarborough, Old Orchard Beach, Saco, Biddeford, Arundel, Kennebunk, Wells, Moody, Ogunquit Village, York Beach and Kittery."*

"Sweet God, it's going to be a long afternoon," he groaned.

"Oh, Kevin, would you do me a favor and watch my things while I go to the ladies' room? I'd like to make one trip there before we have to get on the bus."

"Sure, go ahead."

She jumped to her feet, then stopped abruptly in her tracks. "Now, I hope you won't start going through my luggage while I'm in the bathroom. My clothing, including my underwear, is in there."

"What do you take me for?" he asked, not sure if she was serious.

"Well, with you reading *Ulysses* and all—I'm not sure what I take you for."

He locked eyes with an elderly lady sitting nearby who was taking in the entire conversation. He watched as her eyes left his, scanned down to the copy of *Ulysses*, then returned. Mortified, he stuffed the book into his luggage and stared up at the ceiling.

"Please—please watch your own things," he said before she reached the end of the aisle.

"I was only kidding, Kevin, just joking around."

"No, please take your stuff."

He rose to his feet and brought the shopping bag to her. His limp was extremely pronounced. She smiled up at him when he reached her, but his face had regained the sad look from hours earlier. He was unresponsive to her smile.

Sheba rushed through her necessities in the ladies' room, returning to the terminal lobby as passengers rose to their feet and began filing toward the bus leaving for Portsmouth. Scanning the lobby for Kevin, she did not spot him among the two dozen or so people shuffling toward the waiting bus. Convinced he must be outside already, she hurried toward Trailways Bus two-sixty-two, managing to skip ahead of no less than half a dozen other would-be passengers. Reaching into her breast pocket, she pulled out her ticket and presented it to the driver. Sheba looked down the aisle of the coach, her eyes scanning from side to side in search of Kevin. Finally, she spotted his sandy, neatly-combed hair next to a window halfway to the end of the coach. She moved toward the back, only to find him seated next to a man dressed in dirty work clothes.

"Kevin, I thought you and I would sit together," she said plaintively in a soft voice.

He had been staring out the window, as though trying to avoid eye contact with her. "No, this will be fine. I'm going to try to get a little shuteye on the way to Portsmouth. I really didn't sleep all that well last night."

"Okay, Kevin. I'll see you when we get to Portsmouth," answered Sheba. She looked around, spotted an empty window seat a few rows back, and quickly laid claim to it.

After sliding the shopping bag under her seat, Sheba settled in. She was uncomfortable with Kevin's sudden withdrawal. It was not her imagination, he was clearly pulling back from her. She was astonished with her own behavior in his company. Inexplicably, she had opened up with this young man, a total stranger. She wondered if, somehow, he saw her teasing as a sign of disrespect. Leaning her cheek against the bus window, she looked out at the gray Portland street and considered her situation. She was now without money, thanks to her carelessness inside the terminal. Later in the day, perhaps early evening, she would arrive in a strange city without funds, a place to stay or anyone to turn to. She looked up to see a heavyset woman give way into the seat beside her, hitting the cushion with a thud. She looked into the woman's face. It was overly made up and seemed to lack even a hint of friendliness or warmth. Again, she glanced outside, her mind wrestling with her dilemma. For the first time since she awoke at the sacred rock, she was extremely concerned, even a little frightened. The stream of passengers ended a few minutes later, and she was stirred from a mindless daydream by the noisy closing of the bus doors. The coach slowly moved away from the curb and headed out of the city.

Aftcr following the progress of the journey for ten minutes or so, Sheba lost interest and returned her attention to inside the bus. The woman beside her was knitting, an activity she found tedious and uninspiring. Occasionally, she looked up toward Kevin, reassuring herself he was still where she had left him. With every stop, Sheba watched for any activity from the grizzled man beside him. Over the first hour, the man barely stirred, appearing to be asleep as the bus rolled down Route 1. Progress was slow as they rattled southward. Eventually, she was jolted from a light sleep as the vehicle passed over a pothole, sending a noisy shockwave through it and causing more than a few passengers to call out in surprise. Staring out the window, she identified her whereabouts. The mill buildings in the upper village of Kennebunk were right outside the window. Wells was only a few miles away. Since Portland, the bus had not strayed from Route 1. It was a safe bet, she thought, that it would pass by Wells High School. She made an effort to drive the drowsiness from her eyes, now eager to catch a last glimpse of her hometown. The bus picked up speed over the next few miles, finally reaching Wells with Sheba's cheek literally pressed against the window.

Sheba found herself taking in more detail than during her hitch-hiking experience three days earlier. She was fascinated by the sight of familiar buildings, many in better repair than from her other life in 1970. Her eyes widened as the bus passed by Burnt Mill Road, know-ing she would return there in a few short weeks to survey the fruit of this adventure. It was afternoon—exactly what time in the afternoon she did not know. On the opposite side of the bus, she caught sight of the Lindsey Tavern as the vehicle approached Wells Corner. The high school was just ahead. However, Trailways had passengers standing by the road at the intersection. Sheba's mind raced with the prospect of catching one last glimpse of her mother. Three passengers came up into the bus and exchanged money with the driver. A group of teenage boys walked by the bus and she searched for the face of her father. He was not among them. The bus driver sat frozen at the wheel, then gradually released the hand brake. The vehicle rolled back onto Route 1. With the gears grinding slightly, the bus slowly picked up speed and headed toward Wells High. Seconds later, she was looking out at high school girls and boys gathered in small groups in front of the school. Her eyes darted from one group to the next, finally spotting her mother standing beside another girl, no doubt her friend Lucille. In that instant, she was overcome with the urge to pull the emergency cord and bring the bus to a halt. If she could not be welcomed back at the house, then why couldn't she hide out in the forest behind the property, unbeknownst to her grandparents, and have her mother bring her food and visit with her whenever possible? Her mind actually nurtured this idea as she looked back at Elaine, her eyes straining to keep her in sight. Then, with the bus rumbling forward, the school disappeared from view. She had not pulled the cord, largely because she had too little time to think through the scheme. She thought of her grandmother's reaction to the loss of family funds. The bus passed the site of Congdon's Doughnut Shop. It was little more than a field. Ahead, though, Howard Johnson's Restaurant was there, looking the same as it had the last time she had dined there. They moved on, and she took her last, fleeting look at the Wells of 1944. Her spirits plummeted. This final glimpse of her mother and her town was more painful than heartwarming.

Sheba redirected her attention inside the bus as it continued on its route to Portsmouth. Beside her, the woman continued knitting. It was only a short distance to Ogunquit, where forty-eight hours earlier she and Elaine had bicycled together, learning so many personal and silly things about one another. She smiled when images of the fat man in the store came to mind. The driver slowly brought them to a halt near the center of the village, although no passengers appeared to be waiting at the designated Trailways pickup point.

"They'll be stopping to leave off the movie reels. They gotta stop in Ogunquit even when no one's getting on the bus—'cause of the movie theaters," said the woman beside her, in a listless tone, not even raising her eyes from her lap. Sheba did not respond. Craning her neck, she looked forward and spotted the back of Kevin's head before closing and resting her eyes.

"York Village," called out the driver as the brakes screeched the bus to a halt. "There will be a fifteen-minute rest period. You may get up and stretch your legs, but be back in your seat in fifteen minutes," he added as the doors folded open.

Sheba opened her eyes to see the grizzled man beside Kevin jump to his feet. She reacted immediately, pulling her bag from beneath the seat, easing past the knitting lady and into the aisle. The man had taken no more than two steps from his seat when Sheba planted herself into it. Simultaneously, Kevin rose.

"Please, Kevin, don't just walk away."

"No, it's not you—I need some fresh air." He fumbled his way by her and made for the open doorway. Sheba followed close behind. The two met with a fresh breeze straight off the Atlantic. Within sight, the ocean crashed up onto a sandy beach less than two hundred yards away.

"Oh, God, I was dying in there," exclaimed Kevin, breathing air in exaggerated inhalations. "That guy beside me stank of fish and body odor, not to mention periods of flatulation. At one point, I was on the verge of passing out—no exaggeration."

"Why didn't you just come back and sit with me?" Sheba asked.

"I didn't want to hurt his feelings."

"It was God punishing you for being mean to me—you do know that?" Kevin rolled his eyes, continuing to walk in the direction of the foaming surf. "Now, when we get back on the bus, we sit together—got it?" He nodded his head in acceptance. "We can't be going too far here. The man said fifteen minutes, and we don't want to be left behind, even in a pretty place like this."

They walked past a movie house and a few shops, none of which were open. They stopped a few feet from the beach where white, foamy surf crashed and streamed over the sand before retreating back into the sea. Sheba caught Kevin staring up at a hotel perched above them on an adjacent hillside.

"Is Lowell this pretty?" she asked.

"It's nice in its own way—not this way, though."

"We better turn back. If we miss the bus, you'll have to pay for your and my rooms in that hotel—and I'll want the penthouse."

He smiled and did an about-face. A number of passengers were still milling outside the bus. Sheba locked her arm with his as they walked back toward the vehicle.

"Now, you will keep your promise and buy me something to eat in Portsmouth, won't you?"

"Oh, so that's what this is all about! You see little Kevin Mary as a meal ticket!"

Sheba let out a laugh. "No, I see my little Kevin Mary as a friend—a trustworthy friend."

"And if Kevin Mary doesn't feed you, what then?"

"Then my poor skeleton self will still be friends with Kevin Mary—even though he would choose to starve his precious Sheba to death." She concluded her dramatics by resting her head on his shoulder.

"Tell me about where you live in Lowell. Do you have your own house? You don't live with your parents, do you?"

"No, I don't live with my parents. In fact, I'm just coming back from visiting my parents. They live in Portland. My grandfather died and left them his house, so they moved from Lowell a couple of years ago up to Portland." Inwardly, she was greatly pleased with this information.

They reached the bus with Sheba's head still resting on the young man's shoulder. On inspection, it appeared Kevin's traveling companion had left the bus. He reclaimed his window seat while she took possession of the seat beside him.

"Your friend may be gone, but his fishy smell is still in the air around us," she joked.

"Are you kidding? This is nothing! You had to be here when he was here to really appreciate this guy's problem."

"Kevin, let me know if it's just me, but have you ever been around someone who is really dirty and decrepit, and wondered how nasty and disgusting their underwear must be?"

He leaned forward in his seat and hooted, causing two women across the aisle to stare at him disapprovingly. "I can't believe you just said that! Does everything that pops in your head just automatically come out that mouth of yours?"

She did not answer his question, choosing to simply flash him a coy smile. She was acutely aware of something blossoming in her. It was something she had observed in other females on countless occasions. In the past, she had seen this behavior as distasteful. However, at this moment, and under these circumstances, she recognized the need to endear herself to this young man, and it was not like she had to work at it. There was something in Kevin's manner, more than his appearance, that drew her to him. In all of her sixteen years, she had seen nothing in the opposite sex that prompted her to trust them. Aside from her father, no male had ever shown her anything to earn her attention or respect. Now, with a housing crisis looming in the next few hours, she saw herself putting all of her reliance and blind trust in this young man from Massachusetts.

It was approaching four o'clock when their bus slowly maneuvered its way through the narrow streets of Portsmouth, finally groaning to a stop directly in front of the terminal. It would be another two hours before they could make their way down the coast and inland to Lowell. That route, too, would be riddled with stops in the towns and cities along the way.

"There's a diner nearby," said Kevin. "I could really go for a couple of hot dogs and some fries. That sound okay to you?" Sheba's face brightened and she nodded her head. She followed his lead, careful not to rush ahead. Kevin's steps were measured as one leg dragged behind the other.

Inside the diner, they grabbed an empty booth and waited for the waitress. The booths were weathered and hard with grooves worn into the wood from the countless backsides coming in contact with them over the years. The waitress, a middle-aged, tired looking woman, arrived quickly and stood over the couple.

"Menus?"

"Not for me—I'll have a couple of hot dogs with lots of mustard and relish, and a vanilla frappe," stated Kevin emphatically.

"Can I have a frappe, too?" Sheba whispered across the table.

"A frappe and two hot dogs for the lady, my good woman," he said grandly in his best Errol Flynn impersonation. The waitress rolled her eyes, and jotted down the order. As she left the booth, an uncomfortable silence fell upon them. Then Kevin spoke up in a serious tone.

"Sheba, you know I told you I'd give you a few dollars when we get to Lowell—and I will. In fact, I'll give you enough so you can rent a room for the night and get your bearings in the morning."

"Thank you, Kevin," she answered, her voice scarcely disguising her disappointment.

"I'd like to do more, but I'm not exactly rich."

She made a feeble gesture, acknowledging she understood. In the back of her mind, plans had already been formulated. Her plan was to ride out her remaining time in 1944, a full three weeks, with this young man in Lowell. She had hoped to hear an offer of some sort from him, an offer to open his apartment to her. She thought her total openness, her giddiness and carefree manner would serve as encouragement for such a proposition. She was hesitant to raise the matter of joining him at his house herself, thinking it would come off as pushy and, no doubt, cheap.

With their meals in front of them, the conversation turned to personal matters. Sheba learned that Kevin worked at Kresge's 5 & 10 Cent Store, specifically in the hardware department. He was particularly interested in locks and locking mechanisms. His interest was a direct result of one of his duties, duplicating keys. She listened as he explained how he searched out books and manuals relating to locks of every kind, hoping to self-educate himself in the field.

Following their meal, they took a stroll around the city, knowing they did not have to be back at the bus terminal until six o'clock. Kevin remembered that John Paul Jones had some association with Portsmouth. They stopped a passerby and were given directions to the John Paul Jones House. They walked the four blocks to the historical home and spent nearly half an hour draped over the fence, taking in the site and exchanging each other's knowledge of their country's struggle for independence.

The sun was beginning to drop in the sky when the two arrived back at the terminal, just in time to hear the initial announcement for the last leg of their bus trip. The bus would rejoin Route 1 in town and travel south to Amesbury, Massachusetts. From there, the bus would join Route 110 and track the Merrimack River all the way to Lowell. Boarding the bus, they were struck by the drop in the number of passengers. There would be no more than a dozen fellow travelers on this final stage of their trip. Once settled in her seat, Sheba laced her arm into Kevin's, again resting her head on his shoulder. He offered no resistance—nor any return of affection. Over the next ninety minutes, the Trailways coach rolled through Amesbury, Haverhill, Lawrence, Andover and Methuen, Massachusetts, stopping in each location to drop off and pick up a handful of passengers. All the while, the sun descended toward the horizon, finally sinking beneath it behind the roadway in front of them.

It was dark when the bus reached Lowell and turned off Route 110, across the Centralville Bridge, and into downtown. Sheba's eyes widened at the sight of her prospective home for the next three weeks. Lowell was nothing like Wells. It was a city with brick mill buildings extending as far as the eye could see, nothing like the lone mill building she knew of in Kennebunk. She grew steadily more uncomfortable as the bus creaked and groaned its way through the downtown streets. A set of bright lights proclaimed "Keith's Theatre" off on the left side of the vehicle. This place, so foreign to her, seemed so much more a city than even Portland. As the coach made a slow, exaggerated turn to the right, Kevin prodded her to look out the window.

"That's the Sun Building there. It's the tallest building in the city—ten stories high," he exclaimed proudly. "Over here on the right—that's Kresge's, where I work." She looked across the bus in time to catch a glimpse of the sign. The vehicle moved slowly down the street, suggesting to her that their final destination was near. Her heart pounded within her chest.

Moments later, passengers began to leave their seats and gather their belongings. The bus eventually coasted up to a rectangular block where Sheba made out a waiting area within a modestly lit terminal. There was an almost eerie appearance to the location, with its muted lighting shining out onto the dark sidewalk. Her mind flashed back to the night spent in the forest alone in Kennebunkport just a few days ago. As unsettling as that experience had been, she had not been overwhelmed by it. Now, dropped in the middle of a strange city, she was experiencing an apprehension like none she had ever known.

"Keep in mind, now, I'm not going to just dump you here in the middle of Lowell. What I'll do is walk you to a place where you can rent a room for the night. How does that sound?" he asked.

She looked up at him and produced a faint smile, making no attempt to hide her nervousness.

"Sheba, you'll be fine," he added, in a consoling voice.

"Kevin, I really don't want to put you out. If you could just give me a few dollars and give me directions, I can find the place myself."

"No, that wouldn't be right. I'd worry about just leaving you."

They rose together as the bus lurched to a halt and joined the procession of passengers marching forward, then out of the vehicle. Kevin guided her away from the stream of disembarking men and women. Taking out his wallet, he produced a ten-dollar bill and put it into her hand.

"The hotel's only a couple of blocks from here," he said.

"Please—just go, Kevin. I'm afraid I'll wind up being a bother," said Sheba, not looking at him.

"I'll worry—just leaving you."

"Just go! Thank you for the money, I do appreciate it—but just go!" Her voice rose, arousing curiosity from those within hearing distance. Speechless, he lifted his single piece of luggage and slowly walked away. He shuffled up Central Street, careful not to look back. He reached a dark stretch of sidewalk, away from the dull, yellow light of the terminal and thought he heard steps closing on him from behind.

"Kevin, please don't leave me alone here. Please take me with you." Her voice carried a note of desperation.

"I live in a building where people know me. I can't just bring home an eighteen-year-old girl to stay with me. There are people there who know my parents, who still stay in touch."

"It wouldn't be for anything bad or dirty. Kevin, you're all I have in the world right now. Please Kevin, I'm scared," she whispered, just loud enough to reach his ear. Her words were followed by weeping, accompanied by tears. Her tears were neither forced nor contrived. "Please, help me." Sheba stood paralyzed by her own fear in this city so foreign to her.

"Can you at least tell me something about yourself? Why aren't you in school? Where are your parents? Why can't you just go to the police and let them help you? Give me some reason for not worrying myself sick about this whole thing."

"Kevin, I'm in this situation where I can't tell anyone anything. You just have to trust me a little and know it's not like I'm an outlaw or something—and I haven't hurt anyone, really I haven't."

He stood still with his back to her. "Okay, tonight you can stay. But tomorrow—we take a whole, fresh look at this situation when you're not so shook up. I just can't be taking in a strange teenage girl to live with me. You do understand that, don't you?"

Sheba ran up to him, throwing her arms around his neck. "I promise—you won't even know I'm there."

Kevin pulled a handkerchief from his pocket and offered it to her. She accepted it and brushed away the moisture from her eyes and face. Reaching down, he lifted the shopping bag containing the sum of her worldly possessions. As the two walked through the canyon of office and retail buildings making up the city's downtown area, Sheba took in details from shop windows and store fronts. Kevin, again, pointed out Kresge's, where he worked. They were on the city's main street where a large number of pedestrians were servicemen.

"Fort Devens isn't that far away, and a lot of the soldiers come here to meet girls—at dances and everything," he explained.

Sheba was taken by the number of men in uniform who's eyes made their way to her as they passed the couple on the sidewalk. In response, she clung to Kevin's arm, at least giving the outward appearance of a romantic relationship. Eventually they left the downtown area behind. They were moving toward a steel bridge.

"I live in Centerville—up ahead across the bridge. Now, even though it's only for one night, I hope you're not expecting some fancy house or six-room flat. I live in a studio apartment."

"Like an art studio. Do you paint or something?"

Her question caused him to laugh.

"No—a studio apartment—meaning one big room. The kitchen, living room, bedroom, it's all in one room, wide open."

"The bathroom too? Do we have to take a bath and go to the bathroom in that one big room?"

"No, of course not," he replied, not sure if she was being serious.

"Then it's not one big room, is it?"

He rolled his eyes. They had reached the sidewalk on the bridge. Sheba let out a shudder as a north wind, cooled by the Merrimack River, came whistling through the bridge's steel frame. She clutched on to him, letting out a gasp.

"That's Centerville up ahead of us. I live two or three blocks up Bridge Street. Oh, and while we're on the subject of where I live, maybe we should talk about what we do once we're in the building. I live on the third floor, and seeing that I'd like to keep your visit as private as possible—no talking on the way up the stairs. Is that clear?"

She nodded yes. "What if someone comes out of the door and sees us—what then?" she asked.

The question caused Kevin to stop in his tracks, pondering a strategy. "If that happens, then, let me walk ahead of you—as if we weren't together."

"And if the person who's in the door asks me where I'm going or who I'm looking for?"

He looked off into the sky, as if trying to conjure up his response from a distant star. "If that happens—if that happens, you say—you say you think you may be in the wrong building—and turn around and go back down the stairs."

"God, Kevin, this plan really blows."

He shook his head, dismissing her. "No one will stop us. We'll be real quiet." They reached the far side of the bridge, leaving the worst of the chilly wind gusts behind them. "We'll be at the front door in a couple of minutes, so remember what the plan is—no talking and quiet going up the stairs."

"You've got me feeling like a Nazi or Jap spy, for God's sake. Don't worry—I'll be quiet."

"I'm going to leave the kids with Roberta overnight. I'll get them in the morning," he said, appearing to be thinking out loud.

"Kids! What kids?"

"They're not really kids. You'll meet them in the morning."

They had walked midway up the third block when Kevin motioned her to a doorway and ushered Sheba inside. The hallway and stairs were poorly lit and dreary. Quietly, they made their way to the second floor and then the third. Kevin walked to the door at the end of the upstairs hallway and produced a key. He had the door opened and closed, and his guest inside and out of sight, in a split second. Sheba found herself standing in total darkness while he clumsily moved across the room. Finally, the sound of a switch and illumination.

While her eyes adjusted to the brightness, Sheba took in her new surroundings. As promised, Kevin's apartment consisted of a single, spacious room. The far wall, which ran adjacent to the street below, had two windows. A full-size bed faced them from the far end of the studio while the kitchen area, an oil stove, modest refrigerator and dining table were on her left. The room was Spartanly furnished but clean and tidy. If anything surprised her it was the sight of a large wooden crucifix behind the bed and a statue of the Blessed Virgin sitting on the table by the window.

"I like it," she said, stepping further into his home.

"You can have the bed. I have a cot in the closet that I can use. I use it all the time when my parents come down from Portland to visit."

"No, Kevin, I couldn't."

"Please Sheba, you're company. You can throw your fancy luggage down on it and make yourself at home." He smiled and patted the top of the bed.

"You know, none of this would have ever happened and you wouldn't have a crazy houseguest on your hands if you'd only kept your big mouth shut back in the bus terminal and not made that stupid comment about my fancy luggage."

He smiled and shook his head. Following an examination of the stove and the inside of the refrigerator, she crossed the room and began settling in by the bed. Kevin walked to the radio and clicked it on. It did not produce any sound.

"I think you might want to turn it up," she instructed.

"Nonsense, give it time." He locked eyes with her for the next few seconds, then broke out in a grin as female voices faded in from the

Philco. "Give the tubes time to warm up before you start barking out orders," he chided.

"Who's that singing?" she asked.

"The Andrews Sisters, of course. God, you don't know much about music, do you?"

"No—I guess not," she replied while slowly emptying her clothes from the grocery bag.

For the next hour, little in the way of conversation took place between the two new friends. Sheba thought she detected a heightened degree of nervousness in Kevin's demeanor. Vocal exchanges were limited, for the most part, to her asking questions concerning the whereabouts or availability of objects and his responses. It was nearly nine thirty and the apartment was quiet. Then, the phone rang, causing her to look across the room to him. It rang a second time with no movement from the young man.

"Are you deaf, Kevin? Your phone's ringing."

He lifted his head from the newspaper. "It's not for me."

"And how do you know that?"

"Cause it's not my ring—how else?"

"What are you talking about? Are you telling me you're psychic, like Kreskin?"

"Mine's a long ring—not two short ones—you know, like with all party lines. That'd be Mrs. Lowberg's line. What? Are you telling me you have a private line at home? What are you, rich?"

Sheba saw herself being trapped in another circumstance where her 1960s upbringing was proving problematic amid 1940s technology. She shook her head no and dropped the subject.

"Kevin, I'd like to get undressed for bed, if you don't mind. Would you mind turning your head while I slip out of my clothes and get under the covers?"

He rose from his chair, walked around the table, and seated himself with his back to the bed. She hastily removed her blouse, jeans and moccasins, then slipped beneath the covers.

"It's okay now, I'm under the sheets," she called out.

"He stood up and circled the table, seating himself back in his original chair, rededicating himself to his newspaper, the *Lowell Sun*. He broke the quiet about a minute later.

"So—you don't plan on brushing your teeth, I take it?"

"I don't have a brush. You wouldn't have an extra one, would you?"

"Afraid not."

"God, I wish you hadn't brought it up. Now you've got me feeling all grungy and everything."

He was unresponsive, continuing to focus on his paper.

"Kevin, darling—would it be too much to ask you to let me borrow your brush—just for tonight."

"Go ahead, it's in the bathroom."

Sheba remained beneath the covers. "Kevin, my darling and love of my life—would it be too much to ask you to cover your eyes or go out into the hall while I run to the bathroom and get my—our—toothbrush?"

"You can kiss the idea of me going out into the hall good-bye—that's for sure. If you promise to shake a leg, then I'll cover my eyes." He buried his face in his hands, allowing her to jump from the bed, speed across the room, and lock herself in the bathroom.

"No running. All I need is old man Modeski screaming up the stairs about the running. Remember, I'm supposed to be alone up here and he knows I can't run like that."

"Sorry, Daddy," she answered sarcastically.

The next few minutes brought the sound of rummaging through a medicine cabinet, followed by the brushing of teeth, ending with a series of exaggerated gargles and spits.

"Close your eyes again—please," she called out from behind the bathroom door.

"They're closed." The door opened behind him, followed by the sound of bare feet on linoleum. As she sped by his chair, the side of his face was hit with a spray of water droplets.

"What was that?"

Reaching the bed and slipping between the covers, she broke out in laughter.

Sheba rolled onto her side as she lay on the comfortable bed. From outside the windows came the sounds of the city, periodic voices from the sidewalk below interrupted by the racket from passing automobiles. The cars sounded different than the ones she was accustomed to back in her own time. She thought they sounded less fluid, more basic and mechanical.

"You know, for the past few minutes I've been sitting here thinking about what I may have gotten myself into. For all I know, you could be some homicidal maniac ready to put a steak knife through my heart the minute I fall asleep tonight," he said.

"Oh Kevin, stop being so dramatic."

"No, it's true. I don't know a thing about you—Sheba Smith."

"Well, for starters, just yesterday I went to church service with my family. Does that sound like I'm some kind of murderer?"

He stared across the room at her. "You're not Catholic, are you?" The question was practically a formality. He was fairly sure he knew the answer.

"No Kevin, I'm not—but you certainly are. Oh, and for the record, what's your last name?"

"Shanahan." He rose awkwardly from the table and made his way to a closet. He rummaged inside, finally pulling out a cot which he unfolded. "Where would you be more comfortable having me set this up, here on the bedroom side or across the room in the kitchen?"

Sheba peeked over the blankets, scanning the entire room.

"How about over there in the library," she suggested. She pointed to an end table along the wall with a single book resting on it. He smiled and dragged the cot to the other side of the room. Five minutes later, with the window shades drawn and the lights flicked off, he settled in on the cot for the night.

The room was covered in almost complete darkness when Sheba spoke up from the bed.

"Kevin?"

"Yes?"

"I forgot to ask before—where do you keep your steak knives in the kitchen? Are they in that drawer with the other silverware?"

"Yes, they are. Be careful not to cut yourself when you're taking one out later tonight, okay?"

"I'll be careful, Mr. Shanahan. Thank you, Mr. Shanahan."

"Think nothing of it."

"Kevin?"

"What?" He answered, pretending to be annoyed.

"You do know it was God who made sure I found you—to keep me safe."

"Maybe. Can we go to sleep now?"

"One last thing—I've got to tell you something 'cause I can't stand having lied to you."

"Will this thing you're about to tell me make me want to laugh or make me want to cry?"

"I'm pretty sure it won't make you want to laugh."

"What is it?"

"I lied when I told you I was eighteen."

"And?"

"And—I'm really only sixteen—and a half."

"Merciful Mother of God! I could go to jail!"

"Kevin, I would never let that happen."

"That steak knife in the heart is starting to sound better and better all the time."

"Good night, Kevin—and thank you."

18

September 26, 1944

Sheba, prompted by a car horn from the street two floors below, emerged gradually from a comfortable sleep. Opening her eyes, she stared up at the unfamiliar ceiling. There was only subdued light around her, the product of slivers of sunshine spilling in along the edges of the green window shades. At the other end of the room, Kevin stood in front of the stove, his back to her. About to shout across the room to him, her attention was grabbed by faint sounds and movement from the floor below. Glancing downward, she focused on two faces, one feline and one canine, staring back at her. The cat was first to draw her undivided attention. The solid black creature looked up at her from a single eye, its other socket simply void of an eyeball. Sheba stared intently at the animal, studying the cat's abnormality at length. Her fascination was broken only when the dog let out a single bark, causing her eyes to shift in its direction. The dog was multi-colored and mongrel with a tail wagging excitedly behind it.

"Tripod, what are you doing waking up our guest," called out Kevin from across the room.

"It's okay, I was already awake. By any chance would these be the kids you talked about last night?"

The young man laughed and turned back to the stove.

"What are their names?"

"Tripod, he's the loud one, and Patch, she's the sneaky, quiet one."

"Patch, well that makes perfect sense—and Tripod, you'll have to clue me in on where that name comes from."

He half turned and called out to the dog, causing it to spin away from the bed and scamper across the floor to its master. It was then she noticed the missing hind leg on the animal as it awkwardly scrambled to Kevin's side.

"Any more questions?" he asked.

"You wouldn't be making us breakfast, would you?"

"That's exactly what I'm doing. A bowl of Quaker Oats—or as my dad calls it, porridge. Then, toast, right from the top of the stove to your plate and topped with molasses—seeing that butter is so damn hard to get these days. Wash it all down with a Kevin Shanahan specialty, blended coffee, yes, blended coffee—that means yesterday's and today's. There's a war on, don't you know! Waste not, want not!"

Sheba laughed as the young man showed signs of letting his hair down and relaxing in her company. "Kevin, I'd like to get out of bed without you seeing my ugly body. If you promise not to turn in the next half minute and you put your dog in the bathroom so he can't look either, I'll join you at the table."

"You're afraid of Tripod looking at you?"

"He's a male—that's all I need to know," she answered assertively.

"But it's okay for Patch to look you over?"

She nodded yes. "She's female—and therefore above reproach."

He shook his head in disbelief while ushering the dog into the bathroom. True to her word, thirty seconds later Sheba rushed to the table and readied herself for breakfast. She found two bowls of oatmeal already cooling. Within seconds, her host was scraping three slices of toasted bread from the top of the stove and onto her plate.

"Take all the molasses you want. I'll have the coffee poured in a minute," he reported.

She held off beginning her meal until Kevin had served himself and was seated beside her. As she reached for her coffee cup he stopped her, lowering his head and closing his eyes.

"Dear God, thank you for the food on this table—and thank you for seeing fit to bring such a wonderful guest to our door—amen." Kevin concluded his prayer with the sign of the cross.

"Amen," added Sheba, somewhat startled by his actions.

Both breakfasts were practically gone when whimpering sounds began to emanate from behind the bathroom door.

"Oh, poor Tripod—let me get you out of there," called out Kevin before hopping to his feet and freeing the mongrel.

"Were the animals both born that way?"

"I'm not sure. I think Patch was—but I'm not that sure about Tripod."

"So you haven't had them since they were puppy and kitten?"

"No, neither of them."

She leaned back in her chair, leaving her coffee cup balanced at the edge of the table. "I'd be interested to hear how you came to have them."

Kevin rolled his eyes in mock disbelief, his elbows balanced on the table in front of him. "Okay, you asked for it. Well, it all started when I spotted a mouse scurrying across the floor here. I know it's hard to even imagine vermin in such a palatial palace as this, but it's true. In all honesty, I could have actually lived with the little critter, or so I thought, but then I saw two at once—and that was it. My next day off, I hightailed it down to the city pound in search of a kitty cat. At first they tried palming a kitten off on me, but I explained I wanted a mature cat 'cause—well, 'cause I had mice in my apartment. So they took me back to a holding area where there were a couple of large cages full of cats of every size and color. When I think back on it, it almost seemed like they knew what I was there for—to take one of them home from, well, you know what. It was strange though—I looked to the back of one of the cages and saw this beautiful black cat resting on a ledge by itself. When I asked the attendant about the black cat in the back he said how I didn't want that particular one— that it was abnormal—with a missing eye. By now the cat was look- ing out at me with one eye—well, I guess Patch would have to do that, wouldn't she? Anyway, Patch was looking at me in this sad way, like she had just given up—and I wondered to myself how many times she'd endured seeing people look at her in a funny way—and cringe and maybe make fun of her. It must have been a lot of times 'cause I could see she just didn't want to see or hear any of that stuff again. She'd just given up, you could see it in her face and in her attitude. Anyway, I told the man I was interested in the black cat and could he bring her out for a closer look. He tried talking me out of picking her a final time—saying she had a bad disposition and would be hard to bring home. I wouldn't listen. So, anyway, he brings Patch out to me for a closer inspection and tosses in that she's already been spayed, so that wouldn't be a problem. I just had to stroke Patch on the head for a few seconds and I knew she and I would get along just fine."

"Did she just go to you?"

Kevin nodded his head. "I cradled her in one arm and started back to the office to fill out some form. The attendant couldn't believe his eyes 'cause here Patch was letting a total stranger carry her in his arms—no struggle or anything. On the way out, we passed the dogs and they're just barking to beat the band. There's over a dozen in the cage and, I swear, they're all jumping up, trying to get my attention. Now, I'm there with Patch in my arms and I feel her tense up—but still not exposing her claws or anything, at least I couldn't feel them. I was careful not to go too close to the cage, so not to spook Patch—but I spotted this beautiful collie. I asked the attendant about him and he told me that the collie was almost assuredly a purebred. Of course, they had no papers to prove that. So, what I do is crouch down a bit and talk directly to the collie—telling him how beautiful he was. No sooner did I do that when he started to growl at Patch—real vicious like. This made me think right away that bringing home a dog with a cat was probably a bad idea. Anyway, it wasn't even a second later when I look right next to the collie and I see this undersize, scruffy mongrel who's jumping up and barking to beat the band—his tail wagging a mile a minute. But, he's jumping sort of funny and I look down and notice he's missing a hind leg. Sheba, it was amazing, but of all the dogs, this one's got more vitality and spirit than any of the others—even though fate has dealt him this bad hand. I asked the attendant how long the three-legged dog's been there and he indicates he's been there for some time now—and that he was going to be put down in the next wave. Now, no matter how hard I told myself how I didn't need a dog—that I'd just come to the pound for a cat—in the back of my mind I knew that no one else was going to take this runt of a dog that's damaged goods on top of everything else. But—he was damaged goods—like me. So I left the pound that day with a one-eyed cat under one arm—leading a three-legged dog on a leash. They must have had a good laugh at my expense once I cleared the front door," concluded Kevin, his eyes thoughtful and focused on the rim of his coffee cup.

"If they were idiots they did." Sheba's comment caused him to lift his eyes to her. "Kevin, I need to ask a favor of you. I need to call my grandmother and tell her I'm okay. She was expecting me to go stay in Boston at some boarding house. If she hears from the lady there and finds out I didn't arrive, she'll be worried sick."

"And you want to call her from here?"

"If you wouldn't mind?"

"Go ahead."

"There's also something else. She may want to talk to you—you know—to make sure her granddaughter is being taken care of. Don't mention the fact that I have nowhere to stay tonight, okay? She's a good woman and it'd bother her to no end." With the words out, Sheba managed to raise the question of her fate. She was afraid to ask Kevin in a forthright manner. However, the prospect of being set loose in a strange city continued to frighten her. "I'd be lying if I told you I wasn't afraid of what I'll run into out there on the streets tonight."

"Go to the nuns up at Saint Michael's and ask them for help."

"I'm afraid they'd call the police and I told you I can't have that. Besides, I'm not Catholic."

"They'll still help you, even though you're not Catholic. They'll try to convert you—oh how they'll try to convert you! But, they'll help you."

"I'll take my chances on the street. There are always men who a woman can turn to. They want things, really disgusting, dirty things, but I'll survive somehow. Not a word to Nana though, when I call."

Kevin's head dropped in frustration. "You're only sixteen—I think they could arrest me."

"The dirty men never seem to worry about that. Kevin, you just have to ask yourself what Jesus would do in this situation."

"Jesus never lived in this building—or had to worry about the Lowell Police Department kicking in his door, 'cause an underage girl was sleeping in his bed." He leaned forward over the table, propping his head up with his hands. The room grew quiet for the next few minutes while the young man wrestled with his fears and his demons. Sheba did not speak, knowing she had given it her best argument. At the moment, she could almost see the jury deliberating inside Kevin's skull.

"No matter what I do here, there's a chance I may live to regret it. But—I can't let you go out and face the city alone. You can stay."

"Thank you, Kevin!" Sheba shouted, jumping from her chair and throwing her arms around his neck. "Do you have any idea what an incredible guy you are?" She held her embrace until the young man became visibly flustered.

With the morning meal behind them and the breakfast dishes already washed, wiped and put away, Sheba went to the telephone and, with Kevin and the operator's assistance, dialed up her grandmother in Wells. Only twenty-four hours had passed since she left the woman and the protection of her home, but to Sheba it felt like an eternity.

"Hello," sang out the woman at the other end of the line, her familiar Maine accent sounding more pronounced to her granddaughter after exposure to Kevin's Massachusetts inflections. The quality of the phone line was poor, reminding the teenager of the distance between them.

"Nana, it's me, Sheba. I just wanted to call and let you know I'm all right—except I won't be staying with that lady in Boston. There was some trouble in Portland after grandfather left me off—I'm afraid the money you gave me was stolen. I'm sorry, Nana, I know how hard you and grandfather worked for it—I'm so sorry." She waited on a response from Dorothy. Following an elongated period of silence, her grandmother responded.

"And you're all right, child?"

"I'm fine. This guy I'm with—he's a real gentleman. He helped me out and now I'm staying with him."

"You're staying with a man! Child, are you out of your mind?"

"No, Nana, he's a wonderful guy."

"You don't know that—you don't even know this man!"

"Yes, I do—his name is Kevin Shanahan and he lives in Lowell—Massachusetts." Sheba looked across the room to Kevin, a look of fear and astonishment plastered on his face.

"Not my name and where I live," he exclaimed frantically.

She stood poised, the phone to her ear and gazing out the window, listening to her grandmother's words. Then, her eyes shifted back to Kevin. "Nana wants to speak to you," she announced.

He crossed the room and took the phone. "Hello—Nana," he said guardedly.

"For starters, I'm not your Nana. Now, am I speaking to the young man who has taken my granddaughter—my sixteen-year-old grand-daughter, under his roof? You did hear that young man—sixteen!" Dorothy's tone was cynical and cold.

"Yes ma'am, Sheba stayed here with me last night."

"And you don't see anything wrong with that?"

"Ma'am, I tried talking her into going to the police or asking the nuns at the nearby church for help. She'd have none of that. It was only when she started talking about walking the streets here and meeting strange men to help her get by—well, I told her she could stay here with me—where it's safe."

"Safe, is it! And what can you tell me that will let me know she's safer under your roof than under anybody else's?"

"I wouldn't harm her, if that's what you mean. Last night I gave her my bed—she being my guest—and I already told her she can stay as long as she wants—within reason. She slept soundly last night in a nice, clean bed. I even made sure she brushed her teeth before going to bed. You have to understand, I tried and tried to talk her into going to the police, but she's dead against it."

"Well, Mr. Kevin Shanahan—hear what I have to say to you. My granddaughter is special, very special, and those aren't just words. There are things about her that have to be kept secret, but I'm warning you, you'll be calling down the wrath of God if you harm her in any way. Do you follow me, young man?"

Kevin responded in the affirmative and gratefully returned the phone to Sheba.

"Sheba, honey, what kind of place is it you're staying in?"

The question brought a chuckle from the girl. "It's small, but very holy. There's a crucifix over the bed and a statue of the Virgin Mary on one of the tables."

"That comes as no surprise. With a name like Shanahan and him talking about taking you to the nuns, I didn't have to be a genius to figure out he was Catholic. Don't let him try any hocus pocus on you with holy water and rosary beads, understand?"

"I'll watch this one very closely, Nana, I promise. There'll be no hocus pocus," joked Sheba, winking in Kevin's direction. She was relieved to hear a degree of acceptance creep into Dorothy's voice. "I can't stay on the phone much longer, Nana. Kevin's going to have to pay for this call."

"Take care of yourself, child—you'll be in my prayers—you and Mr. Shanahan."

"Good-bye, Nana, I love you—I love you all. Make sure Momma doesn't forget me or anything I told her."

The upbeat conversation came to an end with tears flowing down the girl's face as she placed the receiver back on its cradle. Sensing his new friend's emotional state, Kevin let her be. Retreating to the far side of the apartment, he made the bed and put away the cot. Sheba sat with her back to him all the while. With the tidying up completed, he rejoined her in the kitchen area. Walking up behind the girl, he placed his hands down on her shoulders. She whirled around, grabbing his hands at the wrist and applying pressure. He lurched backward.

"Hey, calm down," he called out. "Relax, I didn't mean to upset you. It was just an innocent touch. I didn't mean anything by it."

She released his wrists. He stared down at her, stunned and offended, then retreated to the chair by the window.

Moments later, Sheba hurried across the room and deposited herself on his lap, straddling him, her knees tightly wedged into his waist. Startled, he looked up at her.

"Most of the males I've come in contact with in my life were lewd—I can think of one fat, disgusting one in particular. I don't react well to surprises from boys."

"I'm almost twenty-six years old. I'm hardly a boy."

"Kevin, darling—you are still a boy—a wonderful, wonderful boy."

"Did any of these men ever get their way with you?"

"What do you think? Take your time answering and think back to my little scuffle with that red-headed guy in Portland and what his face looked like when you pulled me off of him—and he was a grownup—a male grownup."

"So, do you hate all men?"

"I don't hate my daddy, or my grandfather—and I don't hate you. But, that's about it." She remained perched on top of him. For his part, Kevin showed no sign of annoyance. With only the slightest shift of her head, she glanced in the direction of the bed.

"I noticed you took the time to place your shoes neatly in the corner but left my moccasins in the middle of the floor. Does this mean you think you're too good to pick up my moccasins? You had no problem picking up your own shoes and putting them away. Maybe you think you're too good to pick up after me? Is that what you're trying to tell me?" She brought her face closer to his, eventually touching the tip of his nose with her own. "Well, is it?" she asked in her best tough-guy voice. His response was limited to a nervous laugh.

The room grew quiet with neither knowing where to guide the conversation. Their eyes met and remained trained on the other's, each searching for an explanation of their budding relationship. It was he who eventually dropped, then closed his eyes, replacing eye contact with a succession of deep breaths. He appeared to be relinquishing control of himself to urges deep within him. Deducing that Kevin's growing passion was being fueled by the weight of her body straddling his, she peppered his face with a half dozen baby kisses and dismounted him. Sheba backed away and returned to one of the kitchen chairs. Her retreat gave him time to re-establish his composure.

The remainder of the morning saw circumstances return to normal as the two spent time sipping down reheated coffee and listening to the radio. With noontime almost upon them, Kevin decided to take his houseguest for a walk to familiarize her with the neighborhood. Bridge Street, where he lived, ran the length of Centralville like the stem of a leaf. On the east side of the street the land rose into Christian Hill and some of Lowell's highest terrain. The other side of Bridge Street, the west side, was flat and gradually became West Centralville, a distinctly different section of town. Kevin explained to Sheba that Centralville was largely Irish, Irish Catholic, and West Centralville was largely French, French Catholic. There was no dividing line between the two sectors of the city. Consequently, you knew you were in West Centralville when you heard French spoken instead of English, or when you literally saw Saint Louis Church. Finally, he took the time to point out that this section of the city was officially named Centralville. However, no one in his entire experience had ever called it that—to locals it was Centerville. They walked north along the sidewalk, Kevin calling out instructions.

"If I send you out for meat, you'll go across the street to McCarron's. If the radio needs a new tube, you'll just come down here to Pete's Radio Shop. If we're buying a lot of groceries, we'll go to the First National up the street there," he instructed, pointing to a large building on the next block. Sheba took in her new surroundings, making mental notes as they strolled away from the apartment house.

"I notice the streets are in sequence—we passed Fourth Street and now here's Fifth," she commented.

"Yeah, it's like that almost all the way to the Dracut line. The other side of the street is West Fourth Street and West Fifth. Oh, and just ahead is Wendel's Pastry. If I can save a few cents here and there, maybe we can treat ourselves next weekend."

Reaching the end of the block, Sheba's eyes were drawn up the street.

"That's my parish, Saint Michael's."

"That's a big church."

"Yeah, the parish owns a lot of the property around here. The white mansion across the way is the rectory where the priests live—and up the street is where I went to grammar school—and in front of the school is the convent, where the nuns live."

"Oh yeah, where you wanted to take me last night—close by, nice and convenient." Sheba's comment brought a laugh from him. "You're not taking me to your church now, are you?"

Kevin gripped her arm with both hands. "Oh, yes I am—just like your grandmother said I would—to throw some of that religious hocus pocus at you. Yes—it's hocus pocus time for you missy and no one does hocus pocus better than us Catholics." They wrestled together on the street corner for a moment with Sheba laughing hysterically at her friend while he distinctly showed his sense of humor for the first time in two days. "Or, we could go a little further up the street and stop at Dairy Farms for an ice cream or something. It's hard for me to make up my mind—you decide. Will it be hocus pocus or ice cream?"

"Ice cream," she cried out. "Please sir, ice cream!" She hooked her arm through his and drew him close.

Inside the ice cream parlor, he splurged and purchased himself a hot fudge sundae while going all out for Sheba, treating her to a banana split. She was reminded he would have to return to work the next day and would not have another day off until Sunday. Over ice cream he explained the house rules, as he saw them. She could come and go as she pleased after he made an extra key to the apartment for her. All Kevin asked of her was to perform some light housework in the morning and be back in the apartment by six o'clock when he returned home.

"There's also going to be the matter of Roberta," he added while scraping the last of the hot fudge from the side of his glass.

"Who?"

"Roberta Gilbride—she lives downstairs on the second floor. She's the one who took care of Tripod and Patch while I was in Portland."

"What about her?"

"Well—her and I are friends—not romantically."

"Is she ugly or something?"

"No, she's not ugly. Actually, quite the opposite—she's no Veronica Lake, but she's very pretty."

"There's that name again—Veronica Lake."

He looked at her curiously but did not follow up on the comment. "What I'm saying is—I like her—and maybe under different circumstances she'd like me. Now, she's going to see you and quickly find out you're staying with me—and I'm wondering if we can come up with some story where I won't be absolutely killing my chances with her— as slim as they may be—because of you. Not to mention the fact that you're sixteen years old!"

"What exactly do you want me to say and do?"

"For starters, you're eighteen years old—and you're my niece. You're my older brother's daughter—and you're from Virginia."

"Can't I be from West Virginia?"

"What's the difference?"

"I want to be a coal miner's daughter from West Virginia."

Kevin paused and stared at her in astonishment. "Fine, you're from West Virginia."

"And I'm here 'cause my daddy's trapped in a mine—and I can only go home when they pull him out of the mine."

"You're not taking this seriously."

"It's because this plan is so stupid."

"What am I supposed to say? Well, you see, Roberta, I met this sixteen-year-old girl in a bus terminal—and I don't know a thing about her—and she was punching this middle-aged guy in the face when I met her—so I decided to have her come live with me and sleep in the same room with me—even though she very well could carve me up like a chicken with a steak knife while I'm sleeping. But aside from that—it's all quite innocent."

Sheba raised her eyes to the ceiling and let out a sigh.

"Why can't you do even the simplest thing for me without making such a big deal out of it?" Kevin asked.

"Maybe because you're capable of a better lie than this stupid niece thing."

"Please, just go along with the niece thing—for me."

"Okay, okay—I'm your niece from West Virginia—and a coal miner's daughter."

"Please, Sheba, drop that crap about your father being lost in a coal mine. We'll just say your family back there is going through some hard times and they sent you to me until they can get back on their feet."

"So you're my rich uncle who lives in Lowell in a real small studio apartment?" she added sarcastically, still not content to accept the story in its present form.

"God, you can be such a little brat."

There was no response from her. She was content to scrape the last trace of ice cream from the inside of her glass. With her banana split gone and her mouth wiped clean, the teenager resumed the conversation. "So you sort of like this Roberta, but there's nothing between you—why?"

"She has a boyfriend, actually a fiancé, but he's off fighting. Actually, he's MIA, missing in action. Roberta hasn't received any word or mail from him in over a year."

"Oh, that's really sad—not knowing and everything."

"She's devoted to him. I don't think she'd even consider going out under the circumstances. We're very good friends, though—and spend a lot of time together."

Knowledge of the circumstances concerning Kevin's friend dampened Sheba's mood. They left the ice cream parlor and continued to walk north. It was a picture perfect autumn day, showcased by a refreshing breeze from the north that had the trees along their route rustling noisily over their heads. Neither felt inclined to return to the apartment. They eventually turned eastward and began the climb up Tenth Street toward the top of Christian Hill. Walking uphill was difficult for Kevin, given the condition of his leg. They stopped and rested on a half dozen occasions. Once the two reached the summit of the hill, they walked back in the general direction of the apartment. When they reached the top of Third Street, the friends looked out over the city with Kevin pointing out various landmarks in the distance below. He also gave Sheba a poor man's history lesson of the city, explaining its role in the industrial revolution. It was nearing four thirty when they descended Christian Hill.

Kevin pushed in the front door to the apartment house and the two made their way upstairs, driven by sharpened appetites from the afternoon walk. They were discussing the prospects for supper when a voice interrupted them at the landing of the second floor.

"Hello, Kevin," sounded a female voice from behind them.

They turned together. "Oh, hi, Roberta," he answered, his voice cracking slightly.

"I'm glad to see you're home," added the woman. Roberta Gilbride stood just over five feet in height and appeared to be in her mid- to late twenties. Her long, dark hair draped down beside a thin, pretty face. Her words prompted no response from him, causing the hallway to fall into an uncomfortable period of silence. Throughout, the young woman's eyes never left Sheba, seemingly in the hope of receiving an explanation for her presence.

"Yes, and this is my niece Sheba. She's visiting from Virginia—for a while. She's my brother's daughter—my older brother."

Sheba stepped forward, approaching the much shorter woman with her hand extended. "Actually, it's West Virginia. Uncle Kevin never seems to get that straight."

Roberta stared up at the teenager curiously while the two shook hands in front of the woman's door. "And you're visiting—because?" asked Roberta, halting her words in mid-sentence to form the question.

"Trouble at the mine—lots and lots of trouble. Daddy thought it best to ship me up north and out of harm's way."

The woman looked over to Kevin who stood frozen by the stairwell.

"Well, then, why don't we get upstairs? I'm sure the animals are starving," he added, already turning away from the females.

Sheba let go of the petite woman's hand and ran toward Kevin. A second later she jumped onto his back, wrapping her long legs around his waist. "I want a ride up the stairs, Uncle Kevin! High-oh Silver— away!" she hollered, injecting a particularly juvenile quality to her voice.

Kevin's legs sagged beneath her weight while he gasped for air, her arms squeezing tightly around his neck and restricting his breathing. "Goodnight, Roberta," he called back, barely managing to force the words through his windpipe.

19

September 28, 1944

It was Thursday, payday for Kevin. He left for work on this morning with specific instructions to Sheba to meet him downtown, in front of Kresge's, at twelve thirty. Their plan was to visit the bank and have lunch together at the Waldorf, a cafeteria style restaurant close by. Following his departure on this day, she fed the animals, made the bed, put away the cot, and picked up the apartment. By ten o'clock, the flat was in perfect order. On instructions from Kevin, she let the dog and cat out for the day, then made her way up Christian Hill. At the summit of the hill was a reservoir that provided much of the city's drinking water. Two days before, Sheba had made a mental note of the place. Now, with her downtown rendezvous a full two hours away, she returned to the well-guarded reservoir. Ignoring a 'No Trespassing' sign, she found a soft, comfortable spot on the grass close by the water and settled in with a copy of *The Great Gatsby*, a novel plucked from Kevin's limited personal library. For the rest of the morning she enjoyed the third consecutive day of spectacular autumn weather. The high ground caught gust after gust of wind, causing the girl's hair to swirl around her head and face, sometimes blocking her vision as she stretched out on her stomach, entertained by the storytelling of F. Scott Fitzgerald. At some point, she placed the book on the ground beside her and took in her surroundings while the water nearby slapped against the edge of the reservoir. This was a peaceful place in the city, she thought. Eventually though, her mind drifted to thoughts of her circumstances. She wondered if at least a small part of her good fortune was being provided for her. Was the Great Spirit, who so loved Mowalk, still providing for one of his descendents? She thought of Kevin and the wonderful host that he was. In her sixteen and a half years on the planet, no male, outside of her father, had ever earned even a fraction of the faith and trust Kevin Shanahan had already earned from her. Somehow, he had made her feel comfortable and at ease in a strange house and city, he and his odd pets. In truth, this young man, a total stranger only three days before, was providing for her and asking little or nothing in return.

Without a watch, Sheba was relegated to estimating the passage of time by her internal clock. Intuitively, she knew over an hour had passed since her arrival at the summit of the hill. Climbing to her feet, she took a moment to adjust the clothesline rope, functioning as a belt, around her waist. After tightening it, she detected a change in her waistline. Drawing in her stomach muscles, she was struck by the exaggerated, concave line around her waist. There was little doubt she had lost a few pounds in the past few days. Whether it was her extended walks and bike rides back in Maine, or the limited food supply from wartime rationing, something was having a slimming effect upon her. As the teenager scrambled down the mound of earth surrounding the reservoir, the sound of distant church bells chimed from below. She reasoned it was noontime and told herself to make haste in the direction of downtown.

By the time Sheba made her way down Christian Hill and followed Bridge Street over the Merrimack River, there was a sense of urgency in her step. She hurried past the Paradise Diner and Keith's Theatre, knowing Kevin might already be waiting for her in front of the store. Turning onto Merrimack Street, she was relieved to see the municipal sidewalk clock reading twelve twenty-six. This was her first visit downtown since the evening of her arrival. It had been dark at that time and difficult to get a clear picture of the city named Lowell. With Sheba's hair tossed around her face, dressed in an oversized pair of men's jeans tied at the waist with clothesline rope, and moccasins on her feet, the pretty teenager attracted more than her share of curious looks from both men and women. The sidewalk around her was alive with a beehive of activity as working people scrambled to manage their affairs during their lunch breaks. The girl watched the flow of pedestrian traffic as she waited for Kevin. Particularly interested in the city women, she was mesmerized by the best-dressed ones, in all likelihood secretaries, as they flitted by her in their fine dresses and nylon stockings. These were not the sort of women she saw on a daily basis back home in Maine. Her attention was riveted on a middle-aged blonde waiting to cross the street when a tug came on her belt. She turned to see Kevin standing beside her.

"Come with me while I cash my check at the bank. Then I'll treat you to lunch."

"Lead away," she replied, pulling herself against him. He responded by draping his arm over her shoulder and guiding her up the street. It was only a few steps to the Union National Bank of Lowell. Inside the bank were five tellers on duty, all of whom had sizeable lines extending back from their windows.

"Let me get my check signed and paperwork done before we get in line," said Kevin, making his way over to a customer desk on the back wall.

"Don't take all day. We'll lose our place in line," she prodded.

Kevin sped through his paperwork, only to be cut off at the last second by a well-dressed gentleman in a suit and tie.

"Nice going, slowpoke," she whispered to him. They were lined up directly behind the businessman. Kevin and Sheba stood side by side in line, five customers between them and the teller. She looked up at the back of the head of the man who had nudged his way ahead of Kevin seconds earlier. His hair was impeccably groomed and his aftershave permeated the air around them.

"How long's your lunch?"

"An hour," he answered.

"We'll need every minute of it at this rate," she sniped.

However, both were pleasantly surprised when one, then the next, of the customers sailed through their transactions. It appeared they had picked the fastest of the customer lines. Unfortunately, their exuberance proved to be short-lived. Reaching the teller's window, the well-dressed businessman pulled out a short stack of checks. Then, after asking the teller—her nameplate told customers she was Noreen—for a pen, he proceeded to begin the task of methodically signing each and every check, all the while engaging Noreen in lighthearted banter.

"Do you believe this clown?" piped up Sheba, prompting Kevin to raise his fingers to her lips.

"Jesus, Sheba, do you know who that is? That's Attorney McMichael—he's very important and well-known here in Lowell. Keep it down."

"Am I hearing right? Did you say the clown's a lawyer?"

Her words did not go unnoticed by a dozen of the surrounding people or by Attorney McMichael. The lawyer turned back and eyed her. He extended her a look she was familiar with, a look she had experienced in her days as a waitress. In her mind, this man, this pillar of the community, viewed her with disdain. To him, she was nothing more than a mouthy teenager dressed in clothing little better than rags. He turned back and resumed signing his signature to the back of the checks.

"I guess some people think their time is more important than everyone else's—too important to have their stuff signed and ready to go before they get in line. They must think it's some kind of friggin' honor to wait in line behind them," said Sheba, raising her voice even higher than she had earlier.

McMichael chose to ignore her.

Kevin was becoming flustered. "For God's sake, Sheba, cut it out!" he whispered, this time grabbing her by the wrist and yanking.

"I'll be needing a tidy sum from this for the weekend. The wife and I are heading down to the Cape. We haven't had nearly as much time down there this year as we wanted," stated the man, speaking loudly enough to be heard by a sizeable portion of the bank's patrons.

"For anyone who missed what he said—and it's hard to imagine anyone could have—the lawyer wants us all to know that he owns a house on Cape Cod and we're all supposed to be so, so impressed," came back Sheba in a voice amplified above McMichael's. The crack made the lawyer's body go rigid.

"Shut up, I mean it," said Kevin, tugging at the girl's arm again. By now, Sheba, Kevin, and McMichael were the center of attention within the walls of the bank lobby. The well-dressed man turned and addressed his tormentor.

"You are a rude, ignorant, young woman," he snarled.

"And you are a chiseling, not-so-young, low-life lawyer—but then, we are what we are," she responded defiantly.

The visibly flustered teller spoke up in an attempt to disengage her quarreling customers. "You're very fortunate to be able to get the gas you need for the trip—with rationing and all," quipped Noreen. McMichael turned back to the teller, still visibly agitated by Sheba's outburst.

"You have to know the right people, that's all," came back the attorney absentmindedly, still appearing distracted by the unruly teenager behind him in line.

"Oh, that's just great. It's just wonderful to know that while my brother and a lot of other boys are risking their lives in the South Pacific, we have people like this clown in his fancy suit using up our valuable gasoline taking trips to Cape Cod. It's enough to make you sick," spat out the girl. The bank turned as quiet as a church on Good Friday.

Kevin grabbed his friend by her shoulders. "I mean it, Sheba—

shut up!" he said directly into her face.

McMichael hurriedly concluded his transaction while a per-plexed teller hastily counted out his cash. Every set of eyes in the bank were locked on the man as he turned from the window. He sensed, and correctly so, that the brash teenager's last outburst had turned the onlookers against him.

"If you were a man—I'd punch you right in the mouth," he said, unable to hide his rage. He turned and made his way across the floor of the lobby toward the door.

Sheba would not allow the lawyer to have the last word. "Back to your office now—there are grandmothers to be chiseled and orphans to be robbed," she called out to his back, her voice exhibiting a degree of satisfaction. Her parting volley brought a spontaneous cackle from an elderly man with whiskers standing by the back wall.

"Please wait for me by the door," ordered Kevin in the next breath, before bringing his paperwork to the teller. He was barely able to restrain his anger. While she walked in the direction of the entrance, a man in a brown suit approached her.

"Excuse me, young lady, I want to speak to you," he ordered, tak-ing her arm and pulling her aside. "Do you or your parents have an account here with us?"

"No, I'm new to Lowell."

"Well, based on your little performance out on the floor a few seconds ago, I want you to know that you're not welcome in this bank—and I strongly suggest you stay out of here in the future," he said, curtly and under his breath.

"What! You're asking me to stay out of your bank—just because I got upset at someone who has no problem undermining our war effort?" Her voice projected the question throughout the lobby, the words causing heads to turn. The bank manager froze, sensing him-self being drawn into a "no-win" situation. Now, Sheba smelled blood. In the next instant she was crying.

"My brother writes me letters telling me how scared he is and how horrible fighting is, so when I hear someone who's not totally behind the war effort—I can't help it—I get upset," she cried out, wedging her words between sobs.

Once again, the teenager had made herself the focal point of attention. The bank manager lowered his voice further, going so far as to offer the sixteen-year-old his handkerchief. Thirty seconds passed with Sheba rubbing tears from her eyes and bringing her cry-ing under control. Kevin approached the two, throwing his arm around her shoulder.

"My niece's been under a lot of pressure. I'm sure you understand."

The bank official accepted the simplistic explanation and gratefully retreated from the floor. That left Kevin to dutifully escort the girl from the lobby while customers passed and nodded encouragement to her. Reaching the sidewalk and away from the ears of others, he turned on her.

"There is something seriously wrong inside your head. You do know that, don't you?"

"Will you still buy us lunch?"

"Not until you swear they'll be no more of this craziness going on," he said.

"Cross my heart and hope to die," she answered, then began pulling him up the street.

"The Waldorf's back there."

"I know, I know, but ever since we went to the Dairy Farms I've had a hankering for ice cream—and I see there's a drug store just up the street. And besides—I'm getting skinny!" She reached inside the waistline of her jeans and showed him the extra room. Five minutes later they were sitting at the counter on stools in Bailey's Drug Store, lunching on strawberry sundaes.

Their lunchtime together was drawing to a close as Kevin and Sheba strolled along Merrimack Street, stopping in front of the windows of Pollard's, Gagnon's and Bon Marche Department Stores. Sheba stopped in her tracks at Cherry and Webb, mesmerized by the fashion creations of another generation. With minutes fleeting by, they browsed the aisles of Prince's Book Store and joked outside the Prince-Cotter Jewelry Store over which bracelet he should purchase for her.

"Soon it'll be our first anniversary," she clowned. "A week of bliss together, together with our three-legged son and one-eyed daughter." By one thirty when he returned to work at the 5 & 10 cent store, she had charmed all memory of her confrontation in the bank to the back recesses of his mind, or so it seemed. For a moment, they stood awkwardly at the front door of Kresge's, neither quite sure how to draw their hour together to a close. It was she who snatched the initiative by leaning forward and pecking him on the cheek.

"Supper will be on the table at six—sharp," she announced, before whirling around and beginning her walk back to Centralville."

"Do you really have a brother fighting in the South Pacific?"

called out Kevin.

She glanced back, raising her forearm across the bridge of her nose, allowing only her eyes to show above her sleeve. "I'm sorry, but I must remain a woman of mystery, Mr. Shanahan."

20

September 30, 1944

Kevin rose early with the sun on Saturday morning and prepared himself and the animals breakfast. With the sound of running water and the noise from kitchen utensils, it was not long before his houseguest was awake. Sheba pretended to be asleep, all the while observing him from behind a slightly raised eyelid. He hurried about, whispering comments to the dog and cat, as he rushed through their morning feeding before scooting them toward the front door. With the young man poised in the door to leave, she spoke up.

"I recall someone telling me that they'd make me breakfast in bed this weekend—the same man whose slithering out the door on me. Whatever happened to the idea that a man's word was his bond?"

"Oh, you're awake. The kids are fed and I'm letting them out now—for the day. And that crack about my word being my bond—the last time I checked, Sunday was still part of the weekend. Tomorrow morning—after mass—breakfast in bed, count on it! Meantime, it's to the salt mines for me." Kevin tossed her a halfhearted wave and closed the door behind him. Sheba yawned, stretching her body to its full length beneath the bed covers. After closing her eyes, she spent the next few minutes listening to the sounds of the city from Bridge Street below. It was almost eight fifteen by the time she hauled her body off the mattress. She slipped out of a pair of Kevin's pajamas, something she had taken up wearing for modesty's sake, thanks to her own lack of a wardrobe. It took only seconds to pull on her familiar jeans and work shirt. Sleepy-eyed, Sheba staggered across the apartment to the stove where she began reheating her morning coffee. With her morning caffeine heating on the stove, she took a seat at the table. She looked down at one of Kevin's books on locks and security. Apparently, he had been reading it during breakfast. It was then she heard a series of weak raps on the door.

"Yes?" she called out.

"Is it too early for a visit?" It was a woman's voice.

"And you would be who?"

"It's Roberta from downstairs."

Sheba jumped to her feet and made her way to the door. "Oh, Roberta, please come in—by all means," she said apologetically while ushering the woman inside.

"It's been a little lonely downstairs since you arrived. I've brought you up a little something. Consider it a 'welcome to Lowell' gift. It's a small loaf of banana bread. Maybe you'd like some with your coffee."

"Join me, Roberta. It'll give us time to get to know each other better."

The woman smiled, then moved forward.

With the petite woman seated at the kitchen table beside her, Sheba assumed the role of hostess. Once heated, cups of coffee were served along with the banana bread. A meandering conversation followed, touching on everything from President Roosevelt's health to the fine stretch of sunny weather and ending with Sheba and the woman's impressions of life in the mill town of Lowell, Massachusetts. Finally, it was Roberta who guided their talk to matters of a more personal nature.

"Before you showed up at your uncle's door, we'd been spending a lot of time together." The woman posed the comment as if looking for more specifics behind Sheba's presence. The teenager decided she would have none of it.

"Yes—I think I remember Uncle Kevin saying something along those lines. Now, if I remember correctly, he told me that you're engaged, and your fiancé is overseas." Like an accomplished tennis player, the girl had lobbed the ball back to her opponent's side of the court.

"Yes, that's right. His name is Jimmy."

Sheba looked into Roberta's eyes. Her face took on a sad look, as if the mere mention of her Jimmy's name brought pain to her.

"Now, Roberta, just because I'm here, I don't want you feeling like you can't come up and see Kevin like before. It's not like me and Uncle Kevin have to, or want to, be alone." She thought her words appeared to cheer the woman, her face forcing a thin smile.

There was a hush in the room while Roberta took a deliberate sip from her cup of coffee. "You know—lately—I've been giving some thought to going back home to live with my folks—at least for a while."

"Where's home?"

"Gorham."

"You're from Maine?"

"No, Gorham, New Hampshire. It's a small town up in the White Mountains. I've only lived in Lowell for five years. I came down from Gorham to find steady, year-round work. I work at 95 Bridge."

"What's 95 Bridge?"

"Oh, that just means the mills—that's their address—95 Bridge Street. You know, on the other side of the bridge." Her explanation was followed by another break in the conversation, sending both females back for a sip from their cups. "Now, do you see yourself settling here, and maybe enrolling in school—or taking a job?"

The questions caught Sheba off guard, causing her to retreat behind a wall of uncertainty. "You know, Roberta, everything's happened so fast with me and my family back home—and Uncle Kevin's been so nice, I think we're all kind of just sorting things out right now and no decision's been made yet."

"What's your family like?" asked the woman.

Roberta's question sounded an alarm in the teenager's head. To Sheba, Roberta was straddling the line between genuine curiosity and prying. The actress in the girl took center stage. "I'm sorry—but just talking about my family makes me sad and depressed. If you don't mind, I'd rather not talk about them—at least not right now," she answered, staring across the table at her guest behind a wounded expression. The girl's sad countenance caused the woman to nervously look away and survey the apartment, as if uncomfortable. "Roberta, seeing that you're here and all—and I wouldn't want to hurt Uncle Kevin's feelings: Do you know how he got his leg the way it is? Was he born with it that way? My father's never told me about it and I feel funny asking Uncle Kevin directly."

"What he told me—and he's only brought it up once—what he's told me is that when he was a youngster, he fell out of a tree, landed on a stone wall, and shattered his knee. I can't remember how we got on the subject of his limp in the first place, it was such a while ago, but that's what he told me."

Sheba winced at the account of her friend's mishap and quickly moved the conversation on to more pleasant topics.

* * *

For the next hour, they shared stories of their lives with Sheba cautiously leaving out details that could raise suspicions about her circumstances. The topics of conversation moved from their mutual jealousy of all women with blue eyes to the beautiful clothes in the windows of Cherry and Webb. When Roberta caught sight of Sheba's feet under the table, she declared they were the largest she had ever seen on a woman. Sheba took the slight in stride, extending her hands, with their elongated fingers and pronounced knuckles, further evidence of the joke played on her by God at birth. Following two cups of coffee, the woman excused herself and returned downstairs to her apartment.

The sun, descending in shades of pink and gold, was casting beams on the apartment's far wall when Kevin kicked open the door and entered the flat behind Tripod and Patch. Sheba looked up from the kitchen table, the comic section of the *Lowell Sun* opened in front of her. His arms were full of packages along with a grocery bag.

She jumped from her chair to assist him. "Don't tell me—it's all for me."

"One thing anyway," he answered, handing her one of three parcels. She reached inside the light paper bag and pulled a soft, blue night shirt from it. Her first instinct was to bring the fabric up to her face.

"I love the smell of new clothes. Thank you Kevin," she said, simultaneously planting a kiss on his cheek. "I'll try it on right now."

"Not until you've taken a bath—a real bath—in the tub," he retorted. "We'll start heating the water on the stove right now. You should be able to get in by the time I leave for confession. And you should be clean by the time I get back."

The ritual of heating water on the top of the stove was born from the apartment's absence of hot, running water. It was a cold-water flat, meaning hot water was the responsibility of the tenant. This meant bringing water to a boil on the top of the stove, a pan at a time. The process called for filling the bathtub half full of scalding, hot water, then—and this was the easy part—adding cold water to it from the faucet until the desired water temperature was reached.

Kevin filled a half dozen pans from the tap and placed them on the stove. He instructed Sheba to pour the pans of water in the tub the instant they reached a boil and then repeat.

"The plug's already in the drain. When you think you have enough hot water, then turn on the faucet. Make sure you keep checking. When it's just a little too hot—just a little—turn off the cold and get in. There's a bar of soap on the sink. Oh, and we're having franks and beans for supper. How many dogs do you want?"

"Three would be good."

"You'll get two—there's a war on, you know. Fill up on beans. Now I've got to get to church."

"Are you going again tomorrow?"

"Yes, to mass."

"That's an awful lot of church, if you ask me."

"That's all right, 'cause no one did—ask you." He slipped on his jacket and ducked out the door.

* * *

Sheba's head was leaning back on the rim of the tub when she heard the door open. The apartment, quiet for the last hour, came to life with the sound of Tripod's barking, followed by the crash of items falling onto the Formica table.

"Is that you, Uncle Kevin?" she called out.

"No, it's Attorney McMichael—I've come with an armful of red roses for my Sheba—the only woman I will ever love—and want to spend the rest of my life with," called back Kevin.

"Not until you shed about forty pounds of lard from your rear end and change jobs."

"Then the heck with you." The words were followed by the sound of the door slamming. Sheba sat up in the tub, waiting on her friend's follow-up. Seconds passed, then the bathroom door squeaked open slowly and Kevin's head appeared from behind it.

"Was that Attorney Thomas McMichael I passed in the hallway?"

Sheba slid forward, allowing the soapy water to completely cover her breasts.

"Yes, it was—and he asked me to marry him. Think of it—I'm going to have my own house on the Cape."

"You won't forget your friends, will you? When you're living on the Cape with Tommy, I mean."

"Of course I won't—but that doesn't mean I'm going to invite all kinds of Lowell riff raff like you down there. The McMichaels, Tommy and Sheba, have to keep up appearances."

"Don't take all night in there. I'm putting on supper right now," added Kevin, putting an end to their juvenile exchange.

The teenager dried herself, accompanied by the clang of pans from the next room. Emerging from the bathroom, she found their supper cooking on the stove and two settings laid out on the table.

"The night shirt suits you," he observed, standing by the stove, stirring the pan of beans.

* * *

The evening meal was spent in quiet conversation with Kevin

recounting a few lighthearted stories from the store. A cool breeze blowing in from the street added to the simple pleasure of the evening. With supper behind them, they teamed up to wash and dry the dishes, elevating the apartment to a condition of absolute order. It was true. With Sheba filling her day cleaning, coupled with Kevin's natural tendency for order, the flat radiated neatness; the floor was swept, towels folded, dishes washed, furniture dusted and bed made. After eyeing the room approvingly, the young man retreated to the couch and turned on the radio. True to form, in just under ten seconds, the sound of an orchestra wafted from the Philco and over the room.

Across the apartment Sheba sat on the floor, rubbing Patch beneath her chin, causing a purring sound loud enough to cause Kevin to comment on it from fifteen feet away. The long bath produced a good feeling in Sheba. Her body smelled of soap and her hair felt wonderful to the touch. Her sense of cleanliness was enhanced by the feel of her new night shirt. It was soft, cotton, and draped down her body to a point halfway between her knees and ankles. While Kevin retrieved a *Look* magazine from a table close by, Sheba rose from the floor and joined him on the couch, positioning herself by an armrest and propping herself up with a toss pillow. Her move caused him to glance up at her for a second. Their eyes met briefly, whereupon he smiled and returned his attention to the magazine.

Sheba was filled with a sensation, a mood, a feeling she was not totally familiar with, but which was profoundly affecting her. Lifting her feet from the floor, she brought them close to her body, folding her legs until she was able her rest her chin upon her knees. She stared at Kevin intently, studying every line and pore in his face. He glanced up from his reading and noticed the attention he was receiving.

"Would you like something else on the radio?"

She shook her head no, choosing not to speak. She surveyed the young man even more closely. The lines of his face were fine and straight, but short of handsome. His brown eyes were, by far, his strongest feature. He was blessed with healthy, white teeth, a few of which broke ranks with the others, causing small gaps in his smile. Following a period of contemplation, the teenager extended her legs, dropping them across Kevin's lap. His eyes again left the magazine and met hers. Again, his response was to smile. He followed this by tugging down on her night shirt, the hem of which had risen to just below the knee. With the hemline returned to midway down her calf, he returned his attention to the magazine. Sheba saw herself in a contest with the magazine for his attention and was now determined to return his attention to her.

"I've always been ashamed of my feet," she said, lifting her right leg and placing it down on the issue of *Look*.

He peered down on her foot curiously, as if noticing it for the first time.

"What for? They're fine feet, heavily calloused, but fine feet."

"Heavily calloused and huge, you mean."

"If my mother was here she'd say; *Dearie, you come from good, peasant stock—and that's nothing to be ashamed of.*" Kevin gave his voice an elderly, cracking tone.

"You're making your mother sound like she's ninety-five with that voice," she laughed. "I have callouses from walking on cement pavement—that's how I got them."

"Then stay off of the pavement and—problem solved," he suggested.

"Better yet, I'll only walk on soft things—like on Shanahan Street." She accompanied her words with a series of tiny steps, starting at his belt line and progressing up his arm until both feet rested just below his shoulder. Simultaneously, the hemline of her night shirt rode back up her leg, now leaving her knees exposed.

He shook his head, feigning disbelief. "You must be really bored," he added.

She did not respond, content to study his reaction to her game. Suddenly, in the last few moments, he seemed unfocused, unable, or perhaps even unwilling, to call a halt to her silliness. She withdrew her left foot from his shoulder and let it slowly slide down his chest. Eventually, she let it fall to his lap, all the while studying the young man's reaction to her. Kevin's eyes were closed and there appeared to be a change in his breathing. It seemed more pronounced. At present, Sheba felt a sense of power, power in a way she had never experienced before. If anything, she thought Kevin looked paralyzed, incapable of calling a halt to her game, a game she was getting immense pleasure from playing. He opened his eyes, immediately focusing on and studying her bare legs. Now, her night shirt, the night shirt he had purchased for her only hours before, had slid up, exposing her entire calf and knee. Intrigued by her success, she was resolved to explore the limits of this new-found power.

"Do you see the booboo I have on my knee?" she asked, extending her right knee upward.

He smiled and indicated yes, touching his finger lightly on the contusion.

"You know what you're supposed to do to booboos—so they'll get better. Now give my booboo a kiss. Kiss it and make it better."

Without hesitation, he leaned forward and kissed the bruise, not once, but twice. Sheba looked on with curiosity and amazement, intrigued by the mental state she had caused in her friend through her coy, little game. Kevin, a mature, well-adjusted adult, seemed almost hypnotized by her and unable to control her antics. An increased feeling of power surged through her. His breathing, if anything, grew stronger by the minute as he sat before her in a state of near helplessness. Closing his eyes, he let his head fall back until it came to rest on the top of the couch. She responded, moving the heel of her foot back and forth across his lap until his breathing became even more labored, interrupted occasionally by low moaning.

"Kiss my other knee, Kevin. You just can't kiss one and leave it at that," she ordered, albeit softly.

"Please, Sheba, don't do this to me," he whispered back, sensing the teenager was little more than playing with him and making him act the fool.

"I insist, Kevin, kiss the other knee." Following only a slight hesitation, he leaned forward and complied with her request. The sixteen-year-old sat back, taking stock of the situation and the condition of her male friend. Sitting passively beneath her outstretched legs, he was visibly in a state of sexual arousal, her subtle manipulations having drained every vestige of willpower from his being. The sight of this grownup man in his present condition, a condition brought about by her, exhilarated her, giving her a feeling of power and control she had never experienced before. Pulling herself up from a reclining position, she lowered the weight of her body onto his, her knees converging on his waist and pinning him back against the couch. She expected and received no resistance from Kevin. His head was bowed, as if embarrassed by the ongoing developments. His eyes avoided hers.

"Look at me, Kevin," she demanded.

He did not comply. Reaching beneath his chin, she forced his head upward until her eyes were peering into his.

"You're a good guy—a really good guy. I like you, Kevin—I like you a lot, otherwise I wouldn't screw around with you like this. I trust you—so please don't be embarrassed." She leaned forward, pressing her lips against his mouth. He returned her affection, extending their kiss while he moved his hands to the back of her head, circling his fingers through her hair. There was an indescribable taste introduced into her mouth when their lips came together. It did not belong to her, or him, but instead a compound made up of the two of them.

"I've never had a girl with me up in the apartment—or anywhere else for that matter. Now I'm here with a sixteen-year-old. It's because of the way I am—my knee and my damn limp. Mister 4F, that's me—unfit for military service—unfit for any woman."

"If that's true, then how come I picked you from all the other men I'd come in contact with since last Monday?"

Sheepishly, he shrugged his shoulders.

"I picked you from everybody because I liked what I saw—that's it."

"And you're not embarrassed being seen with someone who's dragging one of his legs around like an old man?"

"Big deal—that's nothing!"

His eyes left hers and focused on something across the room as he ran her words over in his mind. "I love having you sit here on top of me—you do know that, don't you?"

She laughed, placing another kiss on his lips. His breathing had slowed from moments before but retained a measure of its earlier intensity. She brought her hand up to his forehead. "Someone's still a little heated here," she said.

"Who taught you how to do that to a man?"

"Pure instinct. We women are just born with it. It levels out the playing field—with you men having all the strength and muscle."

"Strength and muscle—try telling that guy back in the Portland bus terminal—the poor soul whose face is still probably swollen from those oversized fists of yours."

She lifted her hands and clenched her fists. "The man was simply in the wrong place at the wrong time," she added behind a pretty smile.

"You ought to smile more often. You've got a really, really, pretty smile."

The teenager responded by pressing her lips back on his, then fueled its intensity by moving her hips up and down while remaining atop him. Kevin's response to her manipulation grew more heated as her weight continued to press down on him. Her actions had given rise to a return of heavy breathing when a series of knocks on the door split the air.

"Who is it?" Sheba called out, after separating herself from Kevin.

"It's Roberta. I was wondering if you wouldn't mind a little company. I brought a dish of treats."

"Just a minute," she answered, still balanced on Kevin's lap. "Can't a girl even make out with her uncle without being disturbed?" she whispered into his ear.

The neighbor's arrival set Tripod into a short fit of barking. Sheba opened the door to see the petite woman holding a plate of cupcakes.

"I hope this isn't inconvenient or anything. It's just that you said I should feel free to come up when we talked this morning and I found myself getting a bad case of the blues downstairs. I was hoping that a little company might help snap me out of it."

Kevin and Sheba invited the woman in, practically in unison, with the teenager escorting her to the kitchen table.

"I'll see if I can scrape together a little coffee or some tea bags," said Sheba. "In the meantime, Roberta, I want you to take a look at my Uncle Kevin. To me, he seems a little flushed and maybe running a slight temperature. Would you take a look at him?"

The woman put down the plate and scurried across the room to the young man. Placing the palm of her hand on his forehead, she quickly came up with a diagnosis. "He's definitely warm—probably running a fever."

From behind the woman's back, Sheba signaled to Kevin, playfully mocking Roberta's findings.

"Plus, you're wet with perspiration! What are you doing sitting up on the divan? You should be lying in bed!"

"No, Roberta, it's okay," he argued.

"Nonsense—there'll be no coffee for you. Ice water to battle the fever—that's what you need, Kevin. What's more, I don't think you should be even thinking about the cupcakes. You know what they say—feed a cold and starve a fever."

Roberta's visit on this Saturday evening extended over three hours. During this time Sheba learned that the young woman from Gorham in the White Mountains of New Hampshire was actually a year older than Kevin. Now, as senior member of the threesome, it was her discretion carrying the most weight in dealing with whatever it was ailing Kevin. This resulted in the young man being sent to bed for a night of recuperation and his niece being relegated to the cot until his complete recovery.

21

October 14, 1944

It had been more than two and a half weeks since Sheba found refuge in Lowell, Massachusetts, in the apartment of Kevin Shanahan. The friendship, the bond, between the two grew closer and stronger with the passing of each day. In periods of contemplation, a number spent by the reservoir atop Christian Hill, she relived recent events in her life in the year 1944. She took great comfort knowing she had directly impacted a minimal number of men and women outside of the one she came back to assist, her mother. Since leaving Maine, her only lasting exposure to others was limited to Kevin and Roberta. Whether it had been out walking the streets or visiting the stores in Centralville, all contact with human beings had been minimized, for the most part. On occasions when individuals attempted to start conversations with her or draw information from her, Sheba had adeptly ended dialogue with closed-ended responses. At the moment, she stood studying the calendar as the 17th, the night of the new moon, approached. On more than one occasion over the past week she had raised the subject of her upcoming departure to Kevin, only to have him change the topic immediately.

It was Saturday afternoon. Earlier that morning, Sheba and Kevin put together a plan over coffee for an evening out following his work shift at Kresge's. The arrangement called for her to join her friend downtown where they would grab a modest dinner. Dinner would be followed by a twin bill at Keith's Theatre.

* * *

At five o'clock she locked the apartment door behind her and headed out. She carried with her a certain sense of excitement, partly from the anticipation of seeing a movie. However, in addition to the motion pictures, she was enthused about getting out of the house and among people. Sheba had taken the time to clean and press her dress, the one she had acquired through Reverend Littlefield in Maine. So, with her hair washed, shampooed and combed, and her body smelling of flowers from an hour-long soaking in the tub, she proudly strode down Bridge Street, across the bridge, and finally onto Merrimack Street where she waited on Kevin's dismissal from work. Standing on the sidewalk in front of Kresge's, she felt the eyes of a number of men surveying her. This created a marvelous feeling in her, further heightening an already elevated spirit. Sheba was not put out in the least when Kevin did not materialize at the prearranged time. She was enjoying the attention from passing males, many of whom were in uniform. At long last, Kevin appeared in the doorway of the 5 & 10 cent store, his face transmitting a look of frustration. The look gave way to one of awe and delight when, after scanning the pedestrians near the store entrance, his eyes settled on Sheba standing by the curb. She walked up to him with her eyes locked onto his.

"Not bad for a girl you picked up at a bus terminal, huh? Just don't let anyone know that this classy girl—reeking of sophistication—is wearing moccasins."

"It'll be our secret," he replied, pecking her on the cheek.

Following Chinese food, the couple made their way to Keith's Theatre where *The Impatient Years* with Jean Arthur and *Lum and Abner Goin to Town* were playing. The movie house was only half full, prompting management to cordon off the balcony. This disappointed Sheba, who had never gone to a picture show in a building sophisticated enough to offer seating above the main floor. After picking up on the teenager's preoccupation with the empty balcony above and behind them, Kevin escorted her to the back of the theatre and quietly whisked her under the velvet restraining cord and up the stairs to the balcony, where they sat through a newsreel, cartoon, and the two motion pictures, alone. It was shortly after ten o'clock when they left the movie house and made their way home to Centralville.

Arriving back at the apartment, they were confronted by two animals desperately needing to relieve themselves. They decided to take Tripod out for a walk while Patch was permitted to attend to her own business in the alleyways out behind the building. Reaching the sidewalk, Sheba made a gesture toward crossing the street. Kevin stopped her in her tracks.

"Where are you going?" he asked.

"I've never been down that street. I thought we might go down there, that's all."

"I'm not so sure that's a good idea. West Fourth Street's sort of a rough place. It's always been a little on the rowdy side."

"Oh, come on, Kevin. What? Do I have to take Tripod down there all by myself?" She did not wait for a reply. Without hesitation, she pulled on Tripod's leash and scampered across Bridge Street and down West Fourth. Following a pause, Kevin called out to her and shuffled up from behind. By the time he caught the sixteen-year-old, they were well down the poorly lit street. In spite of the late hour, West Fourth Street was alive with sounds and activity. The sidewalk was dark and neither had their night vision yet. At one point, a stream of young children came through an open gate, screaming unintelligible words at the top of their lungs.

"Shouldn't they be in bed by now?" questioned Sheba.

"Let's just get down to the end of the street and make our way home the long way around," he suggested. Ahead of them, a street light faintly illuminated an intersection.

Reaching the poorly lit corner, they were startled when two figures appeared out of the darkness from across the street and made their way toward them.

"Well, well, well—what the fuck have we got here?" The words seemed to come from the larger of the two strangers. On reflex, Kevin came to an abrupt halt. The two toughs moved out into the light.

"The gimp's out takin' his fuckin' girlfriend for a walk," wise-cracked the larger man.

"Hey Benny—check out the fuckin' dog. The fuckin' thing's got three legs!" The statement caused both to burst out in a fit of high-pitched laughter.

"Yeah, we'd better check the paper—Ringling Brothers must be in town cause we got the fuckin' freak show right here on our street." The verbal assault brought on another series of howls.

"And you, doll—what the fuck are you doin' with the gimp?" The question came from Benny, the tall stranger and, no doubt, the more dangerous of the two punks.

Sheba gave Kevin's hand a squeeze, then stepped forward.

"We're just out walking the dog—and getting some fresh air."

The two men steadily closed the distance between themselves and the couple. "Jesus, you are one fuckin' dish," called out the shorter punk.

Sheba sized up the two as they stopped within a few feet of her. Both were unkempt and greasy. The taller one, he was six feet or more, clearly represented most of the danger at hand.

"You know, doll face, we've got enough Harvard Export, enough for the three of us to drink all night. Say the word and we'll give the gimp and 'Freak the wonder dog' the bum's rush."

"And what would the word be?" Sheba asked, speaking seductively and moving forward to within striking distance of the larger punk.

"Oh, I don't know—maybe just tell the fuckin' gimp he's—aaarrghhh!" The punk grabbed for his crotch as he folded forward and crashed to the pavement. Sheba had unleashed a kick to the groin that struck its target with an overwhelming impact. A grotesque sound came from the man, as if his lungs had exploded.

"You little shit," snarled the second punk, lunging at her and taking hold of her throat. With one hand grasping her throat and the other with a fistful of dress, he swung her toward the ground. Sheba resisted, remaining on her feet but off balance. The young creep tightened his hold on her throat as she unsuccessfully tried to deliver a punch to his groin. Twisting her body downward, he came out with a nervous guffaw at the sound of her dress ripping. She lunged back at him, sinking her teeth into his leg. She heard him cry out just as his body crumbled down beside her. He fell beneath the weight of Kevin, who had joined the melee. She rose to her feet while the two men battled next to her. She examined her dress. It was ripped from the neck to across her chest, exposing her bra.

Beside her on the ground, Kevin and the smaller punk exchanged punches while in a clinch. A few feet away, the larger tough had risen to one knee, showing the first sign of recovery from the kick to the groin. Without hesitation, Sheba drove a knee to his forehead, sending him reeling backwards onto the hard surface of the road where the back of his head hit the cement with a horrible thud. She turned back to see Tripod join the conflict, sinking his teeth into the other man's upper leg while his master delivered punches to his face.

"I've had enough!" screamed the punk. "Get the fuckin' dog away from me."

Kevin pushed the tough to the ground and pulled Tripod away from the hooligan.

"My dress," moaned Sheba, holding up a dangling shred of fabric.

"Let's just go," urged Kevin, already pulling back from the confrontation. The three retraced their steps up West Fourth Street while the smaller punk attended to his friend.

A few minutes later, they were back at the apartment. Kevin removed two bottles of Harvard Beer from the refrigerator and poured them into a pair of glasses.

"Before we go any further—I want to make something perfectly clear here," he said, his voice deadly serious. "I'm the adult in this household—not you. Furthermore, I happen to know my city a lot better than you do. Now, listen to me, young lady—the next time I say something, particularly if it's on matters of our personal safety— you listen! Am I making myself clear here? We could have gotten hurt out there—or worse! Okay?"

"Yes, Kevin, as much as I hate to admit it—I screwed up. Next time, I'll listen to you."

He stared across the table at the girl, almost seeming shocked at her quick acceptance of his command. "Okay, matter closed. Now, I don't care if you are underage—we fought together—we drink together." His words were followed by a salute, raising his glass to the six-teen-year-old.

"To the man who came to my rescue," toasted Sheba, extending her glass to arm's length.

"You hardly needed my help," he added.

"That's not true, Kevin—and we both know it. And to creep number one—who should be coming to just about now—may the fleas from a thousand camels infest his armpits." She raised her glass a second time whereupon Kevin completed the toast by touching his glass to hers.

"And to creep number two—the first man I've ever punched in the mouth—and whose genitals Tripod may have literally sunk his teeth into."

"Here, here," added Sheba.

They lifted their glasses in unison before taking another swig of beer. The two warriors looked across the table at one another, their mutual respect beyond any further expression in words.

"Kevin, I swear to God, that first kick I got off on the big creep— well, I got all of him—right in the friggin' balls. I've never hit any *one* or any *thing* so hard before in my life."

The young man rose from his chair and stood beside her, still holding his glass of beer. "A final toast," he announced. "To the things a man will do and endure for a pretty face." He touched his glass to hers bringing about a vibrating ring. He pecked the sixteen-year-old on the cheek and retreated to the couch.

Her instincts told her Kevin hoped to return to the playful carry-ings on from two weeks earlier. However, Sheba was wary of the dwin-dling number of days she had before the new moon arrived on the 17th of the month. In seventy-two hours she would return to 1970 and learn how her and her family's lives were changed from this experience.

Already, her thoughts every night before dropping off to sleep centered on the potential success or failure of this adventure.

"It's been a long day for me, Kevin, but thank you for the dinner and movie—it was wonderful—and thank you for being there when I needed you."

"It's what any self-respecting freak would have done."

"You're anything but a freak," she countered, bending down and innocently touching her lips to his. She left his side and crawled between the covers of the bed. "Goodnight, Kevin."

22

October 17, 1944

Sheba opened her eyes to a darkened room. It was the day. It was the day of the new moon, the day she would be returned to 1970. She felt a weight on her feet at the bottom of the bed. It was Patch, sleeping contentedly. At the far end of the room, light was escaping from behind the bathroom door, telling her Kevin was already up and preparing himself for work. Here it was, she thought, time for dreaded good-byes. There was no forestalling it any longer. The teenager slipped out of bed and crossed the room, seating herself at the kitchen table. For the past week, she had given her departure from this time and place a great deal of thought. She reasoned it would come overnight, just as her journey back had, but there was no way to be sure. Sheba knew she must not risk leaving without speaking to Kevin. She looked up from the table as the bathroom door swung open and he appeared. The scent of his Old Spice escaped the bathroom with him and filled her nostrils.

"You're up—what's the occasion?" He smiled down on her, a smile now familiar after three weeks.

"Kevin, as hard as this is to say—I'm going to be leaving very soon—and in case it comes quicker than I think—I wanted you to know how much I'm going to miss you—and how much you mean to me." Sheba spoke, her head bowed, having no desire to see the impact of her words on his face.

"What are you saying? Are you saying you won't be here when I get home tonight?"

"No, not exactly. It's just that I know I'll have to be leaving real soon—and I didn't want to go without telling you this."

"Then you will be here tonight when I come home?"

"It's hard to explain. I'm pretty sure I'll be here—but it's something I don't have any control over."

"Is someone coming down from Maine for you? Is that what you're saying?" Kevin spoke while continuing to prepare himself for work. There was anxiety in his voice.

"No, no one's coming down from Maine. I'm afraid it's something I just can't explain. You'll just have to take my word for it—and know I'd never lie to you."

He glanced down at his wristwatch before taking a chair next to her. "Listen, I know I've changed the subject on you every time you brought it up—you know—of you leaving—but it was just because I couldn't face it. Now, I've got to say something. I want you to stay. Do you hear? You being here with me has been the best thing that's ever happened to me in my entire life. You belong here. You were meant to be here with me. I don't think it was chance that brought us together, I think it was God. Now, I'm asking you not to leave me. I'll do anything if it means you'll stay." Kevin pulled himself up from the chair and buried his face in her hair, finally kissing the top of her head before pulling away.

"We'll see," she replied, unwilling to forward the conversation.

"And you will be here—promise me—when I get home tonight."

She looked up, offering a faint smile, her eyes moist with restrained tears. "I'll be here."

* * *

Sheba sat by the window as the afternoon sun dropped lower in the sky and behind the buildings lining the far side of Bridge Street. The sky shone a majestic blue, bordered by a stream of clouds illuminated in white and marbled in dark wisps of mist. With the coffee supply in the house exhausted and a fresh ration book still two weeks away, she made herself a cup of tea. She sipped on it, waiting for the sound of the front door to close from two floors below. It was the approximate time Roberta usually returned home from work. It was a few minutes shy of four o'clock when the sound and shudder of the front door slamming vibrated through the building, telling Sheba of the woman's arrival.

Allowing Roberta a moment to settle in after her eight-hour shift, Sheba glanced around the flat. As always, it was in complete order, the only exception being the new dress Kevin had purchased for her the day before. On Monday, he put his male ego on hold and marched into the Martha McQuade Shop at Dickerman and McQuade's Clothing Store and bought a woolen dress for her at a cost of $8.95. It hung at length on a metal hanger from the top of the closet door. He surprised her with it, bringing it home as a replacement for the dress torn beyond repair on Saturday night. She looked with fondness at the humble studio, her home for the better part of her odyssey in the year 1944. She took this time to take in every ornament and piece of furniture, hoping to commit as much to memory as possible.

The girl descended the stairs and crossed the hall, finally freezing in front of the door. Inwardly, she questioned herself on the wisdom of her mission. At the end of a prolonged hesitation, she knocked.

"Who is it?"

"It's Sheba. Are you busy?" Her question gave rise to a series of footsteps from behind the door.

"Oh, come in, Sheba," called out the young woman. The teenager made her way inside and waited on the woman's hospitality.

"Can I get you a tonic or anything?"

Sheba waved off refreshments. She was now accustomed to the people of Lowell's peculiarity of identifying soda pop as tonic and no longer commented on it. "I just thought I'd let you know that I'll be going home soon. I didn't want to take off and not say good-bye."

"Oh, I'm sorry to hear that. I'll miss you—and I'm sure your uncle will, too."

Sheba paused, unsure how to direct the conversation toward her intended topic.

"You know, I've seen a change in Kevin since you arrived—a change for the good. I never thought it was good for a young man like him to be by himself as much as he was, sitting around and reading those books about locks and keys day and night. Your coming here to visit seemed to prove my point."

"Uncle Kevin is one of the finest gentlemen I've ever met—bar none. One of the reasons I'm down here—besides wanting to say good-bye—is to ask you to watch over him for me. Maybe you two could keep each other company, I mean, even more than before—now that Uncle Kevin's used to having a woman around the house."

Roberta nodded, seeming to be in full agreement with Sheba's statement.

"You know, Roberta, Uncle Kevin's told me a lot about you and your fiancé."

"Jimmy—his name's Jimmy."

"And it sounds like you two were really very much in love."

"Yes—we *are* in love."

"I'm just saying—when two people are that much in love—one will always find a way to let the other one know they're okay—if they possibly can. I know Jimmy'd never let you go on and on not knowing what's happened to him—if he possibly could." She spoke softly, letting her voice grow softer with each passing sentence. "My uncle up there—he's more than fond of you—in fact, I think he's in love with you. He's just afraid to say it or show it because of Jimmy—and maybe a little because he thinks he's not good enough for you because of his leg and all. Now I'm not saying you should up and forget about Jimmy—just that you should keep your mind and heart open for Kevin—in case Jimmy's never able to come home." Sheba looked up, only to have Roberta turn away and walk to the window.

"Thank you for thinking of me and taking the time to say good-bye," she said. It was not the response Sheba anticipated. "I hope your trip home to West Virginia is a safe and pleasant one," the woman added, a statement the teenager saw as a dismissal.

"Good-bye, Roberta," she answered as she rose from the chair and made her way from the apartment.

The sun had already set when the door to the studio opened and Kevin shuffled inside, letting out a sigh of relief at the sight of Sheba spread out on the couch. In one hand he carried a bag of Chinese food he had picked up a few doors down the street.

"Did you spend the whole day on the divan?" he asked while removing his jacket.

"I spent the whole day cleaning—and thinking."

"Thinking about staying on here with me, I hope."

She offered him no response. He hung his jacket in the closet after placing their supper on the table.

"Kevin, I'm facing a scary thing tomorrow—that's going to affect my life a lot—a real lot—and as it gets closer, I'm getting more and more scared and nervous."

"Tell me what it is. Maybe I can help you through it."

"That's the thing, I've got to do it alone. I can't even talk to you about it—it's that secret."

A look of disappointment came over his face as her words took hold of him. "Then you're leaving, even though I asked you not to." His tone carried a degree of agitation.

She rose to her feet and approached him. "Please don't be cross with me," she pleaded, placing her head against his shoulder.

"Here—spoon out your food before it gets cold." Kevin spoke to her as if addressing a child.

Pulling down two plates from a nearby shelf, she portioned out their chop suey and took her place at the table. There, they dined in relative silence, directing most of their words to Tripod and Patch who sat close by awaiting handouts.

Supper was followed by the customary practice of washing and drying dishes and utensils. With the kitchen table cleared and every item returned to, or stacked in, its proper place, Sheba retreated back to the couch where she sat quietly, her head tilted downward as if mourning the loss of a loved one. The sound of an unfamiliar big band tune wafted across the room as Kevin deposited himself next to her. He stared across the apartment, appearing to gather the words or the courage to speak to her from the surface of the far wall.

"I might as well just come right out and say this—'cause if I don't—then I'll be second-guessing myself for the rest of my life. Sheba—I don't want you to leave—and I'll do anything, I mean anything, if it means you'll stay here with me—even if it's only for a little longer. I love you, Sheba, even though you're legally only a kid. I knew that first morning when we woke up here together, I mean, I loved you already then—and as the last three weeks went on—I've only grown to love you more."

"Kevin—you don't understand—and I can't tell you why—but I have to leave soon—very, very soon." Her head remained down. She could not bear to meet his eyes.

"Sheba, think back to that night on Central Street, at the bus terminal. You begged me not to just leave you there—'cause you were so scared. I couldn't do it, I just couldn't do it to you. Well, now it's my turn to beg you back—'cause I'm scared of trying to go back to living without you. I need you to save me from this. For the last two years I've been praying and praying for God to send me someone, a girlfriend, someone to love. I'm so alone in my life. Then you showed up, and I just knew my prayers had been answered."

Sheba threw her arms around him and wept. She wept for the kindest, most trustworthy man she had ever known, and she wept for herself. "I love you, too, Kevin—believe me I do—but I can't stay." With her words still hanging in the room, she pushed her fingers through his, taking hold of his hand and leading him from the couch to the table. She pulled a tablet of paper from a cabinet drawer and began to write. "I'm giving you the names of a few successful companies you will want to invest in over the next ten to twenty years. Do what I say and you'll be able to put away enough money to leave that job downtown and maybe open your own store. You're always talking about how you love locks and keys and safes and stuff—and you spend so much time reading about that stuff. Watch for these companies I'm writing down here and buy shares of stock in them. They will be really successful. Oh, and watch for a fighter named Cassius Clay when he fights for the heavyweight championship against a guy named Sonny Liston. No one will give him a chance to win, but I'm telling you to bet on Clay. And when a fighter named Rocky Marciano comes along—bet on him all the time—'cause he will never lose a fight. I'm writing all of this down so don't you go and lose this paper! I know these things. I can see the future." She continued, frantically writing down every tidbit of information she was able to remember from her life in 1970. Finally, she stopped, and placed the pencil down beside the tablet of paper. Kevin sat quietly beside her, observing her odd behavior with a blend of curiosity and disbelief. Although dumbstruck by her pronouncements, he accepted the paper from her.

Minutes later, after returning with Kevin to the couch, the teenager experienced a slight, but persistent, chill and announced she would be retiring to bed early where she could warm herself under the covers. Retreating to the bathroom, she donned her night shirt and made her way across the linoleum floor to the bed. When a downcast Kevin slid along the couch to his customary place under the lamp and beside the radio, she beckoned him to her side.

"Kevin, if it wouldn't be too much trouble and you wouldn't mind, I wondered if you would sleep next to me tonight. I'm very nervous and it would help if I could have someone close to me—and there's no one I'd rather have there than you."

He knelt down beside the bed, kissing her on the forehead, then the bridge of her nose. He circled the bed to the far side and began peeling off his clothes. After a five-minute ritual where he methodically removed, then carefully folded each article of clothing, he pulled himself under the bed sheets and beside her.

"Oh, my God, you're so warm next to me," she commented as their bodies came together. "I must feel like an ice cube."

He did not reply, content to run his warm hands down her arms, creating warmth from the friction. She shifted her feet, bringing them up between his knees.

"Sweet Mother of God! Your feet are like blocks of ice!" he called out.

"I can move them away," she answered apologetically.

"No, don't—I'll get used to them. I want every part of Sheba Smith next to me—even her frozen feet."

She let out a contented sigh and tightened her grip on him. "You know, Kevin, I read a ghost story once about this guy who picks up a girl in a beautiful yellow dress hitchhiking and takes her to a dance and everything—and he notices that she's really cold when he's dancing with her. When he asks her about it, she blames it on poor circulation or something. Well, to make a long story short, these two hit it off really well this night, but when he's driving her home she suddenly yells to stop the car—and she dashes out into the night and through the gates of a cemetery. So, after he parks the car, he follows her into the cemetery, calling out her name: Jane! Jane! There's no answer. He keeps wandering around the graveyard looking for her—then spots her yellow dress a little ways off. When he finally gets close to it—he sees it's draped over a tombstone. The tombstone reads: Jane Smith, born October 17, 1920, died June 28, 1938. He's been calling her Jane all night and it's October 17th, 1944—her birthday! She came out of the grave to celebrate her birthday—and that's why she was so cold. He'd been dancing *with* and talking *to* a dead girl all night!"

"You're giving me the creeps," he said.

"Don't worry —I'm not a ghost."

"You know what—to be completely honest with you—there's been a couple of times when I started to wonder about you—the way you seem to have come from nowhere—and no one looking for you or anything. I even started to wonder if you might be an angel or something."

His disclosure brought a burst of laughter from her. "An angel from heaven or an angel from hell?"

"I thought about that, too," he added.

"Put it this way, I'm closer to an angel than I am being a teenybopper from Lowell High."

"See, right there, the way you talk sometime—and use words I've never heard before—like you did just then—teenybopper. What the heck is that?"

"Listen, just don't fret about this stuff—and make sure you keep that stuff I wrote down for you—and use it."

He went to reply but she brought her finger up to his mouth, coaxing him not to speak.

Sheba tucked her head under Kevin's arm, resting it on his chest. Lifting her leg atop his body, she laid beside him, drawing from his warmth. Her mind was overrun with thoughts of the pending return to 1970. She was becoming afraid. Soon she would learn of the success or failure of this incredible undertaking. Waves of anxiety moved through her. A thought came to her: If she were to divulge everything to Kevin, the pact between Mowalk and the Great Spirit would be dissolved, leaving her stranded back here in time. She told herself that she must return to her own time, to 1970. If she was successful, her mother and brother would be there on her return. If she was unsuccessful, her father would need her nonetheless. Another cold shiver ran up her body, causing her to pull Kevin closer. She was sure the drop in her body temperature was an indication of her imminent return to her other life in 1970. He responded by eliminating all distance between them. Their bodies were aligned as one. The feel of his warm breath on the base of her neck would be her last recollection from 1944.

23

October 18, 1944

Kevin awakened abruptly to the sound of ticking from the Bulova alarm clock beside the bed. The room was pitch black, not allowing his eyes to focus on any single object. Reaching across the surface of the mattress, he swept his arm beneath the sheets, searching for Sheba's body. When his probe came up empty, he fumbled for the lamp and eventually found the chain. The bulb flashed on. He was alone in the bed. Instinctively, his eyes searched the room for her. Patch and Tripod stirred but did not come to him. Pulling back the bed covers, he saw Sheba's night shirt stretched out beside him. Kevin jumped to his feet and called out for her. His eyes scanned the room a second time, this time noticing her moccasins still neatly positioned along the side wall. The new dress he had purchased for her on Monday still hung from its hanger. He scurried across the room, satisfying himself she was not hiding in the bathroom.

After throwing on his clothes, he raced to the door. A final check of the room found the rest of the teenager's clothing still folded in the bureau, telling him she was somewhere outside the apartment completely undressed. The alarm clock read five minutes past three o'clock. Frantic, he descended the stairs and began the search for her. After making his way down Bridge Street to the river, he circled back, walking north to beyond Dairy Farms before climbing Christian Hill where he traced their route from weeks earlier. The streets of Lowell during wartime were dark and quiet, many only illuminated by lamp posts fitted with fifteen-watt bulbs.

* * *

After more than three hours of fruitless searching, the sun broke above the horizon, beckoning Kevin to return to the apartment. After dragging himself up two flights of stairs, he boiled hot water for tea and sat at the kitchen table, awaiting a call from Sheba. He played with the idea of calling the police and reporting her missing. However, he reasoned there would be questions arising from the bizarre circumstances. What was an adult male doing living with an underage female? Why did he lie to his neighbors, telling them she was his niece? Could there have been foul play associated with the disappearance? He quickly dissuaded himself from making a call to the Lowell Police Department. He called in sick for work, complaining of a high fever.

Kevin remained in the apartment throughout the morning and afternoon, staring alternately at the front door and the activity two stories below on Bridge Street. The room no longer vibrated with the sound of Sheba Smith as it had for the past three weeks. He sat clutching her night shirt. He lifted the garment to his face every few minutes, breathing in the faint scent her body had left in the fabric. It and a half dozen other clothing items were the only tangible evidence of her existence to him. Kevin thought back to their emotional conversation the evening before. He had told her that he loved her. He drew consolation from this.

When the last glimpse of sunlight disappeared from the far wall of the apartment early that evening, he slumped sideways onto the couch and wept aloud. Kevin knew she would never return.

24

Elaine's eyes opened to a sun-drenched bedroom on a warm Sunday morning. Lazily, she shifted her head in the direction of the window where fine, white curtains hung listlessly from their rod. It would be another in a series of hot days, she thought, a perfect day to visit Moody or Ogunquit Beach after church service, yet, something of greater importance would come first. For nearly a year, an envelope made out to her from her cousin hung taped to her bureau mirror. The instructions scribbled on it were clear: Do not open until August 5, 1945. Now, the day had arrived. She pushed herself from the bed, walked to the bureau, then crossed the room to the chair by the window, the chair her cousin so often had sat in during her three-day visit the prior year. She tore open the envelope.

Dearest cousin,

By now my visit must seem like a distant memory. You can be sure that I have missed you more than you have missed me. My few days visiting you and your parents were some of the happiest days of my life. I know this letter will find you in good health and you can be assured that I am the same. The reason for this note is to remind you of my warning from last year and to give you one last piece of evidence that I can see things in the future and that you must follow my instructions. Remember, you must never let a dog or anything else that could block your vision be in the front seat of your car. You must always be very careful when driving anywhere near Four Corners over in Kennebunk and especially careful on August 14, 1960. I'm saying you shouldn't drive your car and put yourself in danger that day. You must do what I say in this regard.

As a sign to you to show you I know what I'm talking about, I will tell you this. The war with Japan will be over very shortly. Tomorrow, America will drop something from the sky on Japan that will change the world for-

189

ever. It will happen twice. The first time in a city called Hiroshima. After the second time, the Japanese will surrender quickly and our soldiers will be coming home. When you hear about what has happened, you will almost not be able to believe it. I'm telling you all of this so you will believe me in my warnings to you. You must do what I say and follow my instructions. Is that clear?

Finally I want you to know that I would never have gone away like I did unless I positively had to. No cousin has ever loved or cared for another cousin like I care for you. You must believe me. And until I see you again—and I will—be good to yourself and your parents.

I love you,

Sheba

For the next few minutes, the fifteen-year-old read and reread the note from the mysterious girl who unexpectedly had entered and exited her life a year before. She sat back and revisited the frustration of not having a photograph or any other tangible reminder of her cousin, aside from the note in her hand. Already, the image of her cousin's face was blurring in her memory. From the far side of the house came the hushed voices of her parents. She decided not to show the letter from Sheba to her mother until after church.

25

Sheba took a deep breath as she slowly emerged from a bottomless sleep. Cradled in a fetal position, she became conscious of cold air as it gusted around her. She lifted her face from a mat of moist leaves, immediately brushing them from her cheek as she rose. There was suppressed light surrounding her. She was encircled by trees. Her eyes focused on the ground far below her, telling her she was back on the surface of the great boulder. However, the holy rock was not in the same condition she had left it on the evening of June 20, 1970. A pair of tree limbs she had cleared months before lay balanced and broken on the surface of the boulder. Sheba took stock of herself. Again, the passage through time had rendered her naked. Running her hands over her body for warmth, she found her nipples erect and her legs covered in goose pimples. She let out a shiver, an audible expression of the frigid condition of her body. Although hesitant to move around in the poor light, she forced herself to her feet and carefully stepped toward the low end of the rock. Moving cautiously over the bough of one fallen tree, she eventually found the familiar grooves where she had climbed and descended the great stone so many times before. Moments later, her bare feet found the soft soil of the forest floor. Her first act was to drop to her knees and thank God for her safe return, followed by a prayer for success, asking Jesus for a new life that would include her mother and brother.

Rising to her feet, Sheba walked around the great boulder until she found the side that provided her with the best protection from the chilly morning breeze. There she crouched, rolling her body into a compact ball by bringing her knees to her chest and wrapping her arms around both legs. For the next ten minutes she sat still, watching the woods gradually fill with the dawn's light.

Sheba spent the time nestled by the edge of the boulder planning her next move. Given her success under identical circumstances back in 1944, she decided to walk to the edge of the roadway and follow the road from behind the tree line until she came in contact with houses. Perhaps, she thought, good fortune would smile on her again and a full clothesline would materialize for the plucking.

Reaching the edge of the road, she turned right and made her way in the general direction of Cape Arundel. Again, just as before, she was forced to retreat further into the woods when houses came into view. By the time she reached the grounds of the property where clothes had been removed on her maiden jaunt, she fully expected to be rewarded with a clothesline sagging beneath the weight of a full wash. Her spirits plummeted when the backyard came into view and the lines were empty.

Close to an hour had passed since the start of her journey and she took this opportunity to give herself a short rest. Nearly a month earlier, this exact spot was where she had put on her stolen clothes, but now all she could do was stand in the direct rays of the sun to warm herself. Sheba reasoned she would now be forced to push her route further from populated areas, away from the ocean and the harbor at Kennebunkport. She could not let herself be spotted while still in the nude. If she could not find an unattended clothesline, then she hoped to happen upon an unoccupied summer cottage on her way back to Wells and Burnt Mill Road. If an unguarded cottage showed up in her path, she would force entry and, hopefully, come up with enough clothing to expand her options.

With a plan in place and her body warmed from the rays of sunlight penetrating the forest, she pulled herself up from the ground and headed away from the Atlantic. Ten minutes into this leg of her hike Sheba crossed a dirt road and concluded she no longer knew her exact whereabouts. She had grown accustomed to her nudity. However, her immense desire to remain hidden from all other human beings kept her in a constant state of alert, her eyes scanning a full one hundred and eighty degrees of the woodland in front of her while her ears attempted to pick up any and all sounds produced by humans, no matter from what distance. The one plus created by this new overland route was the softness of the ground and leaves beneath her, in contrast to the cement pavement that tore at the soles of her feet on the earlier walk.

* * *

Sheba had just climbed to the crest of a modest hill when she stopped short. Beneath her, no more than thirty feet away, a doe and her fawn drank from a rill, unaware of her presence. The sound from the water gurgling its way through the woods and Sheba's position downwind from the doe had allowed her to close to within a short distance of the animals. She stood, quiet and motionless, for a short time, taking in the sight. Then, in a sudden, rapid movement, the head of the doe sprang up. It had picked up on some element of danger. After directing its attention on the forest in front and to the sides of it, it turned, focusing on the form of the human standing on nearby high ground. Sheba watched the mother's eyes grow large with fear. The doe froze for a moment, as if by instinct hoping to go undetected by camouflage.

"Don't be afraid, mama," she called out in a voice just loud enough to carry to the deer. The fawn turned and joined its mother in a frozen stare.

"Finish your drink, I'm in no hurry," she added.

The animals, led by the doe, sprang from the tiny stream and raced away into the deep forest. After losing sight and sound of them, the girl walked down to the fast-moving stream and scooped water into her mouth. She could not even venture a guess on how long it would be before she would eat solid food and filled her stomach with as much water as possible.

The sun had traveled higher in the sky when she wandered into the yard of a small cottage. This was the closest to any house Sheba had ventured all day. Crouching down in tall, dry grass, probably left uncut from the prior year, she deliberately inched her way toward the front of the property. Finally, from a vantage point in the grass and a short distance from a gravel road, she saw the cottage showed no signs of occupation at the moment. From her position, she could spot only one other building, and that was more than fifty yards up the road. Sheba retraced her steps, alternately scampering and crawling until she found herself at the back of the building. She listened closely, placing her ear against the wall of the house, for any sound of human or canine activity. There was none. Following two unsuccessful tries at prodding open a rear window, she lifted a stone from the overgrown walkway and broke the pane of glass directly above the window lock. Seconds later, the window was unlocked and opened and the teenager hoisted herself up and over the sill and onto the kitchen floor of the cottage.

Sheba brushed aside pieces of shattered glass as she rose to her feet, careful to keep the splintered edges of glass from penetrating her skin. Across the kitchen, a clock hung quiet and motionless. It was one of the familiar black cat clocks with eyes and a tail that ticked out the passing seconds. Cautiously stepping around tidbits of broken glass scattered halfway across the room, she made her way past a pot belly stove and into a small hallway. Inspecting the layout of the knotty pine structure, she saw a seasonal cottage comprised of three additional rooms, two of which were bedrooms. Hurriedly, she searched the bedrooms for closets. Sheba found one in the larger of the two but was disappointed when, on inspection, she came up with no clothing hanging there. One by one, the bureau drawers in the master bedroom were opened, only to find each one void of any clothing. The beds in both rooms were stripped to the mattress but Sheba let out a cry of delight when a smaller bedroom drawer produced a set of faded, blue linens.

Stepping back into the kitchen, she located a broom leaning in the corner of the room and put it to use, sweeping every visible piece of glass into a neat pile beneath the window. Next, an inspection of the kitchen cabinets yielded four sharp knives and a pair of scissors. Her spirits grew as she assembled the tools needed to clothe herself. Retrieving the linens from the bedroom, she laid them out on the kitchen table, taking inventory of what fabric she had at her disposal. She had two bed sheets and a pillow case. She paused over an outstretched bed sheet, pondering her options. In the back of her mind was the nagging thought of the cottage owners pulling up to the house. Through this distraction, the teenager made a decision. With the scissors, Sheba cut a hole in the center of one sheet, adding two more on opposite sides of the original. Sliding her head through the middle opening and an arm through the remaining two, she created a makeshift poncho. She let out a spontaneous sigh of relief, relieved to have finally covered her body. The only remaining hindrance was the floppy, loose fabric hanging on all sides of her. She scoured the rooms for rope but with no success. At last, her eyes trained on a roll of electrical cord in the far corner of the kitchen. She detached a six-foot extension and tied it around her waist, constricting a major portion of the loose fabric.

She was in the process of making her final pass through the cottage when her eyes fell on two objects wedged between the front door and a wooden, storage box. She could not believe her good fortune when, on closer inspection, she beheld a pair of rubber boots collecting dust, no doubt left there for use during Maine's annual mud season. After brushing the loose soil from the bottom of her feet, she slipped on the boots. Although a size or two too large, they were still a welcome addition to her limited wardrobe and accessories. She froze. Outside, the sound of an approaching vehicle caused a jolt of nervous energy to shoot through her. She listened on high alert until the car passed, the sound of its engine gradually losing itself along the tree-lined, back road. Sheba climbed to her feet and made her way back to the kitchen. She stopped in front of the cabinet mirror and beheld her own image. She looked ludicrous in her roughly designed linen poncho, accessorized with an electrical cord belt and brown mud boots. Somehow, she envisioned herself walking up to the front desk of the Grande Manse clothed in this very outfit.

"Sir, I'll have your best room for the night—no, make that for the entire summer—and be sure to have the pool emptied of your riff raff before I come down every afternoon. I'll be swimming from two to four every day," she said out loud. She smiled at herself in the mirror, finding humor in her silly daydream. "Young man, I see that you cannot take your eyes off my one-of-a-kind belt—direct from Paris, you know. Yes, young man, they have electricity in France, too." Sheba held her hand out to the mirror, as if expecting an imaginary concierge to bow at the waist and kiss the back of it. "You're crazy, Smith, you do know that—right?" she asked herself before unlocking the back door, running from the cottage into the deep grass, and disappearing into the forest.

26

Resuming her journey with renewed determination, Sheba surmised she must be somewhere near the Kennebunk River just when its muddy shoreline came into sight. Although fully clothed, she set out to remain completely out of sight. She felt her ridiculous wardrobe would reduce her to laughing stock in the eyes of anyone who caught sight of her. Up until now, she had managed to direct her route largely through wooded areas, crossing roadways in quick dashes and cutting through backyards amid vegetation and behind hedges. She was fortunate to catch the river basin largely empty of water. The Atlantic, which fills the basin to capacity twice daily, was past low tide and now just beginning to refill. With the drawbridge connecting Kennebunkport to Kennebunk in the distance, she plodded across the muddy floor of the river, through the cold, knee-deep tidewater, feeling the push from the current of the incoming sea water. Reaching the far side of the river, she emerged without hesitation, sprinting out of the water and into a crop of trees before detection. Then, like a dedicated commando, Sheba scampered through yards and around houses in Kennebunk's lower village until she was able to cross over Route 35 and find refuge in the woodlands just beyond. The sun was practically overhead. Her mind was now focused on getting home to Wells, her spirits buoyed with the knowledge she was only a single town from home.

Not allowing herself the luxury of a rest period, Sheba plodded onward. Hoping not to stray too far off course, she expected the next landmark ahead would be Sea Road. Her march toward Wells seemed to stretch on and on, causing her, in time, to question her route and whether she could have veered off course. Eventually, the teenager breathed a sigh of relief when, first, she heard vehicular traffic and, then, made out what had to be Sea Road directly in her path.

Reaching the roadway, she turned left and headed toward Four Corners. If she was off course, she reasoned, a walk back to that intersection would set her back on a direct line toward Wells. She walked along the side of the pavement, scurrying into the woods and out of view at the sight or sound of an oncoming vehicle. In one instance, while off behind a tree, she caught sight of a VW bus as it whizzed by, assuring her she was definitely not trapped back in 1944. On another occasion, two youngsters, a boy and girl, approached on bikes, forcing her into the brush until they passed. Lying still in the vegetation, she was reminded of her first day back in 1944, waiting on her mother's school bus in the deep grass off Tatnic Road. That day seemed like an eternity ago, she thought. Ultimately, the intersection at Four Corners came into sight. She estimated the jaunt along Sea Road had added a solid half hour to her journey. A hundred yards before the intersection and the inevitable attention of passing traffic, the teenager left the road and re-entered the woods and overgrowth.

Sheba had lost all sense of time and place when she slumped back against a pine tree and slid down to the ground. The forest around her grew darker by the minute. She was hungry. She was using the sound of passing cars on Route 9 to help keep her on course to Wells. Glancing upward, there was no evidence of the blue sky from just an hour earlier. Now, the sky was crowded with dark, threatening clouds and the air began to carry a light drizzle. An uncomfortable wind forced its way through the thick cluster of trees surrounding her. She was growing tired. Forcing her weary body to its feet, she resumed her overland trek.

After enduring what seemed like a never-ending walk through woodlands, the dense trees appeared to end less than a hundred feet ahead of her. She had walked a mile since leaving Sea Road. Sheba reasoned she must have reached the shore of the Mousam River. This meant open ground, and in all likelihood, a swim to the far shore. Proceeding carefully to the edge of the tree line, she looked toward the bridge on Route 9, approximately two hundred yards away. Grouped there, a handful of fishermen were weathering the light drizzle. Straining her eyes, she made out two facing inland toward her and the rest looking out toward the sea. She paused, considering her limited options, then chose the obvious. Sheba dropped to a prostrated position on the ground and proceeded to crawl out into the long, marshland grass that collared the riverbank. The rising tide had filled the river's bed to capacity and was now making its way into the grass. She had only crawled a few yards when the combined river and ocean water made contact with her skin. She moved ahead, careful to remain low and out of sight. Stopping in the frigid water for a breather, she stole a look over at the bridge. There was no change there. Following a momentary rest, she plowed onward. At last, Sheba felt the marshland grass disappear from beneath her, telling her she had reached the actual riverbed. Without hesitation, she broke out into a breast stroke, propelling herself forward in the water, her nose barely an inch above its surface. Focusing on the opposite shore, she pushed ahead, trying to displace as little water as possible, hoping to go undetected, and battling the influence of an incoming tide that steadily pushed her off course. As far as she knew, she had traveled undetected since leaving the great boulder earlier that morning. She continued to stroke, her body cold but, for the moment, free of cramps.

Reaching the point in her swim she estimated to be halfway, Sheba noticed a few droplets of rain striking the water around her head. It was only seconds before the droplets gave way to a more consistent rhythm of rainfall. Before the teenager could even begin to process how the change in weather might impact her swim, pellets of rain began to explode on the surface of the river around her. Furiously, she stretched out her arms and her strokes, propelling herself through the choppy water, now fully employing her legs for propulsion. The churning water around her disturbed her breathing, causing her to resort to deep breaths through her mouth for the first time. Closing her eyes, she concentrated on making her strokes more efficient and ignored the remaining distance to shore. Reaching forward, she repeatedly pulled herself ahead with long, deliberate strokes. Finally, to her relief, her knee made contact with terra firma. Sheba gasped, spit saltwater from her mouth, and stumbled up onto the marshland. She ran toward the trees through water halfway up her calf. From the heavens, the rain no longer merely fell but poured down to earth. Ducking behind a row of pines, she looked back toward the bridge, wondering if the men fishing there had seen her. The bridge, barely visible through the deluge, appeared abandoned. No doubt, the fishermen had sought shelter inside a vehicle, she thought.

If Sheba's memory served her correctly, the terrain over the next two miles was wet and swampy. Back walking through a forested area, she glanced down at herself. Her makeshift clothing, soaked from her swim and the perpetual downpour, clung to her body, leaving her breasts and pubic area open to casual scrutiny. If anything, her position now was less flexible than before the heavy rain. She would have to remain out of sight, she had no options. After stopping to pour a few ounces of water from her boots, the teenager entered an open field. It was less than a mile from Parsons Beach. Route 9 was in sight. To her surprise, no more than a hundred yards in front of her, a barn sat at the far end of an open meadow. Sheba cautiously approached it as the wind and rain buffeted its roof and walls. She could not believe her good fortune. She raced the next thirty yards across the open meadow and found the entrance. Savoring the prospect of shelter from the downpour, she pushed in the barn door. Within the darkened interior of the structure were scattered wooden boxes and a small pile of hay. The hay was trampled and matted to the wooden floor, as if people or animals had lain upon it. She stepped inside the door, just out of the reach of the rain. It felt good to momentarily keep the falling precipitation from her skin. As inviting as the hay pile looked, she felt uneasy. It was a cheerless place. Within the stark walls existed a foreboding quality she found troubling. However, after considering the ongoing inclement weather and her state of near exhaustion from the swim, she decided a fifteen- or twenty-minute rest on dry hay was too tempting to pass up. That is when a pressure, from nowhere, formed in her chest, her breath taken away by what could almost be described as a pair of invisible hands bearing down on her. The pressure was joined by a sense of lightheadedness. Sheba stepped back and opened the barn door. The fresh, albeit moisture-laden air, instantly cleared her head. It was then she decided she wanted no part of this isolated, gloomy building. Stepping back out into the soaking rain, she swung the barn door shut and trotted back into the woods.

Determined to remain out of sight, Sheba moved among the trees parallel to a dirt auto path until she reached a paved road. With Route 9 no more than two hundred yards away, she disappeared into a wall of swampy, low-lying vegetation. Out of sight and temporarily wrestling with an immense craving for food, she thought she picked up on the sound of approaching voices. Confident she was completely invisible from the road, she crouched in a shallow, overgrown gully and listened as male voices drew closer.

"I'm tellin' you, assholes—I saw it with my own eyes. The dickhead's not bullshittin' you. Some dumb bitch was actually swimmin' across the river when the fuckin' sky opened up. She came runnin' out of the water and into the trees."

Sheba looked out from between the wet branches, spotting the figures of five or six young men on the road no more than thirty feet from her. Her heart pounded when they slowed, then stopped, within earshot.

"In case you haven't noticed—it's fuckin' pourin' out!" exploded one of the group.

"Listen, pussy—listen to me. I know it's fuckin' pourin' out! What's more, the bitch knows it's fuckin' pourin' out. Think about it, morons! The little whore is cold and wet—and headin' right towards the barn. Where do ya think she is right now—dryin' off her wet, little ass? It's a free fuckin' show and we're all fuckin' invited." Two or three let out with a howl.

"Shut the fuck up, you assholes! Keep your voices down. She can't hear us comin' or she'll bolt. We gotta surprise the bitch—and what a surprise it'll be." Armed with a strategy, the group moved off up the road in the direction of the barn.

Allowing them time to clear the area, Sheba leaned back on the slope of the gully, a spike of fear tearing through her stomach. The words from the men and, worse, the savage tone of their voices sent chills through her. She pondered her fate had she decided to stay in the barn and out of the rain. They were five and she was one. She shook these thoughts from her mind and rose to her feet. Just ahead, the landscape grew more swampy and treacherous. There was no chance the lowlifes on the road would venture into this terrain, even if they knew she had escaped to it. Knowing she was safe, she disappeared into the underbrush.

Sheba felt the next two miles of her overland trek would be the most difficult and they proved to be. Careful to keep Route 9 within earshot, she waded and slogged her way through mosquito-infested swampland and prickly underbrush. The rain moderated, allowing insects to regroup and make the girl's walk back to Wells, at best, uncomfortable. However, the reality at hand, knowing she would shortly learn the success or failure of the trip back to 1944, kept her preoccupied. Her body now carried a thin layer of mud and muck, providing some protection from biting and stinging insects. On this leg of her journey, young trees grew in close proximity because of the lack of sunlight. The spindly trunks of these unhealthy trees were obstacles to Sheba's progress. During this same span of time she made a handful of rest stops in spite of the cloud of hungry bugs constantly buzzing around her head. On what proved to be her final stop of this leg, she leaned back against a pine tree, exhausted and famished. She noticed the ground beneath her did not have the same moist quality as the terrain she had passed over the previous two miles. She swatted at two mosquitoes in quick succession. The impact of her hand produced a tiny spurt of blood from both. Pulling herself back to her feet, she continued westward.

With the better part of two hours trudging over difficult terrain behind her, she picked up on the steady sound of vehicular traffic through the trees up ahead. Sheba welcomed the sound, knowing she had finally reached Route 1. Coming to the boundary line of trees, she surveyed the area known to her as Cozy Corner. It was a site under roadwork, complete with large mounds of earth and construction equipment.

Crouching a short distance from where the railroad tracks and Route 1 intersect, it would be nearly five minutes before a suitable break came in the two-way traffic, allowing her the opportunity to sprint to the other side of the major road unobserved. She took cover. The persistent problem from insects had lessened, having put the swamplands well behind her. She rested again, fighting off the pains of hunger and the pressure of fatigue. Following a ten-minute break under a mature birch, she began the last leg of her journey. Passing over a railroad trestle, she looked ahead to a line of track leading into a gradual turn to the right. Following it would bring her to within a quarter mile of her house. She walked on a few hundred yards, looking back more than once to assure herself she was not being observed or followed. Then, a thought came to mind, bringing her to an abrupt stop. A short distance through the trees on her left and down an embankment stood the Maine Diner. She was famished, her hunger strong enough to cause a lingering pain in her stomach. If she were to take a short detour, she would probably see Linda Lee. Then it struck her: Would Linda Lee even know who she was? It was true, at this moment in time Sheba had no way to know how different a world she was returning to. If she had cheated fate, her life could be very different from the one she left. In spite of this, she had still almost talked herself into a detour to the diner when she looked down at herself. Her wardrobe was clownish and her partially wet clothing allowed too much of her body to be visible through the moist bed sheet. She let out a sigh and held back the urge to cry. She was still without options. Turning, she swatted at a particularly bothersome deer fly and continued on. She could eat at the house, she thought.

27

Sheba's heart began to race as she staggered from the side of the railroad tracks and onto Burnt Mill Road. For the better part of an hour she had virtually willed herself onward, her body depleted from no food and her arduous all-day walk from the great boulder. Turning right, she walked up the road, staying close to the edge of the trees in the event of any passing cars. The stress from not knowing the world and the life she was about to return to was having a paralyzing effect on the teenager. When a car approached from the rear she scrambled down behind a tree and out of sight. Already in a kneeling position and clutching the tree for support, she called on the Almighty.

"Please, God, all I ask is that you let my mother be alive. I don't care about anything else. I want her and Billy back—that's it! Please, God." Sheba burst into tears. The stress of not knowing, and her wasted physical condition, both were driving her toward the breaking point.

With the passing vehicle now gone from sight, she pulled herself up and resumed the walk home. The house was close now, she knew that. Ahead, she could make out a break in the trees along Burnt Mill Road, the break constituting the front of the Smith's yard and property. In her mind, Sheba ran over what she wanted to see as the yard and house came into view. She wanted to see most or all of the cars and trucks removed from the yard. Her mother would not tolerate such a thing and the absence of vehicles would represent a very positive first sign she was alive. If the house was painted and in good repair, that too would bode well. Sheba plodded on, slightly dizzy, until the grounds of the property began to appear from behind the trees.

Sheba's eyes widened, her heart beat quicker, as the front half of the yard gradually came into view. Her heart soared at the sight of a landscape free from vehicles. Unfortunately, closer scrutiny showed high, unattended grass, something the teenager saw as troubling. Somehow quickening her step, she moved into position to take her first view of the house. Her eyes scanned to the second floor of the building and the roof. There, the graphic signs of a building ravaged by fire were evident.

"No—no," she muttered, stumbling up the driveway toward the house. The damage to the structure seemed to be concentrated in the right side of the second story, where her father's bedroom was located. Her mind was overrun with horrifying thoughts as she closed the distance between her and the building. Every window in the house was boarded, even those on the bottom floor where no sign of fire damage was evident. Sheba's mind flashed back to the family's use of space heaters and her distrust of them. "I don't know what to do, God. I don't know what to do," she moaned. "What have I done?" She was sick with worry, wondering if her trip back to 1944 could have actually robbed her of a parent instead of bringing back her lost one. She braced herself for a very real possibility, an unthinkable possibility. She wondered if she was totally alone.

Sheba stumbled around the circumference of the building before falling to the ground and leaning back against her house. She felt her body begin to go rigid, as if passing into a state of shock. She propped her head up with her hands and stared straight ahead, her elbows resting on her knees. Through her fingers she caught sight of a police cruiser. Moving by slowly, it came to an abrupt stop, then reversed direction. The cruiser turned into the driveway and proceeded slowly to a point about halfway between the house and road. A few seconds passed before an officer stepped from the vehicle. He looked directly at the house and the young woman seated in front of it. He was middle-aged and tall. Approaching Sheba in a relaxed, informal manner, his eyes now scanned the exterior of the house and the grounds as he proceeded toward her. Conscious of her wardrobe's limitations, she lifted her hands to her chest, covering her protruding nipples with her palms. He was only a few steps away from her when he finally spoke.

"You okay there, young lady?" His tone was not threatening.

Sheba nodded her head, indicating she was.

"It just seems like a funny place to be hanging out on a miserable day like this." The officer had closed the distance between them to under ten feet. "You here alone?"

She nodded yes.

The man looked her over, a curious expression spreading across his face. "Now, the way you're dressed—there's got to be quite a story behind this outfit you've got on. Why don't you just come back to the cruiser with me so we can both get out of this dampness—and maybe fill me in on what exactly is going on here." The policeman extended his hand. Sheba refused it, but did pull herself up and began the walk back to the police car. Reaching the cruiser, the officer opened the passenger door for the girl. Instead of stepping inside, she turned and addressed the man.

"I lived here once. I just came back to see it again."

"And where do you live now?"

Sheba balked at providing an answer. In truth, she did not know the answer. "Did anyone die in the fire?"

"No, no fatalities."

Deep inside, she breathed a sigh of relief. "Does the family who lived here still live nearby?"

"I wouldn't know, it happened over a year ago," answered the policeman, showing the first sign of impatience. "Do you have any form of identification on you, young lady?"

She shook her head no.

"If we're going to make any headway here—for starters—I'm going to need your name."

Following a short hesitation, she answered. "Smith—my name's Smith. How many people were living in the house when it burned?"

"I really don't remember—and why don't we stick with my questions here. I'm not the one sitting in the middle of nowhere—dressed in a torn up sheet."

Sheba dropped her eyes in an obstinate gesture. The cop turned and started for the other side of the cruiser. Stopping halfway, he turned back to address her.

"You say your name is Smith?" He asked the question in a rhetorical manner.

She nodded yes.

Entering the cab of the vehicle, he reached for the radio and began to speak. She watched as he carried on a conversation with a third party, the words indistinguishable to her. Finally, he leaned forward, rolling down the window on the passenger side. "Well, Miss Smith, by any chance would your first name be Sheba?"

The girl's eyes widened in surprise, then closed in resignation. Once again, without speaking, she nodded 'yes' with a head gesture. The officer pushed open the passenger door and gestured her to enter. Sheba glanced down on him, a look of defiance etched on her face.

"That wasn't a request—it was an order!"

Unsettled by the policeman's tone of voice, she dropped down into the passenger seat, slamming the door of the vehicle behind her. The officer climbed out and paid a visit to the trunk of the cruiser, returning with a blanket.

"Here, put this over yourself," he said, handing it to her. "It seems half of Kennebunk is out looking for you. I told dispatch I'd take you back home, but in the meantime I'd like a few answers."

For the next ten minutes Sheba was grilled by the officer on a number of matters. Who had she been with for the past twelve hours? Why was she dressed in the bizarre manner she was? What made her come all the way to Wells, and specifically, to this burned-out house? Did a young man have any role in her leaving home in the middle of the night?

It was not long before the squad car was slowly rolling along Route 35 in the lower village of Kennebunk. The officer leaned forward in his seat, attempting to make out a specific residence or maybe the name on a mail box. Sheba was not forthcoming when he asked for her assistance in finding her home. How could she be? Then, he eased onto the brake, bringing the vehicle to a halt in front of a white colonial home.

"Is this it?" he asked.

She looked back at him, feigning defiance in place of ignorance. She sat transfixed by the developments unfolding before her. A woman rushed out of the front door, bursting out in tears at the sight of the girl seated in the front seat of the Wells Police cruiser.

"I'll take that for a yes," he responded dryly.

Sheba's eyes focused on the woman who had been the fourteen-year-old Elaine Lake, back in another chapter of time. Pushing open the cruiser door, she rushed from the vehicle and over the lawn to her mother. The woman wrapped her arms around her and wept uncontrollably.

"I love you, Mama—and I'm so glad to be home." The two held the embrace for an extended time, as if fearing the other would cease to be there at any moment. Inside her, Sheba felt a replay of the exhilaration she had experienced after hailing down her mother on Tatnic Road in the early hours of her odyssey in 1944.

"Thank God, thank God," her mother repeated. "Sheba, how could you do this to your father and me—waking up in the morning to find your bed empty—your pajamas under the covers—not so much as a note or anything—nothing?" And what is the meaning of this ridiculous getup under the blanket? What do you have on? Is that a bed sheet? And you're not going to tell me that Carlton hasn't got something to do with this!"

"Who?"

"Don't give me who. Carlton Nye, that's who!" The woman's voice now showed bona fide anger following her outpouring of relief.

The teenager pulled back, taking in every detail of her mother's face. Elaine was still a beautiful woman, she thought. The twenty-six years spanning 1944 to 1970 had been kind to her.

"Your father's still out there looking for you—the poor man. He's sick with worry. Get in the house, young lady—and take those ridiculous rags off of you. My God, you're filthy! I'm running you a bath. Go to your room and take off those rags, I said. We'll wait until your father gets back before we decide what comes of this episode of yours! And believe me, we'll be expecting some answers from you when your father gets home!"

Sheba stepped inside into a well-kept kitchen. From all appearances, the Smiths of Kennebunk were far more prosperous than the Smiths of Wells. She was ordered to immediately report to her room and change but had no idea where to find it. She stood idly by, waiting on a clue from her mother.

"Get upstairs to your room and change, I said," commanded the woman, pointing through a nearby doorway.

The teenager quickly followed the woman's command, making her way into a spacious living room dominated by a big-screen television in the far corner. Sheba spotted the stairs along the far wall and hurried to the second floor. Upstairs, the hallway divided the house evenly on both sides. Pushing open the first door on the right, she saw what had to be the master bedroom with a king-size bed on her immediate left and an open door leading into a private bath. Walking across the hall she looked into what had to be her bedroom. The white bedroom furniture was topped with all manner of cosmetic and beauty items, while from the walls hung color photos of various members of the Beatles, Monkees and Rolling Stones. Sheba untied the electrical extension cord from around her waist and pulled off the bed sheet. Her mind swam in a pool of confusion, exhilaration and disbelief as she stood before her bureau mirror and surveyed herself, bruised, soiled and naked. As she turned away, a photograph encased in a brass frame caught her eye. In the photo was Sheba Smith, a more delicate and dignified Sheba Smith, posing beside a tall, handsome, young male. Her eyes shifted back and forth from young man to young woman, trying to decide which looked more foreign to her. Then, a door slammed downstairs and her mother let out a howl of excitement.

"Your sister's home! The police dropped her off no more than ten minutes ago—and she's perfectly okay."

Sheba hastily opened the closet, located a bathrobe, and threw it on. Without hesitation, she bounded downstairs and out to the kitchen. There, a tall, good-looking teenage boy stood next to the table, unable or unwilling to hide his agitation. She ran across the kitchen floor, throwing her arms around the eighteen-year-old.

"Oh, God, I can't believe it," murmured an emotional Sheba into his shoulder.

"Ma, get this mental case off of me," he snarled, extending his arms outward and not returning the hug.

She stepped back and looked him over. Facially, Billy Smith was the spitting image of his father. His hair was close cropped and dark, the exact shade of brown as his mother's. He wore a loose-fitting football jersey that hung down over a pair of Bermuda shorts. He was tall and muscular, standing nearly six inches over his sister.

"Man, you gotta be on drugs. Where the frig were you?"

"I was out walking," she said, attempting to put some degree of repentance in her voice.

"Well, this thing with you and your walk has cost me a day's work, not to mention what Mom and Dad have been put through—but I suppose they'll let it go with a warning—cause it's their little angel!"

"Your sister here has a lot of explaining to do—but that'll come after her father gets back. You, young lady, upstairs and take a bath, or at least a good, long shower," barked out her mother.

She planted a kiss on her brother's cheek and bolted from the room.

Following an extended time beneath her first hot shower in nearly a month, Sheba retreated back to her room and anxiously awaited the reunion with her father. Downstairs, the phone rang and from her bedroom door she overheard her mother filling someone in on the homecoming. The receiver had barely been put down when her mother called out from below.

"That was your father, young lady—he'll be home in less than ten minutes. I want you downstairs when he arrives."

She glanced over at the alarm clock beside her bed. It was nearly six o'clock. She estimated that her walk from the holy rock back to the old house in Wells had taken the better part of twelve hours. Without any doubt, there would be hell to pay for the next few hours, or even days, for the circumstances at hand. She smiled to herself, knowing any form or length of punishment would be a small price to pay for the reconstructed life looming ahead of her. After giving her hair a swift combing, she returned downstairs and took a seat at the kitchen table. Billy had already taken leave of the house, probably off to finish whatever was left of his shift at work. Sheba longed to ask her mother any number of questions. How long had the family lived in Kennebunk? Did Daddy still drink? Who was the boy in the picture with her upstairs? Much had changed in her life and, at the moment, she had no knowledge of how it got that way. However, her best judgment told her that any questions along these lines would be met with immense curiosity, perhaps too much. Her mother was in the early stages of preparing supper and extending Sheba the silent treatment. Oh, how Sheba longed to walk up behind Elaine Smith and ask the woman about her recollections of a certain cousin who visited her in 1944; ask her about smoking behind an old shack at Perkins Cove; ask her about a certain boy named Randy from Connecticut. There was so much Sheba wanted to ask Elaine but could not. Then, from outside, the roar from a vehicle pulling into the driveway filled the kitchen. Her mother took a step toward the window and peeked over the curtains.

"Here's your father."

The kitchen door opened and the figure of Broderick Smith appeared. Sheba looked up at the man and was taken aback by his appearance. Her father was handsome and clear-eyed, looking a dozen years younger than she remembered. More broad-shouldered, he was clearly an individual who treated himself better than the parent she had lived alone with those nine years after her mother's accident.

"Daddy," she called out, jumping to her feet and rushing to him. He threw his arms around her, enveloping her frame.

"Young lady—you may think you're too old for me to put over my knee and give a spanking to—but this stunt is going to put me to the test. How could you do something like this to your mother and me? And I want you to come clean with us about the Nye boy's part in all this." Broderick's voice cracked at the end of his statement as the stress in his body began to slowly discharge. Sheba kissed his cheek and reapplied her hold around his neck. At this precise second, she became aware of a pressure being applied around her leg, as if someone or something was hugging the lower half of her body. She glanced down on the top of a young boy's head.

"And that little guy—you know how he feels about you. He wakes up this morning to find his big sister off somewhere, missing from the house," added her mother. The boy looked up at her and smiled through a face wet with tears.

Sheba's mouth dropped open in astonishment as she knelt down beside the child. Suddenly aware of a brother she did not know, whose name she did not know, she began to fully appreciate the enormity of the gift passed down from her ancestors.

"You know I'm sorry," she whispered to him, kissing the boy on one wet cheek. She wanted to ask him his name and age but could not. This, and most other fragments of her life, she would have to piece together over time. At present, her life was a mystery to her.

"Did you and Robby grab anything to eat while you were out on the road?" Elaine asked her husband.

"Nothing—no appetite with everything going on."

Sheba smiled to herself, her first mystery solved. She embraced her little brother, pulling his face up to hers.

"Robby, I'll make this up to you, I promise."

"Not until your mother and I have gotten our licks in on you, young lady. This stunt of yours went way too far— getting the police involved and all. What in God's name got into you? I want you back upstairs for the time being. We'll talk over this craziness of yours and let you know what's going to come of it. Meanwhile, back upstairs."

Sheba bowed her head and turned for the door.

"Sheba, why did you call me Robby—and not Peanut?"

She turned back to her baby brother.

"'Cause—'cause you're getting to be such a big boy. I feel funny calling you that lately."

"I like Peanut."

"Peanut it is," she agreed, crossing the room and applying another hug.

"Upstairs, missy!" Elaine barked, turning back from the stove.

Back in her bedroom, Sheba spread out on the bed and pondered over the last twelve hours. Conjuring up the memory of the other Sheba Smith, the girl from Burnt Mill Road and Wells High School, she found the thought of her new life overwhelming. She lived in a new town, meaning she attended a new school. She wondered if she had any friends. Sheba reasoned she must, considering everything said by her family and the existence of this Carlton Nye character. She glanced back at the picture of him in the frame propped up on the bureau. The teenager wondered if the Sheba Smith everyone knew was the same girl she was. Laying her head back on the pillow, she closed her eyes and reveled in the feel of her own cleanliness. The hot shower had made her comfortable with herself. She was overjoyed with how good her father looked and, so far, there was no evidence of Jody Pease anywhere. Her thoughts were blissful as she looked forward to joining this new life, even if it meant joining it—in progress.

"Sheba—supper!" The voice calling her down to her first meal since 1944 belonged to her mother, and no daughter could ever appreciate the simple act of being called to the dinner table by a parent more than Sheba did on this Sunday evening.

The four Smiths shared a peaceful meal at the kitchen table. In Billy's absence, his mother put aside a full portion of meat loaf for the eighteen-year-old. About midway through the meal the issue of Sheba's punishment was addressed. Her parents decided on a one-month suspension of all social and work activities. She waited for an announcement or mention of where she worked but none was brought up, leaving her temporarily in the dark. She would be restricted to the house without visiting privileges from friends, and particularly, Carlton. What's more, she would be limited to three personal phone calls per week, effective immediately. In addition, her father insisted that his daughter take a complete physical exam, the results of which would be delivered directly to him while her mother demanded that Sheba attend no less than a half dozen sessions with a psychologist. As her punishment was handed down, the teenager nodded her acceptance, promising, in the form of an oath, she would never subject her parents and family to anything like this in the future. The moment the last drop of milk left her glass and passed her lips, constituting the end of supper, she was ordered back upstairs and back into her personal solitary confinement.

With her bedroom door closed and the shade on her window pulled, Sheba rummaged through her personal effects. From the bottom of her bureau, tucked away beneath a pair of faded jeans, she came across a diary, her diary. The journal was locked shut but she quickly deduced it could be opened with only slight manipulation of the locking mechanism. She could not believe this good fortune! Flipping through the pages, she saw there was over ten months of entries, certainly enough to get her up to speed on the life of the girl who was Sheba for these past sixteen and a half years. She sat back in bed and read. Starting with her journal entry from the prior September, an entry heralding the start of her sophomore year of high school, she entered the mind of a somewhat timid girl. On some entries she laughed out loud at the simplistic, fainthearted outlook of this other teenager. In short order, she realized the girl who was Sheba before this morning, and the person who lay stretched out reading her diary at this moment, were two different females. In her mind, the other Sheba, the one now gone, was only a temporary substitute for the real thing. Following a particularly long burst of laughter, the bedroom door opened and her mother appeared.

"See if you find this funny," she chided, tossing a piece of paper on the bed.

Sheba picked it up and surveyed it. "What's this?"

"It's the property tax bill from the town of Kennebunkport for that parcel of land your grandmother left you in her will."

"What land?"

Her mother rolled her eyes. "That ten acres beyond Walkers Point she mysteriously decided to leave you—God knows why."

Sheba flashed a look of acknowledgement, as if remembering the specifics of the matter.

"Your father and I were ready to just pay the taxes this year for you but—now—with everything that's happened—we think we'll leave that to your trust fund." Elaine flashed her daughter a sarcastic smile and prepared to close the door. She was stopped from leaving when Sheba jumped up from the bed and approached her.

"Before, I don't think I told you enough how much I love you," she whispered, kissing the woman on the side of the face and inhaling her cologne.

Elaine stared at her daughter curiously, then disappeared behind the door. Sheba turned and returned to her place on the bed. A few seconds passed and the door reopened.

"You do know we love you—and we always will. We're just very disappointed in you."

"I know, Mama," replied Sheba behind a sad smile.

The girl's eyes scanned the official looking piece of paper with valuations and dollar amounts typed in on the appropriate lines. It meant next to nothing to her. The true meaning of the document could not be expressed in monetary terms. The reference to the parcel of land belonging to Sheba Smith, all 10.41 acres, complete with boundary dimensions and benchmarks, was of no interest to her. That was because she, and only she, knew the real significance of this property.

"Thank you, Nana, thank you so very much," she said out loud. As high as her spirits had been, they soared higher, knowing the holy rock was hers, not only spiritually and by virtue of her blood link to Mowalk, but also by the letter of the law.

27

July 20, 1970

Sheba let out an exaggerated yawn and opened her eyes to her last day in captivity. Tomorrow was the one-month anniversary of her disappearance from the house, marking the end of the sentence, house arrest as she called it, placed on her by her parents. If the truth be known, it was hardly a punishment at all, at least the way she saw it. After spending the better part of her life without a mother, she welcomed the chance to hang around the house and take in the former Elaine Lake's every move and gesture. Frequently, she caught herself staring at her mother and thinking back to the three days they had spent in each other's company in 1944. More than anyone, she could still see traces of the immature fourteen-year-old in the pretty, well-spoken woman, even after all these years. Sheba lifted her head, picking up on the slight creaking of the door.

"Is that my personal butler coming up to get my breakfast order?" Muffled laughter came from behind the door. "If that's my personal butler, Peanut by name, then show yourself at once."

The seven-year-old jumped from behind the door and into the room. "Here to take your breakfast order—my lady," announced the boy in a well-rehearsed manner.

"Well then, tell my personal downstairs chef, I believe she answers to the name of Elaine, that it will be orange juice and French toast today. Now, off with you—scoot!"

Robby turned and scampered toward the stairs. Shortly after, Sheba heard an exchange between her little brother and his mother. Their voices carried all the way from the kitchen. It was not long before the two were at the bottom of the stairs.

"How many times have I told you to stop treating your little brother like your personal foot servant?"

"I posted the job on my bedroom wall—and he applied for and

got it," she hollered back.

"It'll be good getting you out of the house tomorrow. You've gotten a little too big for your britches lately, young lady," called back her mother before returning to the kitchen.

Sheba arched her back and let out another prolonged yawn.

The girl's thoughts were already shifting to the following day's itinerary. The month in the house, listening and observing, along with long periods spent pouring over her diary, gave her a general grasp of the life of this other Sheba Smith. The other her was different from the one who returned and now occupied her body. She was relieved when the name of Felicia Blackburn never appeared on the pages of the other Sheba's journal. That was to be expected, though. They lived in different towns and attended different schools. Tomorrow she would finally meet Carlton face to face. The plan called for her to meet him in front of the Kennebunk Inn in the upper village. From there, and unknown to Carlton at this time, she would orchestrate their first day together in a month, or in her case, a lifetime. If he resisted, then, she would sing him the old Ray Charles song: *Hit the road Jack, and don't you come back no more, no more, no more no more.* As she saw it, her car—her rules. Carlton—oh yes, she'd be shortening it to Carl—Carlton was about to meet the real Sheba Smith, not the imitation he had grown so fond of, the one who wrote so glowingly of him in the diary.

With her month-long detention drawing to a close, she could only look back on two distasteful things over the entire period. One was a trip to Portland where she received a complete physical examination, mandated by her father. He escorted her to Portland because a doctor's office in Kennebunk, Wells, Sanford, Biddeford or Saco might have clerical staff that knew someone who knew someone who lived next door or in the lower village. Her father counted on Portland's distance to essentially kill the possibility of a wildfire of gossip. So it was, after a forty-five minute ordeal, Broderick got to hear what he came to hear from the doctor: "Mr. Smith, your daughter is intact." Sheba believed the doctor could have followed the pronouncement with, "unfortunately, she has picked up a strain of leprosy that probably means she'll be losing a limb a week by next month." It would not matter to him, because Daddy's little girl was still a virgin. The other distasteful thing she had forced on her was the trip to the psychologist's office, mandated by mother. These sessions were short-lived. Following only her second visit, Elaine was called and told her daughter was uncooperative, evasive, bad-tempered and generally lacking in basic, good manners. However, the psychologist saw no reason for the young woman to continue with treatment. In his judgment and opinion, she was reasonably well-adjusted and would, in all likelihood, grow out of this anti-social stage in her life.

Over her long month's confinement, Sheba had pondered over things in her life, present versus former. One obvious difference, aside from going from a one- to a two-parent family, was how much better a provider Broderick Smith was in this life. After some consideration, she developed her own theory for the change. First, her mother took an active administrative role in the family business's day-to-day operations, functioning as bookkeeper and secretary. What's more, she was good at her job. Secondly, her father was not the same man who admittedly only worked and lived with the hope of surviving until his daughter grew to maturity. For him, the former Elaine Lake was the pillar on which he built his business and his entire life. His devotion was there for all to see, visible in his eyes whenever he looked her way or in his touch when he routinely ran his hands over her as they passed in the hallway or kitchen. Oddly, in spite of the improvement in everyone's life as a result of her actions, a part of Sheba missed being the absolute focus of Broderick Smith's attention. In this new life, she may still have been "daddy's little girl," but the former Elaine Lake was, without a doubt, the center of his universe.

Another mystery Sheba was able to solve during her extended stay at home was the entire story behind her old house on Burnt Mill Road. She was able to learn from her mother that the family moved from the house to the lower village in 1962. Her grandmother then rented it to a family, the St. Jeans, who had moved to Wells from Vermont. A fire in 1968 caused by a discarded cigarette sent the St. Jeans back home to the Green Mountains. Fortunately, none of the family of six was injured in the fire.

Her relationship with her parents, and even Billy, solidified over the preceding twenty-nine days, although each noticed the change in her personality from before her disappearance. Sheba had returned to a better life. The Smiths owned four vehicles, one of which was designated as hers. Broderick Smith Construction was recognized as one of York County's most reputable and successful small businesses. During the preceding twenty-nine days, Sheba learned that her summer job at The Olde Grist Mill in Kennebunkport was no more, thanks to her confinement, and the name of one Jody Pease never came up at the house, leading her to believe the man had no role in her father's life. Sheba surmised, with help from an observation she remembered from her grandmother, that the success of her father was predicated on the love and companionship of his Elaine. With her, the man was capable of climbing mountains. Without her, he was destined for a downward spiral and premature, final act. Lastly, and maybe even more importantly, there was little Robby. In their four weeks together Sheba experienced more adoration and loyalty from the small boy than she thought possible. Perhaps, she thought, he was sent to make up for the loss of her father's undivided attention. She awoke every morning, anxiously anticipating his appearance at the door. The only regret attached to her 'Peanut' was knowing she had missed the first seven years of his life, years she would never be able to recover. As she sluggishly pulled her bathrobe on over her pajamas, she knew she had done her job, and done it well. However, there were two critical things she would need to address in the next twenty four hours to put her mind, and her life, back together.

28

July 21, 1970

The ear-splitting sound of her alarm clock jolted Sheba awake as her own independence day finally arrived. After unsuccessfully swiping twice at the off button, she made contact and relieved her bedroom of the clanging, metallic noise. It was here, the day she both longed for and dreaded. She would pick up and meet Carlton Nye today, in front of the Kennebunk Inn in the upper village. As far as he knew, the two would play the day by ear, which probably meant making their way to Drake's Island or Gooch's Beach. However, she had a completely different itinerary in mind. The family, with the exception of her father, sat down to breakfast on this Tuesday morning. Elaine quizzed her daughter on her plans for the day. Sheba explained she would be meeting Carlton later in the morning but was vague on the day's specific schedule. She did promise her little brother that the two of them, and only the two of them, would go out for ice cream later in the evening. It was just after nine thirty when the girl tossed a few personal items, including a bathing suit and towel, onto the back seat of her 1966 Ford Mustang and headed for Kennebunk's upper village.

As Sheba slowed the car in front of the Kennebunk Inn, she instantly picked out Carlton, thanks largely to the photograph on top of the bedroom bureau. The young man broke out in a wide grin as the Mustang rolled to a stop amid tourist season traffic. Grabbing a canvas bag, he hustled across Route 1 and hopped into the passenger seat.

"I can't tell you how long I've been waiting for this day," he called out, leaning across the front seat and caressing her cheek.

"I can—it's been thirty days."

"Yeah, Babe—thirty days—exactly."

She gently pushed him off and eased out into traffic. Once back in the flow, she took this opportunity to glance across the car, catching quick glimpses of her boyfriend. Carlton was a good-looking kid with blondish hair, blue eyes and a clear complexion. He was taller and more physically developed than she expected. Each time her eyes shifted to him, she caught him staring trancelike at her.

"A month's a long time. I just want you to know that during that time I didn't so much as look at another girl—so help me God." He lifted his hand in true, Boy Scout fashion.

"Well, Carlton—neither did I—look at another girl."

Following her statement, there was a distinct period of silence from the passenger side of the car, then a burst of laughter. "Good one, Babe—you didn't look at other girls either—good one."

Sheba was already formulating an impression of the young man who was her boyfriend, something she had been unable to do over the past four weeks during their abbreviated conversations on the phone. Her first impression of Carlton Nye was of an uncomplicated, but decent, young man. The passenger door rattled when the car hit a pothole in the road.

"Your door isn't closed all the way. Sometimes you have to slam it hard to get it to close," she advised him. He pushed open the door while they continued on, then closed it with a resounding slam.

"Thank you, that jiggling sound really irks me," she added.

She motored southward to the Wells town line, then maneuvered through the continuing road construction at Cozy Corner. When the car passed the turn onto Route 9, the boy was caught by surprise.

"Are we going to Drake's Island?"

"Actually, I'm stopping at the diner for a couple of minutes. I want to take care of some business inside. It won't take that long."

"What! You want me to hang around outside in the car?"

"If you wouldn't mind."

"I kinda do mind. I haven't even got a welcome-back kiss from you yet."

Sheba leaned across the front seat and kissed the boy on the lips. When he gestured for a second kiss, she tangled her fingers in his blond hair and pulled, giving her the leverage to move his head at will. The slightly rough treatment from her caught Carlton by surprise.

"Oh wow—I like that," he said.

She ran her moist tongue across the boy's lips a final time and settled back against the seat. Carlton let out a sigh followed by a deep breath.

"Wow—take as long as you want, Muffin."

"Muffin?"

"Don't tell me you forgot? How could you forget that? You're kidding, right? The canoe ride last October—up the Mousam—and how I called you my little English muffin—'cause we're both English. You thought it was so cute. Sheba, how could you go and forget something like that?"

"Oh yeah, now I remember. Maybe all the time locked up in my room has killed my memory." She hopped from the car, instructing Carlton to wait for her and not wander off. Making her way through the familiar door, she scanned the room, spotting Linda Lee at the far end of the counter. She approached the cash register and waited to be noticed. Eventually, her old friend broke from a conversation and walked in her direction.

"Anything I can help you with, sweetie?"

"Yes, miss, I wonder if I could fill out a job application form. I'm looking for full or part-time work over the summer and then part-time into the school year."

"Is that right?" came back the woman. Linda Lee chuckled, then turned from Sheba. "How's this, Ernie, this pretty little thing wants to apply for her summer job on—what is it—July 21st!"

"Quite the little early bird, ain't she? At this rate she should be tossing out her Christmas tree any day now," hollered the cook into the room.

"Honey, I had people in here looking for summer jobs in April. Where've you been?"

"Oh, here and there," she answered. The circumstances at the moment had Sheba mentally off balance. To Linda Lee, this woman she was so fond of, Sheba was an absolute stranger. "So you're telling me there are no jobs to be had right now—telling me, the best employee you'll ever have the chance to hire—ever—in your entire life."

The attractive woman took a step back, sizing up the brash sixteen-year-old. "Listen to this kid, Ernie. She's got moxie, I'll say that for her."

The cook stuck his head out through the two-foot-by-five-foot portal, catching his first look at the bold-as-brass teenager.

"We have something open—part time—twelve hours a week—but I don't see it as a good fit for you."

"Try me," came back Sheba.

"You'd be cleaning pots and pans—and washing dishes."

"I've done that before—sounds fine."

"And where would that have been?"

"You wouldn't believe it if I told you."

"Try me," prompted the woman.

"Oh, here and there," repeated Sheba.

"Ah, the same place you were that caused you to look for your summer job in late July."

"Precisely." Sheba looked into the woman's face, wanting to scream out she missed her, wanting to ask her about her brother who was hurt in the war, wanting to see if she remembered Elaine Lake's cousin from their brief meeting on the beach, wanting to thank her for everything she did for her in a life only she remembered.

Linda Lee turned and walked to the back room. She returned seconds later with a form and ballpoint pen. Sheba grabbed the end stool at the counter, where she quickly filled in the employment application. Less than five minutes after leaving it with her, Linda Lee turned around, only to be startled by the girl standing directly behind her.

"I'd like to leave here with definite word that I have the job," she stated, handing the completed form back to her potential boss.

"I don't believe this kid," she responded, dropping a pair of reading glasses from their perch on top of her head. The blonde stood against the wall, her eyes looking over the application. Sheba stared at her friend. She thought back to the rainy Saturday in 1944 when Broderick and Elaine drove by her on Mile Road. The woman's eyes suddenly locked onto something on the form.

"In case of accident contact Broderick Smith, Kennebunk, Maine. What is this, Miss Sheba Smith? Does this mean you're Broderick and Elaine's daughter?"

Sheba nodded yes.

"And does your mother know you're coming to me looking for work?"

"No, but that's my business, not hers."

Sheba thought she detected sudden hesitation on the part of Linda Lee. "It would mean a lot to me to get this job. I'm a hard worker—you'll see," she promised, her tone carrying a sense of earnestness.

"Okay, kid, what the hell—you'll work all day Saturday—half a day on Sunday. And in case you haven't figured it out yet, I'm the owner. My name is Linda Lee."

"Linda Lee—not Lynn—not Linda—not Ms. Tuttle—it's Linda Lee. And from this moment on it will be yes Linda Lee, and no Linda Lee, and you don't look a day over eighteen Linda Lee," recited Sheba excitedly.

"Sweet Jesus, don't get carried away. It's not a day over twenty-five, sweetie, not eighteen. Let's not go off into the Twilight Zone here."

Sheba walked behind the counter, pushing open the swinging door to the back room and the back sink. After pausing in the doorway, she returned to the dining area where a half dozen or so customers looked on her with curiosity. She wanted to call out: "It's great to be back." By now, her boss had returned to servicing customers and stood over a booth with a carafe of coffee in one hand. The teenager came up behind her, throwing her arms around the woman's waist and resting her head on her back.

"What's this?"

"Thank you, Linda Lee, just thank you," said Sheba before releasing her arms and moving toward the door.

"It's a lousy twelve hours a week."

"For everything—just for everything," added Sheba.

The woman looked back to the counter where three regulars, all lobstermen, sat turned on their stools, taking in the goings on. "I'm getting hugs and bouquets from this kid for her minimum-wage job. What's she going to do when she gets her first dime raise?" she wisecracked.

With her hand already around the doorknob, the teenager looked back at her old friend. They exchanged smiles.

"Six o'clock—Saturday morning—Sheba Smith," barked out the woman before the girl closed the door behind her.

Returning to the parking lot, she found Carlton draped over the hood of her Mustang, his face directed at the morning sun. On her approach, the boy rolled sideways toward the pavement, landing on his feet.

"So are we finally ready for the beach?"

"One more stop," she answered.

"Aw, come on, Sheba. Where now?"

"Massachusetts."

"No friggin' way—now I've got to put my foot down—no friggin' way!"

"Look at it this way, Carl, we can use some time alone in the car to get caught up on everything. After all, it's been a long month."

"No way, Jose—and when did you start thinking you can call me Carl?"

"I guess this is as good a time as any to bring it up. Your name—Carlton—is like an old farmer's name or the name under some guy's picture in the bank who founded it back in 1820. Carl, on the other hand, is not nearly as creepy."

"What the heck is it with you? You're acting so damn strange. You never talked or acted anything like this before. It's like someone or something has crawled inside your skin."

"Now you sound just like my mother. That's all I heard from her for a month. What's gotten into you, young lady? What's happened to my good little girl?"

"Your mother's right—you're different."

"Look me in the face, Carl—right in the face." She grabbed his chin and yanked his head sideways. "It's my face, Carl. It's your Sheba—your English muffin. Now I'm leaving in thirty seconds for Lowell, Massachusetts—with or without you."

"I really don't want to go," he said, but with limited conviction.

She jumped from the Mustang and circled to his side of the car. She proceeded to open the door valet style, addressing the boy in a no-nonsense growl.

"Then get your ass out of *my* car'—cause I don't have time to be farting around with you."

The well-built teenager remained in his seat, a troubled expression having replaced his bright, beaming face from twenty minutes earlier.

"Don't just sit there sulking, answer me. Are you coming or not?"

"I'll come," he announced, practically under his breath.

She returned to the driver's seat and settled behind the wheel. Carlton seemed lost for words. Their first confrontation was over and Sheba had taken his measure. Reaching across the front seat, she placed her hand on Carlton's leg, just above the knee.

"I'm glad you're coming, Carl, I really am." She had tempered her voice. Squeezing the inside of his thigh, she set out to mend his feelings. "Let's not fight the rest of the day. We should be back in time to get to the beach—but going to Lowell is very important to me. Now, tell me this whole, silly matter is behind us."

He forced a smile across his face, nodding his head in agreement.

With her altercation now behind her, Sheba turned the car south toward Lowell. She decided to use this time in the car to pry information from Carlton. They had traveled less than a mile from the diner when he leaned forward and clicked on the radio, spinning the tuner to the bottom of the dial. "W-R-K-O—Boston," sang out a giddy radio jingle, prompting Sheba to reach over and turn off the radio.

"We've been apart for over a month. I think we should try to get reacquainted instead of listening to music for the next two hours. You okay with that?"

Carlton reached over, pushing a strand of hair from the side of her face to over her ear.

"I'll take that as a yes. So, Carl, do you have any questions about anything—with me I mean?"

"Yeah, one big one. Where were you that Sunday when your parents were going bonkers looking for you? Man, they called my house and called me every name in the book—claiming I'd done something to you or gone somewhere with you. They almost had *my* folks believing it, except I was with the guys the night before and never left my room once I got home."

"Truthfully—I woke up in the middle of the night and decided to go out into the dark woods, like a wild animal. I wasn't a bit afraid—and once the sun came up—I stayed in the woods away from people and stuff, just meditating for the whole day—away from people entirely."

"The cops said they found you over in Wells in front of a old, burned-out house, dressed like a lunatic with your tits showing through these rags you had on. That is so unlike you—at least the you I know, or maybe knew."

"Are you saying I'm different?"

"Hell, yeah! I used to get the feeling you were almost afraid of the world unless you were with me—just by the way you'd hang onto my arm. Now, when I look in your eyes it's almost like a totally different person looking back at me. It's like some wild spirit has inhabited your body or something. I know that sounds nuts—but it's what I see."

Sheba did not respond to Carlton's observation. As she saw it, there was no way to half explain the situation and she was not at liberty to fully explain her metamorphosis. He, even more than her parents, had seen through her façade and detected the intruder.

"So, Carl, which do you like better, the old version or the new, and hopefully improved, version?"

"I don't *like* either one—but, nothing has changed. I love every version of you—every version holds me in the palm of their hands. I'd be lying if I told you that no other girls have come on to me in the last month. They have. But I didn't give a rat's ass because I knew I'd be seeing my Muffin soon. You know, when I got those calls from your parents saying I'd been with you—and I knew I hadn't—I almost got sick from worrying that you were out there somewhere with some new guy. Yeah, Muffin, I've got it bad for you, the old you—the new you—every one of you." Carlton's words carried no forged sincerity. They appeared to be a heartfelt outpouring of his feelings.

She reached over, pulling him by the scruff of his neck until his head rested on her shoulder. If Carlton Nye lacked a quick wit or an overpowering personality, he compensated for these with an openness she found appealing. "I've missed you more than you'll ever know. I only wish I could express myself as freely as you do." Sheba could not return his profession of love, she barely knew him.

For most of the nearly two-hour trip to Massachusetts, Sheba asked Carlton open-ended questions about himself and school, allowing her to learn something about the people and circumstances she would face in just over a month when school reopened. It was not until she pulled off Route 93 in Methuen and picked up the Lowell-Lawrence Boulevard that her thoughts returned to the purpose of her mission. If she remembered correctly, this road would bring her directly into the Centralville neighborhood of Kevin Shanahan. She came with no concrete plan of action. However, in her mind there was a minimum number of objectives to be met. Sheba knew she must learn of Kevin's well-being and whereabouts. Her instincts told her to return to his Bridge Street apartment. Should she just walk up to the door and knock? By her calculations, Kevin was now about fifty years old. What reaction would she get if he opened the door and came face to face with the girl named Sheba standing in his doorway, not looking a day older than the morning she vanished from his life—in 1944! She wondered if it would be consolation enough to simply track him back to the apartment and leave it at that, knowing he had survived the twenty-six years since the October night she left him. She grew quiet as these thoughts flashed through her mind, causing a reaction from Carlton.

"You okay, Muffin?"

"Yeah, I'm fine. You know, Carl, we're almost there, to Lowell I mean. I suppose it's only right to fill you in on what this trip's all about. We've come down here so I can look up this man I know—and that I haven't seen in a long, long time."

"You're here to see a guy!?"

"Carl, relax! This is not some romantic rendezvous. The guy I'm coming to see is older than my dad. You're just going to have to trust me here—that's why I'm being totally up-front with you. He's a close friend that I owe a great deal to. Can you understand that?"

"What's a middle-aged guy doing screwing around with a high school kid?"

"He didn't screw around with me—he saved me. Now I understand how you might get confused with all this, but I won't understand it if you won't trust me. Now, that's it—end of exercise! Understand?"

Carlton folded his arms and peered straight out the windshield, ending all eye contact with Sheba. Her response was to simply stop talking. The Mustang sped ahead alongside the Merrimack River with no words spoken. Her eyes widened as they passed the "Entering Lowell" sign. After five minutes of silence, it was Carlton who interrupted the quiet.

"There is a way you could prove to me that I wasn't just being used like a chump here—if you're willing to do it."

"Carl, let me be honest. I can guarantee you right now that I *will* be using you as a chump sometime in the future. With God as my witness, I promise you I will," she said, raising her right hand in the air as if taking an oath. "But—this is not one of those times!"

"Can I say my piece—please? If you're telling me the truth, and I am still your number one, then kiss me, really kiss me. I'll know from that if you're jerking me around or not."

In the next instant, the car was steered into the breakdown lane of an underpass. Directly above, the sound of vehicles whirred as they circled a rotary. Turning off the ignition, she lifted herself up from behind the steering wheel and mounted the young man, digging her knees into his sides and grabbing hold of his hair with both hands. Carlton responded with a half laugh, half gasp before Sheba pressed her lips down on his. A moment later, her tongue had slid inside his mouth. For each, the taste of the other brought on a rush of pleasure as they exchanged a small part of themselves. Sheba moved her hips over him, heightening their shared passion. Their mouths separated. His eyes were closed as he drew long breaths into his lungs. Sheba, her own breathing intensifying, looked down on the boy. Carlton had taken on a helpless appearance, as if the willing prey to her passionate aggression. She initiated another spurt of kisses, further heating the young man's blood. When he craned his neck upward to meet her mouth, she unexpectedly called a halt to the proceedings. Their ecstatic indulgence had lasted no more than a minute.

"Does that convince you?" she asked.

"Yes," he responded, his answer coming though shortened breath.

With the matter settled, Sheba slowly dismounted him, purposely applying direct pressure to his upper thigh as she rolled back to the driver's side of the car. His breathing remained heavy, prompting her to keep one hand resting on his leg a few moments longer than necessary. She turned the ignition and checked the flow of traffic from behind. Less than a quarter mile away was Bridge Street and the site of Kevin Shanahan's apartment, her home for better than three weeks in 1944, nine years before her birth.

Traffic was light this midday as she turned the Mustang off the boulevard and onto Bridge Street. Sheba hit the brake almost immediately, spotting a parking place a short distance from the corner of Second Street and directly in front of Arthur's Restaurant. They were less than two blocks from Kevin's apartment house. With her mind racing uncontrollably in anticipation, she brought the car to a stop. However, before she could even turn off the engine, Carlton's hand came down on her wrist.

"Before we get out, can we talk about something that's been on my mind for a while now, but that you really got going back there under the bridge?"

"And that would be?"

"And that would be the fact that we've been going out for nearly a year now—and still we've never spent any serious time together."

"What exactly are you trying to say?"

"You know, Sheba—what I'm trying to say is that we've never gone to bed together. All we do is kid stuff—which was fine—but I'm getting to the point that I want more. And I think you do, too."

"Did I hear right? You're thinking for yourself and me, too? And am I getting a threat here—or an ultimatum? What exactly are you trying to say here—Carl?" There was no nonsense in Sheba's tone or in the frigid stare she now directed at the young man.

"You know, it really doesn't help when you pull something like you did back on the side of the road. How do you expect me to be?"

"Oh! So this little problem of yours is suddenly all my fault! Let me get this straight. I'm supposed to become a little slut and let you just use me. Is that how it is?"

"No, we'd be doing it together."

"But it's my reputation that'll get dragged through the mud. Now I want to make sure I'm perfectly clear on this. Are you threatening to go find someone else if I don't get with the program—your program? That's funny—'cause you look just like the guy who told me he loved me just a couple of hours ago."

Carlton let out a long sigh, his eyes searching the nearby skyline as if hoping to find a clue to the mystery that was Sheba Smith.

"I'm not threatening anything, Muffin," he answered.

"You didn't enjoy our little time back there under the bridge? I know I did. Stop rushing things. Now it's getting really hot inside this car. Let's get out so I can start looking for Kevin."

From the sidewalk, Sheba pointed up the street in the direction of the apartment and grabbed hold of Carlton's arm. The air temperature was noticeably warmer here in the city than it had been when they left Maine less than two hours earlier. Stopping at the corner of Second Street, they glanced up toward Christian Hill and were struck at the sight of a line of highly polished Harley Davidson motorcycles lined up along the sidewalk. After waiting out a short line of turning cars, the couple crossed to the next block where two muscular males in leather jackets stood. On their backs, the familiar insignia of a scream-ing skull, "Hell's Angels" and "Lowell" made no secret of their identi-ty. The teenagers were only a few steps beyond the two when a loud, cat-call whistle split the air.

"Get lost," called back Sheba, assuming the annoyance was for her benefit. Her response brought a roar of laughter from the two men.

"Oh, we're just going to have a great time down here," whispered Carlton into her ear. They walked on, distancing themselves from the bikers. Eventually, they were standing directly in front of a familiar door. With her heart beating out of control and her stomach develop-ing a fist-size knot of nervous energy, she turned to him.

"Chances are, even if Kevin still lives here, he's at work. So we're going to have to hang around for a while. I'm going in to check out the mail boxes and look for his name. Then maybe I'll go upstairs to check and see if he's in his apartment—in case he is home today."

"I'll come, too."

"No, Carl, I want you to stay down here—just in case he is home. I'd rather not have him see us together if he should be home."

"I thought this guy was fifty or something. What's going on, Sheba?"

"It's a long story—long and complicated—real complicated. You just have to trust me on this."

She pushed in the heavy wooden door, leaving her boyfriend loi-tering nearby on the sidewalk. The hallway had changed little since her time in the building, a coat of paint the only thing distinguishing it from what it was during the third term of Franklin Delano Roosevelt. She looked up at the individual mail boxes, reading off the names in order; Duhamel, Perez, Contover, Grenier, Morris, McDermott, Moran and Butler. Her momentary exuberance was replaced with disappointment. Not only were the names of Kevin Shanahan and Roberta Gilbride nowhere to be found, but other names she remembered, like Modeski and Lowberg, were also absent.

She climbed the stairs, listening for sounds of activity from behind the doors. There were male voices from the apartment at the far end of the hall on the second floor. Sheba walked to within a few feet of the door, picking up on a conversation between two men, one having a Latin accent. Hesitating for only a moment, she turned and made for the stairs. Reaching the third floor, she walked deliberately toward the doorway and apartment that once sheltered her in another life. There was only silence coming from behind the familiar door. A nameplate reading "Morris" was screwed into the wood three-quarter ways up from the floor. Given the total absence of sound around her, Sheba deduced she was alone on the top floor of the building. She had to speak to someone. There was always a chance of finding someone who knew the whereabouts of Kevin. Hoping beyond hope, she strode to Kevin's former door and knocked. Nothing. She knocked a second time. Again, nothing but the hollow echo from her pounding on the door's wooden surface. She turned and made her way back down to the second floor. After wrestling with the idea while descending the stairs, the teenager walked to the apartment where she heard men speaking and knocked. She heard the sound of a radio from inside. Following no response for a second or two, the voice with the Latin accent called out.

"Bri, get that for me. Find out who it is before you open the door."

"Yeah, who is it?" The voice belonged to a youth.

"I'm in the building looking for someone who used to live here, and I was hoping to talk to someone who might know where he is."

The door opened and a teenage boy peeked out at her. He appeared younger than she, tall and wiry. After surveying Sheba for a moment, he opened the door and invited her in. She hesitated before accepting the invitation. The boy had a fresh, wholesome look about him. He pulled out a chair for her, then returned to his side of the kitchen table.

"My friend's lived here for eight years or something—probably longer than anyone else in the building. If anyone can help you, he can. He's on the phone right now but he'll be off in a jiff." The boy smiled across the table, seeming eager to converse but hard pressed to come up with what to say. "I can get you something to drink if you'd like—Perez wouldn't mind." Sheba shrugged off the boy's offer while beginning to show impatience at being kept waiting.

"Do you go to Lowell High?" he asked, finally coming up with something to say.

"No, junior, I don't go to Lowell High—so asking me to next

year's prom is out of the question. Will your friend be much longer?"

Before the young man could come up with a response, Mr. Perez stuck his head through the doorway to the next room.

"If she's from the Girl Scouts, tell her I'll take two boxes—and get yourself two, that'll be four boxes, and make sure mine are chocolate mint. Brian, you know where I keep my small cash. Why don't you pay her now."

"I'm not from the Girl Scouts! I just need to talk to you about someone who lived in this building once."

The Latin man lifted his index finger, signifying a minute more was needed on the phone. This caused Sheba to raise her eyes to the ceiling in frustration. The boy was becoming visibly upset by her impatience. Again, the two teenagers sat at the table in silence. From the next room the phone conversation went on with no end in sight.

"Keith Hall?"

"What?"

"You don't go to Lowell High—so I wondered if you went to Keith Hall?"

"I don't live in Lowell—so I wouldn't go to either—would I?" Sheba's curt responses to Brian were not triggered by a dislike for him. On the contrary, there was a refreshingly honest quality to him that she found endearing. His reaction to her remarks played out on his face. Meanwhile, she sensed his uneasiness around young females and exploited it while she waited on the man in the next room. Brian had broken all eye contact with her, opting to fiddle with the Coke bottle on the table in front of him. Unfortunately, the fiddling led to a small accident when the bottle tipped and spilled some of the beverage on the table in front of him. Grabbing the bottle, he peered up at the girl.

"Nice play, Shakespeare," she murmured.

Without responding, the boy rose to his feet and made his way around the table. Sheba turned her head in unison with his movement, as if not trusting to have the young man out of her sight. The door to the next room opened and the elusive Mr. Perez finally joined them in the kitchen.

"Sorry to keep you waitin' like that—but I've been waitin' for that call all day and I had to stay with it. Now, young lady—seein' that you're not here to sell cookies—what can I do for you?" The man was short and of average build. His most distinctive features were a pair of intense, dark brown eyes.

"Well, for starters, you could tell your little friend that I can see him making that stupid face behind me in the cabinet mirror," said

Sheba, causing Brian to look up and meet her eyes in the mirror across the room. The man burst out laughing.

"Busted, Bri—you got busted!"

The boy returned to the table and began cleaning up his mess.

"A friend of mine named Kevin Shanahan lived upstairs in this building some years back, like in 1944. It looks like he's not here now and I was hoping to find someone who might know where he went."

"When do you think he moved out?"

"I have no way of knowing."

"Damn, that's a long time ago when you're talking about 1944. I've been here about eight years—and you pretty much get to know people in a small building like this. Jesus, the name just doesn't do anything for me. Mrs. Moran's the only one here longer than me, but her memory is shot. She has a hard time rememberin' me sometimes. I don't know what to tell you."

Frustrated by the developments, Sheba grew quiet.

"Wait a minute, how about the phone book?" asked the man. Hurrying to the front room, he returned with the local phone book and began flipping pages. "You said Shanahan, right? Kevin Shanahan."

Sheba watched the man's eyes scan the columns, then stop.

"No Kevins, no K's either."

She took the phone book and looked herself. Incredibly, with all the Shanahans listed, there were no Kevins.

"You might try the library and the city register or registry—I'm not sure which they call it. That'd have his name in there even if he's got a private number or no phone at all," chipped in Brian.

Sheba's eyes brightened as a glimmer of hope was added to the search by the boy's input. She shot Brian a smile.

"Out of the mouths of babes," she added. She rose from the table and turned for the door.

"Gentlemen, thank you for your time and your help. Brian, think of me at prom time."

"We didn't get your name," called out the young man.

"Sheba."

"Ooh, baby—queen of the jungle," sang out Perez.

"That's Sheena, buddy, not Sheba—but you were close," corrected the boy.

Sheba made her way to the door, wishing her hosts a final goodbye. Brian followed her into the hallway and to the flight of stairs. She was conscious of his presence as she made her way to the ground floor.

Stopping at the bottom landing, she turned and looked up.

"I just finished the eighth grade. It's going to be a while before I'll be going to the prom, I'm afraid," he called down to her.

"Well, Brian, I'm a patient girl—when you do, don't forget to look up your Sheba, right?"

The boy grinned and watched her leave the building.

Stepping out onto the street, there was no sign of Carlton. She scanned the sidewalk and storefronts, eventually spotting his powder blue shirt across the street. He had found a shady patch of grass behind an iron fence and propped himself up against the base of a bill-board. Dodging the Bridge Street traffic, she scurried across the road and called to him from the fence.

"Change of plans, Carl—we're off to the library."

Sluggishly, Carlton pulled himself up from the ground and dusted himself off. Reaching the fence, he hoisted himself over the protruding steel spikes that ran the length of it.

"How far do we have to go?"

"It's downtown, right by city hall." Then, Sheba stopped and looked directly at her boyfriend. She was processing a fresh idea. She looked over at Kevin's former apartment house, then up and down Bridge Street.

"What now?"

"We may not have to go downtown, at least not until I check out one more thing. There's a variety store up the street that may have all we need."

Stepping in front of Carlton, she walked in the general direction of a sidewalk fruit stand. After shaking his head in disbelief, he jogged up from behind and accompanied her. It was only a short distance to Fruean's Farm Stand, a combination mom-and-pop variety store and produce retailer. Sheba distinctly remembered this location being vacant during her three weeks here in 1944. Outside the store, racks of fruits and vegetables sat against the windows on display. The teenagers entered the store where, behind the cash register, a surly man with a cigar protruding from the side of his mouth eyed them suspiciously.

"I wonder if I could borrow your phone book?" asked Sheba. The man rolled his eyes.

"Our phone is private. We have no pay phones in the store."

"I don't need to make a call—just look something up. Please."

The proprietor reached down beneath the counter and produced the Greater Lowell phone book. He flipped it over the counter into her hands. "Don't go too far," he warned.

A customer approached her from behind and ushered Sheba aside. She laid the book down on the surface of a nearby ice cream freezer and flipped forward to the yellow pages.

"Hey, don't be playin' with the fruit unless you plan on buyin' something," snarled the owner.

Glancing up, Sheba saw the warning was addressed to Carlton. Reaching inside her pocket, she pulled out a dollar bill and some change. She walked to the front door and slapped the money in her boyfriend's hand. "Buy us a banana or something—for the ride home."

Returning to the freezer, she reopened the phone book and took up the search. After flipping from page to page, she stopped and ran her eyes back and forth across the printed material below. Oblivious to the activity around her, she continued to review the information until a single item brought a halt to her search. She stared down on the surface of the page where the text provided her with everything she needed to know and had traveled to Massachusetts to find out. Inside her, an emotional swell rose, causing tears to form in her eyes and a bittersweet sentiment to grab hold of her deepest, most guarded feelings. Below her, the product of her trip was spelled out faultlessly in large, block letters.

SHANAHAN'S LOCK AND KEY COMPANY
"Greater Lowell's Largest Lock and Security Company"

Residential — Auto — Commercial

Kevin & Roberta Shanahan & Sons, Proprietors

Following a period of contemplation, Sheba ran the tips of her fingers over the names printed on the page, more than ever wanting to see Kevin. Finally, following an exaggerated pause, she closed the book and set it down on the counter. From the corner of her eye she saw Carlton standing at the edge of the sidewalk, his hand clutching a small bunch of bananas. The man with the cigar noticed the tears welled up in her eyes. Reclaiming the phone book and placing it back under the counter, he softened his tone from earlier.

"Didja find everything you were looking for?"

Sheba smiled at him from behind eyes unable to conceal the tug of war raging inside her.

"Everything, everything—and more. They even have a family. They have—*sons*," she answered before turning away and heading out of the store.

She walked up to Carlton from behind, stopping beside him at the edge of the curb. He turned his head to catch Sheba staring blankly at him, her face forming a sad mask.

"You okay, babe?"

She nodded her head, but the response lacked conviction.

"Can we go now? We don't have to go to the library, do we?"

She hooked her arm through his and started back toward the car. "No, we can go home now—mission accomplished, sort of."

They had only taken a few steps when Sheba stopped abruptly.

"Oh, come on, babe, you said we could take off from here. I'm not real comfortable in this neighborhood." Carlton looked on as a comforting smile slowly spread across his girlfriend's face, her expression brightening before his eyes.

"No, we'll be heading home now—but I'm going to have to come back in a couple of weeks to attend to the Mustang."

"Down here?"

"Yeah, you know that problem with my passenger door—the way it sticks and sometimes you have to slam it to get it to close right?"

"What about it?"

"The locking mechanism—it needs fixing. And it's not like I'll let just anyone work on my Mustang. I found a company down here that I'm sure I can trust with my car."

"I can't believe you'd come all the way down here just to fix your car door."

"Why not? It's not that far—it's less than two hours by car."

If you enjoyed reading

The Odyssey of
Sheba Smith

by

Thomas E. Coughlin

Look for his other works of fiction

Maggie May's Diary

Brian Kelly: Route 1

About the author

Thomas E. Coughlin is the author of *Maggie May's Diary* and *Brian Kelly: Route 1*. He is a practicing certified public accountant and former disc jockey. He considers four locales as home; Lowell, Massachusetts; Wells, Maine; Berlin and Chester, New Hampshire.

Author's Notes

For those readers who are curious about the origin of certain ideas and plot points behind any work of fiction, I offer you some insight into the creation of *The Odyssey of Sheba Smith*. First, the general plot of this book has been lodged in my head for over five years. I know this because I made vague references to this, my third novel, in a radio interview as far back as 1998. My original story outline set the book in Chester, New Hampshire, and had Sheba venturing off no farther than Manchester, a mere ten miles away. In fact, I originally envisioned the Sheba character as a male. I do not recall when I changed my mind regarding her gender, but it was early on. My first attempt at writing the story saw the novel open inside a school bus as it rattled along a back road in rural New Hampshire in mid-winter. Sheba was returning from classes on the last school day of 1969 instead of leaving for them as she would be in the completed novel. The change was made to more effectively introduce her adversary, Felicia Blackburn.

In the early stages of writing the book, I drove the back roads of Wells and selected specific roadways where my character would carry out her adventure. In particular, Burnt Mill Road and Tatnic Road suited my story line and became Sheba's home address in 1970 and the site of her mother's homestead back in 1944, respectively. At about the same time, I approached Myles Henry at the Maine Diner and asked for permission to use the restaurant as a setting within the novel, the business where Sheba Smith would obtain her first job. I wanted my main character to work in a place familiar to residents and vacationers alike. The diner was already open in 1970, although considerably smaller, giving it historical validity. I am a firm believer in placing my stories in locations my readers can visit, allowing them to set eyes on the exact backdrop I envision while constructing my plot. Myles agreed and I instantly had a literary home for Linda Lee Tuttle, Sheba's middle-aged and closest friend.

A character named Irv Rosen shows up at the Maine Diner early in the book and recounts a story concerning his fear of flying. Irv actually made an appearance in my second book, *Brian Kelly: Route 1*. He was a minor character but in my initial draft from that book told a story at Alisson's Restaurant in Kennebunkport about a cross-country plane flight with a rabbi's daughter and three nuns. That story was edited out of the novel for page-count reasons but was brought back in *The Odyssey of Sheba Smith*. The story is rooted in truth and was told to me by a roommate way back in my days as a disc jockey. At the time I was impressed by the fact that my roommate, who was Jewish, clung to all faiths within the walls of a plane terminal. The story proved to me that, at 35,000 feet, clergy is clergy. To this day, I, too, feel better flying with priests, nuns, ministers and rabbis on board.

Unlike the character of Irv Rosen, two characters who make an appearance late in the book, Brian Kelly and his Hispanic mentor, Perez, did not show up in my original plot outline. The novel was nearly completed when I decided to include these two characters in the final chapter. The story brought Sheba back to Bridge Street in Lowell where she had to make contact with someone in Kevin's old building. It wasn't until I brought Sheba to the front door of the building that it dawned on me: Perez had an apartment on Bridge Street in the very same neighborhood. So I brought the two characters from *Brian Kelly: Route 1* together again. Writing these few pages of the book was a joy. It is always a pleasure visiting with old friends.

As stated earlier, Manchester originally was to be the city where Sheba would seek refuge from an unknown world. Early on, I reluctantly moved her from Chester, New Hampshire, the small town that spawned the idea for the book, to Wells, Maine, for marketing and economic reasons. This explains why the prototype for Mowalk's sacred rock can be found on the side of Route 28 in Londonderry, New Hampshire, and not in Maine. The novel was well under way when I decided on a second relocation. After the release of my second book, *Brian Kelly: Route 1,* I received unexpected help and support from the people, businesses, and media in Lowell, Massachusetts. I cannot begin to explain how much this meant to me, in light of the fact that it had been thirty years since I left the city. For this reason, I decided to offer the same warmth and generosity to my protagonist. Hence, Sheba follows Kevin Shanahan all the way from Maine to

Lowell, and my readers ride out three weeks with her in wartime America, sharing in the shortages and hardships of these strong, working-class people.

Finally, an explanation for a brief interlude within the book and the dedication at the beginning of it. While gathering information on York County in the 1970s, I came upon a news story concerning the abduction and murder of a thirteen-year-old girl. Mary Catherine Olenchuk was abducted in Ogunquit while running an errand for her parents in August of 1970. Her body was found approximately two weeks later in a barn a short distance from Route 9 in Kennebunk. Nearly a year after first reading the account of her disappearance and ultimate murder, I am still haunted by the image of her pretty, smiling face looking up at me from the newspaper. The barn, now only a cellar hole following a fire many years ago, is briefly visited by Sheba during a rainstorm. I was mindful to place my character in the barn nearly two months before the actual kidnapping and murder.

I hope these few paragraphs provide you with some small insight into the unbalanced mind of a fiction writer and the process by which ideas are transferred to the printed page.

Tom Coughlin